CAROLINE AWOKE TO the creak of door hinges.

At first, she couldn't recall where she was...and then she remembered. She lay on her side, trying not to breathe too loudly as she watched the tall form of a man backlit by moonlight—Viscount Rexton—opening the double glass doors. He was slow and deliberate in his movements, but clumsy nonetheless.

He stepped out onto the balcony rather unsteadily and undressed with his back to her, leaning for support on the stone balustrade and letting his clothes lie where they fell. Nude, his silhouette put her in a mind of an engraving she'd seen of Michelangelo's *David*—broad-shouldered, lean-hipped, long-legged.

He turned.

Caroline closed her eyes, but not before catching a glimpse of his privates, which shifted heavily as he moved. She heard the faint squeak of a floorboard beneath the carpet as he approached the bed. He stood for what seemed like an eternity as Caroline feigned sleep, her heart jittering.

Something nudged her collar very slightly, which was when she realized he'd leaned over and was touching it, manipulating something. She smelled gin on his breath. It took all her self-control to keep her breathing slow and somnolent as he unclipped the leash and carefully gathered it up.

ALSO BY LOUISA BURTON

House of Dark Delights

Book 2 in the Hidden Grotto series

Bound
in
Moonlight

Louisa Burton

BANTAM
BOOKS

BOUND IN MOONLIGHT
A Bantam Book / December 2007

Published by
Bantam Dell
A Division of Random House, Inc.
New York, New York

Book design by R. Bull

Bantam Books and the rooster colophon are registered trademarks
of Random House, Inc.

Library of Congress Cataloging-in-Publication Data

Burton, Louisa.
Bound in moonlight / Louisa Burton.
p. cm. — (Hidden grotto series ; bk. 2)
ISBN 978-0-553-38413-0 (trade pbk.)
1. Castles—France—Fiction. I. Title.
PS3602.U7698B68 2007
813'.6—dc22
2007020379

Printed in the United States of America
Published simultaneously in Canada

www.bantamdell.com

BVG 10 9 8 7 6 5 4 3 2 1

For my sisters, Janice, Kate, Pam, and Suze—
with special thanks to Suze, proofreader extraordinaire

Tutelage

Take heed therefore, myne eyes, how ye doe stare
henceforth too rashly on that guilefull net,
in which if euer ye entrapped are,
out of her bands ye by no meanes shall get.
Fondnesse it were for any being free,
to couet fetters, though they golden bee.

From "Sonnet XXXVII" of Edmund Spenser's Amoretti

One

NEVER IN HER *twenty-four pampered and cosseted years among New York City's privileged Upper Ten* had Emmeline witnessed acts of such appalling lechery, nor supposed that people of her own class might stoop to indulging in them.

She was determined to find Lord Hardwyck and be quit at once of this shameless château. Surely her distinguished and urbane fiancé had not suspected the nature of this bacchanalian house party when he accepted the invitation.

Such were her thoughts as she opened the door to which she had been directed by the countess in the leather mask. Emmeline was further comforted upon entering the room within and discovering it to be lined floor to ceiling and wall to wall with bookshelves. No doubt his lordship had spent the weekend ensconced in a secluded corner with his nose in some dusty old tome.

Imagine, dear Reader, our heroine's dismay when her gaze lit upon Archibald Dickings, Baron of Hardwyck and heir apparent to the earldom of Upswinge, atop a polished mahogany writing table with his nose, along with the rest of his face, planted snugly between the thighs of one voluptuous blonde and his turgid shaft between those of another.

"I'm coming!" cried the latter as she strained against the silken cords that bound her hands and feet to the four legs of the table. "Oh, yes! God, yes! Oh! Oh!"

Upon hearing Emmeline's gasp of horror, Lord Hardwyck looked up and blinked at her. "Miss Woodbridge. Fancy encountering you here. I didn't even know you were in France."

From Chapter One of Emmeline's Emancipation *by Anonymous, first published in 1903 by Saturnalia Press and reprinted since then in innumerable editions worldwide. A rare first edition from the original eight-hundred-copy print run sold in 2003 for $158,000 at Sotheby's in New York.*

January 17, 1922
Steamboat Springs, Colorado

Dearest Rèmy,

No, no, a thousand times no, I will not marry you. I will, however, ride you like a cowgirl as soon as I see you again. I mean, the moment I lay eyes on you, so I suggest you don't meet my ship when it arrives, unless you want us both to be arrested for public indecency. Or don't they care about that sort of thing in France? Probably not. God, I love the French. You most of all, *naturellement.*

You can't imagine what it means to me in my present wretched situation, hearing from you (most especially when you relate one of your deliciously filthy little fantasies, like the one about you making a stag film starring *moi*). I reread your letters with pathetic regularity, like some moony sixteen-year-old. Thank God for Air Mail. Every morning I sit in my wheelchair in front of this enormous picture window in the front room of the inn, my poor smashed leg in its plaster cast propped up on the window seat, waiting for the mail. It arrives via the strapping, ruddy-cheeked young Nils, who delivers it on skis after picking it up in town, except of course when the weather won't permit the mail plane to land.

Nils, who hails from Norway, is a silver-blond giant. I tend to gape at him, because you just don't see men that tall in France. You tower over most of your countrymen, and you're at least an inch or two shy of six feet. I read somewhere that the reason most Frenchmen are on the short side is that Napoleon turned all the tall ones into soldiers when he was trying to take over the world, and of course most of them didn't live to reproduce. Weren't there something like twenty-five thousand French casualties at Waterloo alone?

This is the kind of thing I start ruminating on ad nauseam while I sit here staring out at the snow and wishing I were back in Paris with you. I know I can't stop whining about how bored I am, but you can't imagine what it's like, watching all the other guests tromp gaily away every morning with their skis over their shoulders while I languish here with my shattered leg, cracked arm, and abandoned dignity. At least it was the left arm I broke, so I can still hold a pen. I've been polishing (actually over-polishing) the article about the Steamboat Springs Winter Festival that Hearst sent me here to write. And composing epic letters to you, of course.

I shouldn't complain so much about being bored. Kitty is wonderful company, as always, and at least I'm not being held hostage in that ghastly hospital anymore. Dr. Horney (God, what a miserable boyhood he must have suffered) will not change his tune no matter how much I plead and cajole. He insists I must wait until both casts are off before I can travel. Kitty says she won't go with me if I try to leave before he saws off all this plaster, and I couldn't possibly travel solo in this condition, so it looks as if I'm stuck here for at least another four weeks.

Your last letter was a delight, *mon amour,* except for that rather tedious harangue about me being a reckless thrillseeker who got what she asked for. You know damn well that I can handle myself on a pair of skis, or you should, after Montgenèvre. You told me I was the most accomplished female skier you'd ever seen—or is that the kind of applesauce you sell to every fresh new skirt you meet? In any event, you know I've been keen to try my hand at ski jumping. Pretty much the only reason I took this assignment was so that I could learn to jump from Carl Howelsen himself—and, of course, to watch the best jumpers in the world compete against one another. For your information, I completed over a dozen successful jumps before that nasty landing, which only happened because I was exhausted.

On a serious note, about your campaign to make me Mme. Rèmy Binet:

Touched as I am by your heartwarming observation that I "look and fuck" like a woman ten years my junior (ah, you romantic frogs), a subtraction of a decade would put me at thirty-four, which is, need I remind you, STILL TWO YEARS OLDER THAN YOU. But that's not the only reason I won't marry you. We've only known each other for a year, and although I can't argue with you about our "extraordinary rapport" and "the deep communion of our souls," there is still much you don't know about me, such as the reason I'm so sour on the institution of marriage.

Suffice it to say that *Emmeline's Emancipation* is something of a roman à clef. Which is to say, the events I described in that book actually happened, more or less. I changed the names of everyone involved, of course, and altered some details to make it more entertaining and more difficult to identify me as the author. The most major change was the setting. It didn't take place in Scotland. It was a castle in France called Château de la Grotte Cachée.

I did, however, show up to find my betrothed giving it to two women, although it was in the dining room, not the library. The women weren't both blond, though, just the one he was banging (who really was tied to the table, but with ordinary hemp rope, not silken cords). He was holding himself over her with his arms braced, eating out a dark-haired woman in a black corset, black opera gloves, and tall boots, who was kneeling in front of him. She had a riding crop, and she was whacking him on the ass, really putting her arm into it, barking instructions as to how he should fuck the blonde. "Pound her! Ram it in! Harder, you miserable weakling. Put your back into it! Squeeze that ass! Squeeze it!" In the book, both women are tasty young tomatoes, but in real life, although the dark-haired one was pretty, the blonde was a little more...real. She sported quite the chunky chassis even by the standard of the times, and I remember she had a really ugly bruise on her thigh.

The faithless fiancé was Randolph Lytton, Baron of Hickley and now the eighth Earl of Kilbury, his old man having turned up his toes between then and now. I must admit, he wasn't quite as unruffled when I walked in on him as was his fictional counterpart, Archie, but neither did he seem particularly distressed. He honestly did seem more perplexed than anything else.

The rest played out much as it does in the book, and yes, there really was a charming young satyr with a rolling pin between his legs who took me in hand, as it were, but his name wasn't Tobias. It was Inigo. And when I say he was a satyr, I don't mean he was a lothario. I mean he very well may have been a satyr.

I can't believe I just committed those words to paper.

It goes without saying that this letter mustn't fall into the hands of anyone other than yourself. The only people in the world who know that I wrote *E.E.* are you, Kitty, and my agent. Can you imagine the damage to my career if it became public knowledge that novelist-cum-journalist-cum-reckless thrillseeker Emily Townsend is, or once was, a secret pornographer? The French would brush it off, but the Americans? These are the people who passed a constitutional amendment making it illegal to wash down your porterhouse with a lovely old cabernet. This country has never managed to rise beyond its Puritan roots, and I fear it never will.

Speaking of which, although I dearly appreciate your offer to ship me a case of Château Montrose to keep me warm through the rest of my sentence here in the frozen American West, Kitty has managed to find a source for a local hooch that comes in big, crude stoneware jugs and tastes, so help me God, better than anything I've ever had in my mouth.

Except for your thing, of course.

I remain, *de tout mon cœur,*

>Your devoted,
>And pitiful,
>Em

Two

EMMELINE STARED IN *bewilderment through the side window of the brougham parked next to her little green Benz in the château's carriage house. In the throes of some delirium fever—for what other explanation could there be for his violent tremors and mad rantings?—the young man cried out,* "Yes! Oh, yes! Lick the tip. Squeeze the balls. Now suck it hard . . . harder . . . Here it comes. It's coming!"

He roared like a lion, convulsing in spasms that filled Emmeline with unspeakable dread. She must do something, and quickly, lest this poor young man succumb to whatever ghastly ailment held him in its grip.

"By Jove, Lavinia, but you are an *artiste* with your mouth," *he said as a woman's head rose into view.*

Dear God, no, *thought Emmeline. She couldn't have actually put her mouth on his . . . his . . .*

Emmeline recoiled in disgust as the depravity of what she had just witnessed sank in. Her vision went gray, and she collapsed in a swoon of horror and disbelief.

ঌ

January 26, 1922
Steamboat Springs, Colorado

Mon chéri Rèmy,

No, no, a thousand times no, etc. etc. etc.

I'm forty-four. You're thirty-two. Why do we even have to discuss this? Rèmy, you know how I feel about you. You're the most perfect man I've ever known, the best lover, the warmest companion. And, oh, the contrast of those big, muscular peasant shoulders with the eyeglasses and the brain...it still makes me weak in the knees.

If there were any real reason for us to tie the knot, I might consider it, but I honestly just don't see the point. Everything's copacetic, is it not? What are we lacking that marriage can provide? We sleep together, we travel together, we share the same friends and the same interests. Yet we have our own homes, so we're not on top of each other constantly, and we have an understanding about sleeping with other people that would be unworkable if we were bound together in holy matrimony. Really, it's the perfect arrangement. I can't imagine why you want to go and ruin it.

Speaking of sleeping with other people, I must tell you about the dream I had last night about Nils, the

Viking. Well, first I should tell you what inspired the dream.

Every morning after he brings in the mail, Nils sits in the dining room and drinks a cup of hot cocoa before setting out again. Yesterday, Kitty, who's got quite the crush on him, asked if she could join him. He was delighted, of course. She's quite the doll. Afterward, she told me he'd asked her if the pretty brunette with the broken bones was her sister. She said he was astounded when she told him I was her aunt, and twenty-three years older than she.

Well, the compliment must have really taken root in my subconscious, because I awoke in the middle of the night from the most exciting wet dream (yes, women have them, too). In the dream, it was I, not Kitty, having cocoa with Nils in the dining room. He was so shy and nervous, and clearly sweet on me. And he was a virgin who had never so much as touched a woman.

I said, "You can touch *me,* if you like," and I lifted my skirt just an inch or so to show him what I meant.

He pulled his chair close and very tentatively slid his hand up my leg—not the one in the cast, the good one. I was wearing my peach silk camiknickers, and of course those are so loose that he had no trouble at all reaching the bull's-eye. He touched me very carefully, teasing apart the hair over the slit with his big gentle fingers and exploring the little folds and furrows between them until I was panting and clutching at the arms of my wheelchair.

He said, "It's getting slippery."

All I could do was nod.

A fingertip grazed my clit, and I sucked in a breath. He thought he'd hurt me, and started pulling his hand away, but I told him it felt good. He told me it felt good for him, too, and I could see that he had a hard-on like a broom handle.

He pushed a finger inside me, and I instantly came. It galvanized him. He started frantically undoing his trousers, but I pushed him away, saying we couldn't go any further, that he was too young for me. (I know, I know.) He tried to talk me into it. My refusals grew more and more halfhearted. At this point, my casts had disappeared, and my clothes, too (dreams are very convenient that way). He threw me to the floor, pinned my arms down, and fucked me like a pile driver.

I woke up climaxing, even though I was lying on my back, with nothing to push against. Usually when I come in my sleep, I'm lying on my stomach and thrusting against the bed. I brought myself off by hand a couple more times just to get it out of my system, and then I drifted back off to sleep.

At breakfast, Kitty asked me why I was smiling that way, so I told her about the dream.

"Do you think he's really a virgin?" she asked.

"You're in a better position to find that out than I."

So this morning she joined him again for cocoa, steered the conversation around to women, and asked him outright if he'd ever gotten any. You know Kitty, she's not much for subtlety.

Well, guess what? He hasn't! Twenty years old, a Norse god with the face of an angel, and he's a virgin. Isn't that the sweetest thing you've ever heard? She asked him if he'd ever touched a woman...down there. He hadn't. She asked him if he'd like to. He was hesitant, something about some girl at church he's been pining over but can't work up the nerve to ask out. Eventually, though, he took her up on it, and she said it was very similar to my dream, Nils gently fondling, the two of them getting hotter by the second. But just as she was about to go off, he tore himself away with an obvious effort, said he liked her too much to treat her like an alley cat, and left. That was eight hours ago, and she's still grumpy.

Yes, darling, I know you're chafing at the bit, wondering when I'm going to get around to "spilling it all" about the château, as you so emphatically demanded in your letter. Your rabid curiosity slays me, as does your outrage that I'd never told you about Hickley or any of the rest of it until now. I'm not the type to live in the past—you know that. Once I wrote "The End" on the last page of *Emmeline's Emancipation,* I was done with that chapter of my life and ready to start fresh.

That said, I can certainly appreciate your point about my "cockteasing" you with that little dining room ménage à trois and the satyr comment. I understand your wanting to hear the whole story, and your point about my having nothing but time on my hands for the next three weeks is well taken. It will require more than one letter to relate it all, but I'll give it the old college try.

I must warn you, though, that I'm not sure how well I trust my memory about the things that happened at Grotte Cachée, and not just because it was twenty years ago. It's a screwy place, and I felt vaguely hopped-up just being there, especially in certain areas, like the cave.

The château is in Auvergne, tucked deep into a valley formed by heavily wooded, extinct volcanoes, one of which houses a labyrinthine cave. The entrance to this "hidden grotto," or the main entrance, is in a Roman bathhouse built onto the side of that particular mountain, "Roman" meaning it actually dates back to the Roman occupation of Gaul. Whatever it is that affects your mind when you're at Grotte Cachée seems to grow more and more powerful the deeper you go into the cave. But you sometimes feel it in the castle itself, or even in the woods around it, which are vast and ancient.

Looking back now at the things that happened there, the things I saw, or thought I saw...well, it's tempting to conclude that I was just completely off my nut the entire time. It was a stressful episode, or it started out that way, and stress can do that to you. Some of the soldiers I nursed during the war were delusional, but it was just shell shock from the trauma of battle, and they got better once they were out of the fray. But the reason I'm not so quick to chalk up what I experienced at Grotte Cachée to stress is that I was actually warned beforehand that it was a strange place populated by demons, and that I was likely to be exposed to unexplainable phenomena.

But I'm getting ahead of myself. To understand why I went there, you need to know how and why I became engaged to Hickley in the first place.

I've told you my father was a banker. He actually owned a bank, and he was a partner in the Vanderbilt railroads. He built a granite castle on Fifth Avenue and a white marble one in Newport that was patterned after the Temple of Apollo, with six forty-foot columns out front. Oh, and we had a big old sprawling country home out on Long Island that was actually sort of homey and pleasant, and where I learned to ride. And Mother kept a little pied-à-terre in Paris for her shopping excursions.

Are you getting the picture, *chéri?* There were buckets of money, but it was just a little too shiny and new, my father having been a self-made man. The Astors and the rest of their ilk looked down their noses at the new rich, even the Vanderbilts for the longest time, but my parents were determined to break into their ranks. The time-honored way to do this was to ~~pimp one's daughter~~ marry one's daughter into a venerable old family. Titled Englishmen were thought to provide the splashiest and most surefire entrée into society.

My childhood friend Consuelo Vanderbilt was torn away from her beloved Winty Ruthurford and married off to Sunny Churchill, a sallow, bug-eyed little weasel with manicured hands who had absolutely nothing going for him except that he was the ninth Duke of Marlborough. I was one of Consuelo's bridesmaids, and my first clue that Sunny might end up being a disappointment was when he skipped the wedding rehearsal to go shopping instead. On the afternoon of the wedding, Consuelo's eyes were red and swollen from sobbing all morning in her room, with a guard stationed outside the door in case she tried to make a break for it. I am absolutely serious. Of course, the marriage was an utter debacle. Sunny treated her like dirt, having only bound himself in matrimony to a dollar princess so that he could afford to restore the true love of his life, that majestic mausoleum known as Blenheim Palace.

That was what they called us, the American heiresses who got engaged to land-poor British aristocrats looking for an infusion of cash in the form of dowries with which to repair the ancestral manse, play baccarat, or support a mistress or two. The terms of my betrothal were negotiated between my father and Hickley during Hickley's wife-hunting excursion to New York in March of 1902. *His* father, the seventh Earl of Kilbury, had squandered what remained of the family fortune, leaving him deeply in debt and desperate for the two million dollars in cash and railroad stock he was to receive upon our marriage in June of the following year.

Why, you are asking yourself, would a smart, self-reliant little bearcat like me agree to such a bloodless and venal arrangement? Perhaps you're recalling my alter ego, Emmeline, so sheltered and class-conscious before her sexual awakening, and thinking I must have been the same sort of girl before breaking out of my shell.

Actually, Emmeline is probably the most fictionalized element in the book. To make her transformation dramatic, she had to start off extraordinarily naïve. In reality, I was what they called, in America, a "New Woman." We played tennis and golf, smoked cigarettes, rode bicycles, drove motorcars, and got educated, although you wouldn't believe the histrionics it took to convince my parents to send me to Bryn Mawr. We wore blouses with burly leg of mutton sleeves and skirts that showed the ankle, though we would have died before lifting them for a man. We felt we had the right to careers, and also the right to remain unmarried if we so chose.

So then, why did I let my parents hand me over, along with two million smackers, to a money-grubbing English baron? First, you must understand that I had no notion of Hickley's true character, or lack thereof, when I met him. We were introduced by a mutual acquaintance named Kit Archer. Kit was an Englishman, but he lived in France, where he served as *administrateur* to the *seigneur* of Grotte Cachée, the fourth generation of his family to do so. He was also the author of two books of classical history, as well as a novel about Atlantis that was obscure but really quite good.

I'd met Kit four years earlier at one of Bertha Chalmers's semimonthly literary salons, which he frequented whenever he was in New York. It was my first time there, and I was shaking in my boots to be in the same room with people like Edith (this was before *House of Mirth*, but I was in awe of her stories and articles). Kit was so warm and garrulous—he made me feel right at home (as did Edith, of course). He and I became fast friends and remained so until his death right before the war, despite the fact that I was twenty and he was a portly, bald, gout-ridden sixty-year-old who lived on the other side of the Atlantic. And lest you conclude that there was anything untoward in our relationship, Kit had a wife, four children, and a grandson, all of whom he worshipped.

In any event, I might have skipped Mrs. Chalmers's salon that night, because New York was buried under

one of those suffocating March snowstorms, but Kit had
sent a note saying he'd just gotten into town and would
be bringing a young baron he'd met on the crossing who'd
read one of my magazine articles and wanted to meet
me. So, I went, partly to see Kit and partly to meet this
English nobleman who actually knew who I was! And
wanted to meet me!

Hickley turned out to be handsome and debonair,
with that classic British imperturbability that we
Americans are too quick to confuse with intelligence,
and he seemed perfectly comfortable mingling with my
unconventional, Left-Bankish crowd. He told me he'd
very much enjoyed my piece two years before in
Scribner's about Marion Jones Farquhar competing at
Wimbledon. He was extraordinarily attentive to me,
which was quite a novelty at the time, and I won't lie to
you. It went to my head.

I was not, and had never been, the belle of the ball.
I was usually the girl who heard about the ball the next
day from her girlfriends, which I had in abundance. It
was boyfriends I lacked—serious boyfriends. I did get
asked out occasionally, and I'd even been kissed a few
times, but it never went anywhere. The main problem
was that I was plain—not ugly, mind you, but not
beautiful, not according to the taste of the times. My
face was all right—in fact I rather liked it. It had a sharp
delicacy to it that may not have been in vogue then, but
which I found aesthetically pleasing. But I was too
slender, too small-breasted, too athletic. To make
matters worse, I'd never gotten the hang of fawning all
over men, giggling at their unfunny jokes, and dreaming

up reasons to praise them. It didn't help that I was semi-accomplished, having already launched a writing career, even if it was still small potatoes at the time. (My publishing credits consisted of two short stories and a handful of articles and essays, but it was my dream to write a novel, and I couldn't seem to get one off the ground.)

One of the reasons I embraced the New Woman thing with such fervor was that it was the perfect camouflage for an ungorgeous, sporty little bluenose like me. At twenty-four, having had not a single real beau, I was starting to worry that I'd never get married, not because I didn't want to, but because nobody would have me. New Woman principles notwithstanding, I loathed the prospect of ending my days a pickled-in-brine old spinster like my great-aunt Pembridge.

It wasn't that I wanted children—as you know, that's never been a priority of mine. If I'm honest, I have to admit, with a fair degree of shame, that my primary motivation for wanting to get married had much more to do with society's expectations than with my own innate desires. Despite my bohemian inclinations and my support for the rights of women, I had been brought up to believe that a woman's destiny was to be a wife, and that single women over thirty were pathetic and unwanted.

As if that weren't bad enough, there was no respectable way, within the confines of New York society, for an unwed woman to have sex. Just because I was a virgin didn't mean I wanted to remain one forever. I was fascinated by sex, but since females of a certain class never spoke of such things, I knew little more than the basic mechanics of intercourse. I'd discovered the delights of self-gratification during a bath at fourteen, so I did know about orgasms, even if I didn't know for the longest time what they were called or that other people had them, too.

Hickley conducted a seemingly sincere, if cursory, courtship before popping the question (on April 1— you'd think that would have tipped me off). He seemed genuinely interested in me, read all my stories and articles. In retrospect, I'm fairly sure he'd chosen me out of the *Sears Dollar Princess Catalogue* and had one of his minions brief him on me so that our meeting wouldn't appear quite as calculated as it was. ("She wrote a piece in *Scribner's* two years ago, my lord....") I wouldn't be surprised if he booked the same ship as Kit because he'd been told we were friends and always saw each other in New York.

Although he wasn't remotely demonstrative in terms of emotions, he did claim to hold me "in esteem," which I took to be his stiff-upper-lip way of saying that his feelings for me would most assuredly grow into love, as I assumed mine would for him. I knew about the dowry, but I just thought that was how it was done with aristocratic marriages. I didn't for one moment put my union with Hickley in the same category as Consuelo's to Sunny. What Hickley and I had was, if not quite a love match, surely destined to become one. The money was secondary.

Okay, so I was a little naïve. By the time Hickley returned to England, promising to visit me once or twice before the wedding, I had a sapphire and diamond ring on my left hand and the memory of a chaste good-bye kiss that represented, in my mind, the lifetime of carnal bliss that I would enjoy as Lady Hickley. I told myself that he surely would have kissed me with more passion if we'd ever been left alone. Perhaps, thought I, he would have attempted even more intimate liberties, which I frankly would have welcomed, fourteen months being a long time to have to wait for the aforementioned bliss. Now that I knew my days as a virgin were numbered, I couldn't wait to find out what I'd been missing. It was all I thought about. I was in heat pretty much twenty-four hours a day.

Toward the end of July, Consuelo sent me a cable telling me that she'd managed to wrangle me an invitation to King Edward's coronation on August 9, at which she was to serve as one of Queen Alexandra's attendants. At the insistence of my parents, Aunt Pembridge accompanied me to London, where we were guests of the Marlboroughs at Spencer House, which Sunny was letting at the time. I'd thought about cabling Hickley before we set sail to let him know I was coming, but then I decided it would be more fun to surprise him. I inquired after him in London, only to be told that he was spending the rest of the summer touring France with friends, beginning with a sort of extended house party at Château de la Grotte Cachée.

Once I got over my disappointment, I realized I didn't have to return to New York without seeing him. For a couple of years, I'd been carrying around a little calling card in my purse that Kit Archer had given me when he'd issued a standing invitation to drop by the château if I ever found myself in Auvergne.

"I warrant you will find it a singular experience," he'd said. "Just show this to the gatehouse guard."

The card, which was in a tiny envelope engraved PERSONAL AND CONFIDENTIAL, was of gilt-rimmed ivory stock so heavy you could hardly bend it. On the front was printed, in French and English, RIGHT OF ENTRÉE IS GRANTED TO THE FOLLOWING. Below that, Kit had inked *Miss Emily Townsend* and his initials. The back of the card explained how to get to Grotte Cachée from the nearby city of Clermont-Ferrand, an incredibly convoluted route along unmarked roads. I asked Kit how his employer would feel about a perfect stranger coming to his home.

"Seigneur des Ombres is too busy to cultivate social connections," he said, "but he enjoys having guests at the château, so he gives me carte blanche to invite whomever I like. I must warn you, Em, it is a place of unbridled libertinage. You will likely witness some very indecorous goings-on, but I shan't think the experience would do you any harm—I daresay it might do you some good."

I'd slipped the card into my purse and forgotten about it. Now I was glad I'd held on to it. After the coronation, I convinced Aunt Pembridge that we should make a little side trip to France before returning home. I had no intention, however, of dragging a chaperone with me for a surprise visit with the man about whom I'd been entertaining libidinous fantasies for four months.

Consulting a map, I saw that Clermont-Ferrand was about a hundred miles from Lyon, where my mother's cousin Biddie owned a château. Biddie's real name, Obedience Blick, couldn't have been more inappropriate, the Blicks being a notoriously wild branch of the family, and Biddie being the quintessential devil-may-care Blick. That was part of the reason I'd always adored her. I knew she spent every summer at that château, so I cabled her, and she invited us to come for a visit.

When we got there and I told her that my fiancé was at Grotte Cachée, she rolled her eyes and laughed, because of course she knew exactly why I'd come. She offered to lend me her motorcar and driving clothes the next day, and told me not to rush back if I didn't care to—although I promised her I would stay no more than four days, returning by Sunday the seventeenth. She also convinced Aunt Pembridge that she should remain at the château and rest up from all that traveling because I had no need of a chaperone where I was going (she conveniently neglected to mention that Hickley would be there).

Biddie told me that she had never been to Grotte Cachée, but that her paternal grandmother had apparently spent a week there one summer in the early part of the last century. She had never discussed the visit with anyone, but after she died, Biddie's mother was sorting through her papers and came across several letters wrapped up in a black silk cravat. Their contents had evidently shocked her deeply, given her reaction to them. Biddie saw the letters only briefly before her mother whisked them away, but she did manage to read the first line of one, which she'd never forgotten: *Did you ever think you would miss being collared and leashed and forced to submit to a perfect stranger for an entire week?*

Biddie had to explain to me that this had to do with sex, that's how ill-informed I was. The letters were written by the woman who had been her grandmother's closest confidante from the time they'd attended Miss Cox's Academy for Girls in New York—my own alma mater. Biddie said that the two of them used to laugh about the madcap exploits of their youth, and what "highfliers" they'd been (meaning sluts, essentially). Over the fireplace in Biddie's drawing room there was a portrait of her grandmother that had been painted by Ingres(!) around 1830, judging from the gown and hairstyle. She was a dainty little redhead with a mischievous smile and a certain snap to her eyes. Biddie said her friend had been a redhead, too, and that at school, they'd been known as "Miss Cox's Red Foxes."

Biddie's mother burned the letters and, for the rest of her life, refused to speak of them. From time to time, however, she would caution Biddie that she must never, while summering in France, accept an invitation to Grotte Cachée.

"Sadly," Biddie told me, "no such invitation has ever come my way. How I envy you! You must tell me everything."

Now comes the part where I was warned about the demonic denizens and mysterious goings-on at Grotte Cachée. Biddie had a sort of mechanic/handyman working for her, a funny old bird named Eugène who insisted on testing my ability to handle her jaunty little lipstick-red Peugeot before he'd trust me with it. He made me motor around the local roads with him in the passenger seat while he held forth, not about driving, but about Grotte Cachée and why I should give it a wide berth.

There were forces in the very earth, he said, in the mountains looming over the secluded little valley, in the ancient stone with which the château had been built, that exercised an *"influence diabolique"* over any human unwise enough to set foot there. He said the force was like that of a magnet, that it exercised a different amount of pull on different people, but that no one was entirely immune. And there were beings (he called them "Follets") who made their home there and performed *"actes obscènes"* on visiting humans. They were incubi and succubi, he said, the sexually voracious demons about which the Church had been warning the faithful for centuries.

Well, it was all I could do to keep that little car on the road. I bit the inside of my lip so hard that it was actually swollen for the rest of the day. He told me the only way to kill most demons was to burn them, which made them virtually immortal, and that the same four demons had lived in that valley for centuries. Three were the kind that violated humans, and in the most depraved ways imaginable. Of those, one was a female succubus who bewitched human men so as to drain their vital essence through sex. Another was, as you may have guessed from my last letter, a satyr. The third was a demon called a dusios who could change from male to female and back again in order to effect a *"transfert de sperme"* between specially chosen men and women, thus producing human progeny with supernatural abilities—although Eugène was careful to point out that dusii usually kept their male form and ravished women just to ravish them, because they were consumed by lust that returned as soon as they slaked it. The fourth dwelled deep in the cave so as to avoid contact with people, because if he touched a human, he was compelled to turn their deepest desires into reality. This particular demon, Eugène said, could transform himself into a cat or a bird, or even make himself invisible.

I asked him how he knew all this, and he told me that his brother Alain had worked as a guard in the château's gatehouse for many years. Like all Grotte Cachée employees, Alain had been sworn to secrecy about what he saw and heard there, in return for which he received a ridiculously huge salary and retirement pension. Alain had always been irreligious, but when he was dying, Eugène brought him back to the true faith. Flush with his newfound piety, Alain told his brother everything before passing on. Eugène went all the way to the archbishop in his quest to have the demons exorcised from Grotte Cachée, but he was dismissed as a loony old fanatic.

I thanked him for his advice, but told him it was very important that I make the trip. I did say I'd keep an eye out for demons. He told me they were more beautiful than ordinary mortals, the better to captivate and seduce their human prey. And he begged me to remember, when I turned in at night, to lock not just my bedchamber door, but every window in the room, even if I was at the very top of one of the towers. He said the demons' insatiable lust maddened them and gave them extraordinary strength, and that the dusios in particular would climb the castle walls to get to sleeping humans.

What with rutted dirt roads, a top speed of forty-five kilometers per hour, and hordes of geese and sheep to contend with, it took me over five hours the next day to drive to Grotte Cachée. All the while, I prayed that the rain clouds gathering overhead would hold off until I got there. Although you're FAR TOO YOUNG TO REMEMBER, those early autos were sans windshield or top.

Luckily, I arrived just as I felt the first few pinpricks of rain. The château was so deep in the lushly vegetated valley, and so dark (having been constructed, I later found out, of volcanic stone), that I doubt someone flying an airplane overhead would even notice it. It was a rectangular castle with a courtyard in the center, a round tower on each corner, and a shorter, squarish one in the middle of each range, that in the front range being the gate tower. As I pulled up in front of it, a gigantic guard came out and crossed a drawbridge over a deep, wide ditch that had probably been a moat at one time.

"*Bonjour, mademoiselle,*" he said as he approached the car. "*Êtes-vous perdu?*"

I handed him the little card and told him no, I wasn't lost, that Mr. Archer had invited me. He informed me that Mr. Archer was in India at present, and that their current houseguests would be departing the next day, but that I was welcome to remain as their guest until Mr. Archer's return. He said the housekeeper, Madame Gauvin, would have a room prepared for me, and that he would call for a driver to take the car to the carriage house. I didn't want to leave it waiting in the rain, though, so I told him I would take it there myself, but that I would appreciate it if someone could fetch my luggage.

The carriage house, which was tucked away in the woods next to the stable, was the largest one I've ever seen, a long, narrow stone building (of lava, like the castle) with about a dozen bays. The bays were open, rather than being walled off separately, so that as I pulled the car into an empty one, I could see the other automobiles and carriages parked to either side.

I had shucked off my driving goggles and was pinning on an uncharacteristically chic black picture hat with silken bows and ostrich feathers that I'd bought especially for my reunion with Hickley, when a subtle movement from within a carriage about five or six bays to the right caught my eye. It was a gleaming landau with a glass window on either side of the passenger section. Through the window facing me, I saw a young man in shirtsleeves with slightly mussed brown hair sitting with his head thrown back, eyes closed. I might have thought he was asleep, except that his chest was moving as if he were trying to catch his breath. He looked pained, and I thought, I've got to help him, but then he lifted his head and said something, looking down. I couldn't hear what he was saying, but I realized he wasn't alone. Perhaps, I thought, there was a woman lying with her head in his lap—those landaus were pretty roomy inside. (Do stop laughing, Rèmy, or I won't go on.)

The young man threw his head back, grimacing. His

back arched, and he shuddered for several long seconds before he slumped back down. By this time, I'd figured out that there was, indeed, a woman in there with him, and that she must have just brought him off by hand. (I said don't laugh!)

He looked down again, heavy-lidded and smiling contentedly, and said something else. A blond head appeared.

It was another young man.

I stuck a hatpin into my finger.

The blond man leaned forward for a kiss, then turned to sit back on the seat, which was when he saw me. He said something to his companion, who looked in my direction with wide-eyed panic.

I mouthed, "I'm sorry," as I stumbled from the car and fled from the carriage house, my car coat flapping behind me. I was about fifty yards down the gravel path when I heard a voice from behind me call out, *"Mademoiselle!"*

The brown-haired young man was jogging toward me, hurriedly shrugging on his coat.

"I'm so sorry," I said, backing up with my hands raised. *"Je suis désolée."*

Hearing my accent, he said in breathless English, "You are *américaine?*"

I nodded. "I'm Emily Townsend. I'm a friend of Mr. Archer's. He invited me here, but he's not here, but I know someone else who's here, and that's why I—"

"Please, *Mademoiselle,*" he said, putting a thankful end to my idiotic babbling. He struck me as so young and vulnerable, standing there hatless in the rain with his hair plastered to his forehead. "I beg you, what you saw..." He looked toward the carriage house, where the blond man stood just inside the first bay, watching us as he lit a cigarette.

I said, "It's really none of my—"

"If my father were to find out..." he began. "He mustn't. Please, I beg you not to say anything to him—to anyone."

"Who is your father?" I asked.

"He is Émile Morel, Seigneur des Ombres. I am Claude Morel. If he knew..." He shook his head desolately, raindrops coursing down his face like tears.

I said, "I won't tell him. I promise."

He nodded thoughtfully. "I believe you. You have a sapphire radiance about you."

"I've never even met your father," I said. "I'm here at the invitation of Mr. Archer."

Looking alarmed, Claude said, "He mustn't find out either."

"Kit wouldn't judge you." There were two men who attended Mrs. Chalmers's salons, a *Harper's Weekly* editor and a playwright, who were known to be lovers. And there was a female poet who smoked a pipe and dressed in men's clothes. No one, including Kit, seemed to think anything of it, although I was probably the only one who hadn't realized that homosexuals expressed their love physically. It had simply never occurred to me that two people of the same sex might be moved to kiss, much less make love.

"He might not judge me, but he would have to tell my father, because if I don't provide an heir..." Claude pushed the wet hair out of his eyes. "It is unthinkable."

I asked him how old he was.

"Eighteen."

"You're young," I said. "Perhaps, by the time you're ready to marry and have children, you'll have outgrown this, this attraction to other—"

"No," he said bleakly. "I won't have."

I assured him that I would keep his secret, whereupon he returned to the carriage house and I continued on to the château. It was raining harder by the time I entered the courtyard, but I could make out six or seven naked people of both sexes cavorting in the pool of a large central fountain. One, a young woman, was dancing around with arms outstretched, her face turned to the sky. A tall man knelt behind a woman who was bent over the pool's stone rim, his hands around her waist. His dark blond hair was so long that I would have taken him for a swish had I not seen his hips pumping and realized, with a fair degree of shock, that they were fornicating—and in a manner I'd thought to be the exclusive domain of animals. More curious still was that, as he coupled with the one woman, he was kissing another, one with black hair who knelt in the water next to him, lightly stroking his back.

A man with dark, curly hair stood on the base of the fountain's central column (which supported a sculpture of a couple going at it, by the way), one hand gripping a bottle, the other the head of the woman who stood before him. The rain made it difficult to see exactly what was going on, but it was clear that her face was at the level of his private parts, the implications of which I didn't want to ponder. Another man stood behind her, hips churning. A dark tail-like object seemed to be sticking out of his rear end. It was hard to make it out, given the rain and my utter stupefaction. So these were the "indecorous goings-on" that Kit had warned me about, I thought, marveling at his typically British knack for understatement.

I took this all in with a curious sense of detachment, almost as if it were one of those dreams where you know you're dreaming, so you become more or less an observer of the surreal. I'd been in a slightly off-kilter state of mind ever since I parked the car. I remember thinking, *Maybe Eugène was right about the magnetic force in this valley.*

The dark-haired man on the column saw me as he took a swig from the bottle, and gave me a delightfully boyish smile, the first of many that he would direct my way, for this was Inigo. *"Ah, une beauté! Joignez-vous donc à nous!"*

With a frantic shake of my head, I turned and scurried into the castle through the nearest doorway, the invitation to join them echoing in my mind.

I found myself in a great hall that looked like something out of a painting. It was cavernous and opulent, with Renaissance tapestries hanging above carved oak wainscoting. Such halls usually have a rather forbidding quality, Sunny's cartoonishly regal Blenheim Palace being a case in point, but this one felt warm and appealing. Perhaps it was the comfortably modern furnishings, but it was quite an inviting room—or it would have been were it not for the gagged and blindfolded woman (naked, of course) dangling from the ceiling by means of chains attached to the fleece-lined leather straps around her wrists and ankles. She was hanging faceup at about the height of the little table next to her, with legs widespread to display her oil-sheened gash. On the table sat a fat, unlit candle, a black marble statuette, a carrot, a squash... You get the idea. Around her neck was a sign that read FUCK ME or FRIG ME.

"My God!" Pulling down the gag and blindfold, I said, "I'll get you down from there."

"The hell you will," she said in a refined British accent. "Do you realize how long it took them to get me like this?"

"You *want* this?"

She stared at me incredulously. "What *is* that bloody thing on your head?"

I patted the hat to find the enormous brim sodden and drooping, with the wet, ratty ostrich feathers hanging limply over the edge.

"Are you going to frig me or not?" the woman asked.

Taking a step back, I said, "Um, perhaps some other time. I'm looking for my fiancé."

"And that would be...?"

"Randolph Lytton, Baron of Hickley."

Brightening, she said, "You're Randy's Yanky Banky? Bloody excellent to meet you. I'm Frances Caddingdon, but you must call me Fanny."

I recognized the name—in fact, I thought I might even have met her in passing a couple of years before at the Royal Opera House. She was *Lady* Caddingdon, a marchioness.

Fanny told me I'd find Hickley in the dining room, gave me directions, and asked me to replace the gag and blindfold.

You already know the little tableau I encountered in the dining room. When he became aware of my presence, my betrothed paused in his humping, extracted his face from the brunette's snatch, and said, "Miss Townsend?" (No, we had not yet progressed to first names.) "I say, is that you?"

I replied that it was, since I could think of absolutely nothing else to say.

Frowning in bewilderment, he said, "What the devil have you got on your head?"

And with that, *chéri,* I must bring this marathon missive to a close, because my hand is cramping up (impending old age, you know) and Kitty has just come to wheel me into the dining room for dinner. She says to tell you she's blowing you a kiss, and that I must write the following or she'll withhold my postprandial moonshine: "Keep on Em about the marriage thing. She'll cave sooner or later, because she really is crazy about you."

She's right on one count.

    Je t'aime à la folie,
    Em

Three

YOU'LL THANK US *for this, my dear,"* said Lady L——, *tying Emmeline's hands behind her as her maid, the robust Fanny, gripped her snugly about the waist.*

"Unhand me this instant, you shameless hussies!" Emmeline demanded as the women pushed her down onto a silk-upholstered footstool, yanking her legs indecently wide so as to lash her feet to its two front legs.

"Prudery such as yours only brings misery and fits of hysteria," explained her ladyship as she gagged Emmeline with the waist sash of her own daisy-sprigged frock. "You are overdue for an education in the ways of the flesh."

She whipped aside the curtain over what Emmeline had taken to be a window in the dark little room. It was, indeed, a sheet of glass, however the view it afforded was not to the outdoors, but into a room the existence of which Emmeline had been entirely unaware until that moment.

"We call this the Ruttery," Lady L—— announced.

It was a windowless but bright chamber, thanks to the light from electric sconces reflecting off white walls hung with tapestries depicting acts of unspeakable licentiousness. Some of the furnishings appeared to be of unfamiliar and cunning design, but Emmeline's gaze was drawn to the naked beauty hanging faceup from the ceiling by means of golden chains attached to her outstretched arms and legs. She was not just gagged, as was Emmeline, but blindfolded as well, and at the perfect height to be ravished by a standing man, which was, in fact, precisely the activity that was transpiring at that very moment.

The gentleman in question was naked but for one peculiarity; sprouting from his nether orifice was what appeared to be a tail of black horsehair. Behind him stood a woman in a black corset, black opera gloves, and tall boots, whipping him on his rear with a riding crop and shrieking, "Harder, you puny gelding! Ram it in! Pound the wench!"

Nor were these three the only debauchers making use of the Ruttery that evening. What Emmeline had taken for a life-size bas relief sculpture of a man on the back wall was, upon closer inspection, an actual man affixed to the wall by means of a coating of plaster. The only exposed parts of him were his nose, his mouth, and his groin, which appeared to have been shaved and painted white. A woman in a severe black dress stood before him, trailing a raven's feather over his turgid manhood and the bulbous sac beneath it as he emitted a low, quavering moan.

In a corner stood something like a tall, leather-cushioned sawhorse, on which a young woman lay facedown with her limbs strapped to the splayed legs of the curious bench and her *skirts thrown up. Behind her, facing Emmeline's direction, stood a dapper man in a black mask made of something hard and shiny, like lacquer, but Emmeline recognized him from his well-oiled reddish hair as Lord Hardwyck, her betrothed. He was having carnal relations with the tethered woman dogways, giving her a smart spank on her pink-stained bottom with each snapping thrust. All the while, he was staring across the room at Emmeline, a lewdly sinister glint in his eye.*

"He can't actually see you," said Lady L——. "What he's looking at is himself giving it to Philomena Quimsby. It is a mirror on one side, and a window on the . . . Oh bloody hell, not again," she groaned as Emmeline, overcome, as you can well imagine, by the indecency she was being forced to witness, slumped into a faint.

Yanking Emmeline's head up by her tidy bun, her ladyship gave her captive two revivifying slaps across the face. "Stay awake and learn something, you little twit. Come, Fanny," she said as she swept from the room.

Oh, dear Reader, the things our innocent Emmeline learned that evening. The strangest sensations arose within her as she watched her fellow houseguests disporting themselves in the Ruttery, sensations she'd never experienced until that moment. Her heartbeat quickened, along with her breath, and the rosy tips of her bosom grew oddly stiff. Most curious, and disconcerting, was the tingling heat pooling at the juncture of her thighs, which felt damp for reasons she couldn't begin to imagine. Her sex was consumed by a strangely delicious itch, prompting her to press that part of herself repeatedly against the footstool in an effort to assuage it, yet it only got worse, maddeningly so.

"Darling Emmeline. What the devil . . ."

She turned to see her only real friend in this place, the hand-some, gentle Tobias, entering the dim little anteroom.

"Are you all right?" he asked as he untied her gag.

"I don't know!" she cried. "They . . . they tied me up and left me here, and now I feel so . . . so . . . Oh, Tobias." Shaking with the urge to sob and scream, she wondered if this was what they meant by hysteria. "What is happening to me?"

He glanced into the Ruttery, nodded to himself, and knelt before her, saying, "I think I know. And I think perhaps I can help you."

"You . . . you do?" she asked, not even caring, as he slipped a hand beneath her skirt, that he had not yet offered to untie her.

❧

February 2, 1922
Steamboat Springs, Colorado

My darling, foolish Rèmy,

First: I happen to like parentheses (except in fiction), and I have no intention of giving them up just because you find them "syntactically sloppy."

Second: Your assurance that I am far from plain, that I am in fact, "the very model of lissome female perfection," is very sweet and very much appreciated, but not really necessary now that looks like mine have become, in recent years, all the rage. Looking back, I'm actually glad that I came of age feeling like an ugly duckling. It's good to be plain when you're young, I've decided. It builds character.

Third: No, I did not do it with Nils, and no, I'm not lying about it to spare your feelings. It really was just a dream. My God, he's twenty! For one thing. For another, if you honestly think nookie's on the agenda for me in my present condition, it's because you haven't seen me, propped up in my wheelchair with my casts and my afghan and my sad, sad hair. A crisp little bob like this has to be trimmed regularly, or it looks like hell, and I was due for a haircut even before I came here. My bangs have gotten so long I've had to pin them to the side, imparting an insouciant Appalachian aura that should ensure my complete fidelity until I see you next.

Not that fidelity is an issue with us, but you know what I mean. And just for the record, because this Nils thing seems to have really gotten under your skin, in the year that we've been together, I haven't yet actually exercised my option to sleep with anyone else. I still, however, consider that option to be fully in effect, which is why I'm frankly a little surprised by your jealous horror at the notion that I might have spread these crippled old gams for Nils. Just because we haven't taken advantage of our right to see other people doesn't mean that right has disappeared.

I should say, just because *I* haven't taken advantage of that right. We never discussed the whole disclosure question, in other words whether we would tell each other about our conquests outside of our relationship. But now that the subject has arisen (and I suppose it's easier to discuss it in a letter than face-to-face), perhaps we should both come clean. Or rather, since I've already done so, perhaps it's your turn. Please don't think I'm going to throw some kind of bourgeois tantrum if you tell me you've gotten some tail here and there. This whole free love thing was my idea, after all, and I should hope I'm not that much of a hypocrite. If I wanted to keep you on a short leash, I'd marry you.

About that: your argument that I could be a "real stepmother" to Jules and Inès if we were husband and wife doesn't really hold water. Jules is eleven, Inès is nine. They know I'm not their mother. They live with her. They only see me when they visit you. It's not as if they're going to suddenly start calling me *Mère* if you put a ring on my finger, nor would I want them to. I much prefer being the eccentric, beloved aunt-like figure. It's a role I've perfected with Kitty, and one that suits me to a T. I love your children so much, Rèmy, and we have such a warm, comfortable relationship. It's perfect as it is. I mean honestly, sweetheart. Don't you think you're clutching at straws?

Moving on, it tickles me to report that Kitty and Nils have a little necking session every time he drops off the mail. Ah, to be sixteen again. Except that they're twenty-one and twenty, respectively, a bit long in the tooth, methinks, to be stalled out at the osculation stage. The problem, of course, is the torch Nils is carrying for this church girl, combined with his conviction, all too common among well-brought-up young men, that if you like and respect a woman, it's hands off. Women encourage this behavior, of course, for reasons quite beyond my ken. Yes, I know, I'm a fine one to talk, having held on to my virginity till twenty-four, but times were different then. Kitty has had a diaphragm since she was nineteen. I know—I took her to get it.

Speaking of my virginity, and this serialized account of how I lost it, your reaction to that whole Claude-getting-head-in-the-landau scene really threw me for a loop. For you to say you felt "emotionally ambushed" because the fellatrix turned out to be a fellator strikes me as just a tad melodramatic, not to mention antediluvian.

Have you forgotten that blue movie we watched with Margaux and Denis in your office at *Pathé-Cinéma* last summer after everyone had gone home? The one where the man discovers the housemaid diddling herself with the vacuum cleaner hose, so he calls the wife in for a little ménage? You told me those two women going down on each other was the hottest thing you'd ever seen, and I well believe it, given how, the moment we were alone, you shoved me to my knees, pulled out your cock, and growled, *"Suce-le."* I get wet just remembering how brutish and commanding you were. When you told me to stop sucking you and bend over the desk, I came without even being touched, the only time in my life that's ever happened to me (awake). If you recall, I had an unbroken string of screaming Os while you were hammering away inside me—plus a couple more when you pulled the car into that alley on the way home, hauled me onto your lap, and drilled me again. You are by far the sexiest man I've ever known, and the most uninhibited lover. I can't believe how lucky I was to find you.

But I'm digressing into sappiness. The reason I brought up that movie is that I don't understand, if you have no objection to watching a woman eat another woman, why it's "disturbing and unpleasant" when it's two men. Are you afraid you'll get an itch in the old *pénis* and have to ponder the implications? Just asking, because I find it perplexing that a man as open-minded as you should exhibit such a pedestrian reaction.

Now, back to this week's installment of *Emily's Adventures at the Château, Partie Deux.*

Hickley and I had the expected confrontation later that afternoon, when he tracked me down and found me weeping in the library. Or rather, I confronted him, while he mostly just stood there looking bewildered by this strange and unfamiliar liquid leaking from my eyes. I had to yell to be heard over the drumming of rain on the roof, because the library, which Kit told me he'd completely redesigned, soared up three stories, with a wide, stack-filled gallery halfway up the front wall. It was the most extravagant and well-stocked private library I've ever seen.

I accused Hickley of faithlessness, perversity, and fraud, that last for having led me to think he cared about me, when all he really cared about was my father's two million dollars. I said he'd manipulated me into believing that ours would be a marriage of the heart, when it was really just another business transaction between a greedy British lord and a gullible American heiress. I yanked off that sapphire ring and threw it at his head, which was when I think he truly grasped the depth of my fury and its implications for him: the Yanky Banky

(I had figured it out) had informed him that his business was no longer welcome.

His demeanor changed then, mild bemusement giving way to a distress that seemed entirely genuine, and probably was—but not for the reasons he led me to believe. He started shoveling it hard and fast, swore he'd never considered our engagement a business transaction, in fact, he cared for me far more than he'd let on, but he'd been afraid to declare himself because we'd only known each other such a short time, and he was sure I couldn't have fallen in love with him as quickly as he'd fallen in love with me, and oh, if I would only give him a second chance...

I told him I wasn't buying it. If he loved me, there would have been more than that one little dry peck back in New York. "I know I'm not beautiful, but if you love a woman, don't you want to...express that love with more than words?"

Hickley told me he was mad about me, but that he'd been keeping himself on a tight rein lest he get carried away and overstep himself. He said all men had needs, but that a true gentleman wouldn't dream of compromising the innocence and reputation of his fiancée. That was why he, like every other bachelor of his acquaintance, relieved his lust with "baggage one never has to see again." (Note that he did not contradict me on the subject of my lack of beauty.)

As for the accusation of perversity, he maintained that I was only shocked by what I saw because Americans are so straightlaced compared to Europeans. Enlightened though I was, he said, my culture had never prepared me for the prospect of anything other than "doing one's wifely duty with the lights off and the nightgown on." So, of course, being a typically guileless, uninformed American girl, I would naturally find the more creative forms of lovemaking repulsive.

Well, of course, I was mortified by being lumped in with the common herd, which was undoubtedly his intention, but having never been exposed to so smooth a schemer, I didn't figure that out until later. I lied and claimed I wasn't repulsed at all, when, in fact, the cunnilingus had appalled me and I hadn't known what to make of the whipping. I said I was just "taken aback a bit" and disappointed by his infidelity. And then, God help me, I told him that I now understood and appreciated why he'd held himself back with me, but that it really hadn't been necessary, since I was anything but straightlaced.

Well, now he was pretty sure he had me, and I'm ashamed to admit that I was questioning my earlier resolve to end the engagement. The bastard actually got down on one knee, took my hands, and told me he'd never been in love before, never even had a real relationship, and couldn't bear the thought of losing me. Since it troubled me to think of him with other women, he promised to "be an absolute monk" until the wedding. As for afterward, he assured me that our "marital relations" would be only as adventuresome as I wished them to be.

I told him I'd always considered myself adventurous.

"I may not know much about such matters at present, but I assure you I have an open mind and am willing to learn—if and when the time comes."

Well, that was all he needed to hear. He jumped up, crossed to the far corner of the library, slid out a book, and brought it back. "They've got an outstanding little collection of bawdy literature here, but this one's my favorite. You might find it instructive, that is if you're willing to read this sort of thing."

I took it, saying, "I'm not much for self-censorship," although, of course, I had never read such literature in my life. The book was the first volume of *My Secret Life* by "Walter." He told me it would teach me a great deal about the sexual inclinations of men. "It can only benefit our marriage."

Hickley tried to get me to take back the ring, but I told him I'd have to think about it—a decision for which I've thanked myself ever since, as it allowed me to salvage some small shred of dignity out of the humiliating episode. He told me that he and his friends would be leaving the next morning for the French Alps, but that they'd be coming back that way in a few days, and that he hoped I would be "in a suitable frame of mind to accept the ring" then. I said I'd be gone by then, weather permitting. (As it happened, I wasn't, but not because of the weather.) I resisted his attempt to kiss me good-bye, which caused him to walk away looking like a whipped puppy.

The housekeeper told me that my luggage had been left in *la Chambre Rouge,* a bedchamber on the second floor of the castle's east range. To get there, I had to climb the winding stone staircase in the southeast tower.

As I did so, *My Secret Life* in hand, an elegantly attired couple dashed up the stairs from behind, pushing past me with a breathless apology.

"Oh, it's Randy's Yank," said the woman over her shoulder as she paused a few steps above me. It was "Fuck Me or Frig Me" Fanny. "Do join us. I hear Lucinda Mumford's upstairs hitting the slit in the Boudoir."

Having no idea what that meant, but filled with curiosity, I followed them to the top of the tower. As soon as I stepped onto the landing, I knew that I'd entered a special place. I'll describe it as best I can. The tower was round and quite large, its thick outer stone wall perforated with arrow slits. The lower levels were comprised of one or more stone-walled rooms, sometimes pentagonal or otherwise strangely shaped in order to fit into the circular space. On this top level, however, there was just one round room somewhat smaller in circumference than the tower itself, leaving a sort of corridor about six feet wide all around the outside of it that was furnished with couches and chaise longues.

The round room looked to be of newer construction than most of the rest of the castle, judging from its exterior walls, which were darkly paneled, but with a tall window every few feet. Through these windows could be seen the interior room, the walls of which were papered in apricot watered silk and lined with gilt-framed full-length mirrors. In the center of this strange "Boudoir," suffused with afternoon sunshine from skylights in the conical roof, stood a large four-poster bed. On the bed lay a beautiful young woman in a black satin gown and glittering jewels, masturbating.

She lay on her stomach with her skirts bunched around her waist in a great froth of black petticoats and her ruffled drawers, also black, pulled down to the tops of her stockings. The only exposed part of her was her ass, which I recall as looking like smooth white marble against all that black. Her hips were slowly rocking, and I saw that she had one arm beneath her, moving rhythmically. Her mouth was open, her eyes heavy-lidded, dreamy. Through the glass, I could hear her shuddery breathing, and I remember thinking, *My God, this is real. She's really diddling herself, and I'm really watching.*

Fanny and her companion reclined on a leather couch against the wall in the semidarkness of the outer corridor, she unbuttoning his trousers as he worked his hand under her skirt, both of them staring into the round room. I heard stertorous breathing and low voices from elsewhere in the corridor, and realized they weren't the only couple enjoying this display. But how were we able to see into the room through what were obviously mirrors?

"They're transparent mirrors," whispered a man I hadn't realized was standing next to me.

He was incredibly good-looking in a sun-gilded Mediterranean way, with a mass of dark, curly hair and sweet, warm, molten chocolate eyes. There was a frankness in his expression and demeanor, an openness, that was utterly disarming. It was the man from the fountain, the one who'd called me a beauty and asked me to join them. Hearing him speak English with an American accent tickled a memory I couldn't quite call up. I had the sense that I'd met him before, or at least seen him, but not there.

"A Russian fellow installed them for us a few months ago," he said as he raised a wine bottle to his mouth.

"Us?"

"Well, he installed them for Seigneur des Ombres. I'm really just a...long-term tenant, you might say." Gesturing toward the mirrors with the bottle, he said, "They're half-silvered, so that if you're looking into a brightly lit room from a darker room, you can see in, but the people in the room can only see their reflections."

"Then she doesn't know she's being watched?" I whispered back. "That's horrible. That's..."

"Oh, she knows. Everyone knows what *le Boudoir des Miroirs* is about. There's a waiting list to use this room. You'd be surprised how many people harbor an exhibitionistic streak. It can be booked for the night, or for an 'afternoon nap,' like this. I'm Inigo, by the way." He extended his hand as nonchalantly as if we were meeting at some Fifth Avenue dinner party.

"Emily Townsend."

"I know."

"I'm sorry, have we met?"

"Not that I know. Fanny Caddingdon told me your name when I asked her who the pretty new girl was. I don't suppose you have any American cigarettes."

"Sorry, no."

A door on the other side of the "Boudoir of Mirrors" opened slowly and a man slipped in. He was around thirty, nice looking, but with a predatory glint in his eye. I felt a very real sense of alarm as he crossed stealthily to the bed.

Patting my back, Inigo said, "This is all part of what Lucinda was hoping for when she asked for this room."

"You mean, it's staged?"

"Oh, no. Once someone has booked *le Boudoir*, there's usually a bit of negotiating between the other guests as to which of them will pay the surprise visit, or which group, if that's the plan. But the person sleeping in the Boudoir has no idea who that might be. The uncertainty is part of the thrill. This fellow is Theodore Newton. He and Lucinda are Americans and former lovers, but I understand she turned him in for an older, richer model a couple of years ago. He's been trying to reignite the flame since they've been here, but she's been giving him the cold shoulder. I say, would you like to sit down?" He pointed to an empty chaise.

"Oh. No. No. I, um…"

"Just to sit," he said. "I didn't necessarily mean… you know."

Necessarily? "I don't mind standing."

Newton unbuttoned his trousers, withdrew his erection, and gave it a few firm strokes. I knew I should leave that instant, but I was riveted. I'd never seen a penis before, erect or not, and it was quite an eye-opener. I remember being surprised at how satin-smooth it was, with that glistening purple glans. He sucked three fingers into his mouth to moisten them and said, "A penny for your thoughts, Luce."

She gasped, but before she could react, he pressed a knee to the small of her back and pushed the fingers up her quiver. She shrieked and thrashed, giving him clumsy backward swats with her free hand, the other being pinioned beneath her.

"A penny's not enough?" he said as he worked his fingers around inside her. "No, I don't suppose it would be. But I can guess your thoughts from how wet you are. You must have been imagining all those rubies and emeralds and pearls you traded me in for. That's what gets you dripping, isn't it?"

"You son of a bitch!"

Unlatching one of her necklaces, a strand of diamonds with fat Baroque pearls at regular intervals, he said, "It's what you think about when you're lying there getting pegged with that shriveled up old tiddler. It's this you love." He shook the necklace in front of her face. "I'll bet you wish you could just fuck the jewelry and skip the middleman. Do you still love taking it in the ass?"

I gaped as he shoved the necklace into her rectum, forcing in one big, irregular pearl after another, until all that was visible was the clasp at the end of a little string of diamonds. It was lewdly beautiful, like jewelry for the derrière. He jiggled it. She sucked in a breath, hips trembling.

Still pinning her to the bed with his knee, he finger-fucked her while tugging and twitching the necklace. She moaned hoarsely.

"Teddy, you bastard," she breathed, thrusting faster, faster… "Cocksucker. Fucking prick…"

He took his knee away. She didn't even seem to notice. Just as she started to climax, he pulled out the necklace—pop-pop-pop-pop-pop…

She screamed and bucked as she came. As she was recovering, Teddy leaned in close and said softly, "Did he know I'd be here, Luce? Did you tell him I was the reason you were coming to France without him, that you were desperate to see me again, fuck me again, even if you're too proud to admit it?"

"N-no," she stammered as she struggled for breath. "God, no. If he finds out..." She shook her head.

With a look of triumph, Teddy flipped her over, tore off her drawers, and mounted her. He grabbed her hips and drove in—so forcefully that I let out a little squeak. He fucked her hard, grunting with each jolting thrust. She climaxed again, clawing at his back and moaning, "Oh, Teddy...Oh, God, how I've missed that big, hard cock. Deeper, Teddy, deeper..."

"Are you all right, Miss Townsend?" Inigo touched my arm.

I jumped. Just that light touch through my sleeve had given me a sexual spasm, that's how aroused I was by that point. "I have to go. It...it was a pleasure meeting you."

He called my name as I sprinted down the stairs, but I didn't slow down till I was behind the heavy oak door of *la Chambre Rouge*. Except for dinner, I pretty much kept to my room for the rest of the afternoon and evening. That night, I sat up for hours in my red velvet-draped bed reading *My Secret Life*. I found it deeply depressing, not because it was long-winded and banal, which it was, but because the sex was dirty, smelly, brutish, and vaguely scatological. And "Walter" himself struck me as both immature and rapacious, a despoiler who preyed upon women, including innocent virgins, with an utter lack of conscience.

Reasoning that an "outstanding collection of bawdy literature" should contain something more appealing, I went back down to the library in the middle of the night to see what else there was in that little corner. I discovered ten (count 'em, TEN) other volumes of *My Secret Life,* but I chose instead *The Autobiography of a Flea* by "Anonymous," because a brief skim revealed a refreshing dollop of wit mixed in with the hot, graphic sex.

On my way back to the second floor, I heard soft footsteps above me in the winding stone staircase. I hesitated, but curiosity got the better of me. I went upstairs more or less expecting to find other houseguests in the observation corridor surrounding *le Boudoir des Miroirs.* It was hard to tell, because it was dark as hell, but I appeared to be the only one there (it was, after all, the wee hours of the morning).

I could see through the transparent mirrors into the Boudoir itself, though not nearly as clearly as I had that afternoon, because the lighting conditions weren't ideal. According to Inigo, the mirrors worked best when looking from darkness into light, and the Boudoir was lit entirely by moonlight. There was plenty of it, given the skylights, but still, moonlight will provide only so much illumination.

My view was dim and a little hazy, as if I were looking at one of those out-of-focus Julia Cameron photos of which you are so inexplicably fond. I saw the big bed, on which a woman lay curled up on her side, clad—or half-clad—entirely in black leather: a wasp-waisted corset, gloves that came up all the way to her shoulders, and a hood that conformed to the contours of her head and neck, covering them completely. From my perspective (I was looking diagonally across the bed from the foot to the head), I could see that the hood laced up in back. I couldn't figure out how she could breathe through solid leather, but then I saw that it moved over the mouth with each breath she took, so I realized there must be a patch of something like black gauze there. I could tell she was fast asleep by the somnolent rise and fall of her chest, although I couldn't, and still can't, imagine falling asleep with something like that over my head.

I was wondering where the person was who had come up the stairs ahead of me when I noticed something move on the other side of the room, near the door. It was hard to see, both because of the distance and because the moonlight shone mostly in the center of the room, where the bed was, but I managed to make out a blurry figure standing there in a dark dressing gown. I assumed it was a man because of the height, probably about six feet, but then the gown slipped off and I saw slender, feminine contours, and realized it was a woman, albeit a tall one.

She dropped to the floor and sat on her haunches, very gracefully. I remember she put me in mind of a big, sleek jungle cat. Her eyes were closed, her mouth moving—although she was whispering too softly for me to hear through the glass. She clenched her teeth, trembling, then lowered her head, her hair spilling onto the floor in a gleaming bronze torrent. For a good minute or so she remained in that position, one hand braced on the floor, the other on her knee, back heaving. Finally she seemed to relax. She used an arm to flip her hair back as she rose to her feet.

I stepped closer to the glass and squinted. Although the figure was still indistinct, it was broad-shouldered, lean-hipped, and taller, maybe six and a half feet. This was no woman, although he still had hair that fell to the middle of his back. It was the blond man from the fountain, I realized, the one who'd been kissing one woman while screwing another.

I remember standing there with my mouth open, trying to make sense of what I'd just seen. Obviously, I couldn't help recalling Eugène's dusios, who could change from male to female and back again—not that I thought I was looking at a sex demon. I'd been feeling a little high ever since I got there. Remember the time we smoked hashish with Gertrude and Alice? It was kind of like that, as if I were watching a skewed version of reality from a slight distance. Given that, and the optical issues I was dealing with, I may very well have been mistaken in thinking I'd been looking at a woman before.

The man looked down and felt his genitals, not in a sexual way, but almost as if he were checking to make sure everything was where it was supposed to be. He rotated his shoulders, stretched his head from side to side, shook out his arms and legs, cracked his knuckles. Crouching down, he retrieved something from a pocket in the dressing gown, a ribbon or a piece of string, and used it to tie his hair back. And then he walked over to the bed and stood there looking down at the sleeping woman, who was facing away from him, in a way I can only describe as hungry.

I could see him better now. He was magnificent. Honestly, Rèmy, it was as if I were looking at a soft focus platinum print of a young god bathed in silvery moonlight. Sorry to wax so embarrassingly poetic, but he was literally breathtaking. He had an amazing face— radiant blue eyes beneath slashing eyebrows, an aquiline nose, a soft mouth. He would have been too pretty were it not for the geometric angles with which his jaw and chin had been carved. He was lean, but it was all muscle, every inch of him—including his cock, which rose and swelled as he stood looking at the woman, until it was standing almost straight up, shiny and hard. He stroked it very lightly with his fingertips, and it seemed to grow even longer and thicker. I was throbbing just looking at him.

He lowered himself onto the bed behind the woman and glided his hand lightly along her hip. She awoke with a start, but he stroked her reassuringly, whispering, "Shh," and she relaxed. She tried to roll toward him, but he pushed her back onto her side and untied the lacing that secured the hood.

When she realized what he was doing, she shook her head violently and tried to pry his hands away. He used his outside arm and leg to contain her struggles as he unlaced the hood and pulled it off, freeing a mass of beautiful, rippling auburn hair.

"Calm down," he said. "Calm down, Helen. It's Elic."

"*Elic?*" She tried to rise up, but he banded his arms

around her, saying, "Relax, Helen. It's all right. You'll see." He had a deep, pleasantly rough voice with a mild European accent I couldn't quite place.

Helen struggled and kicked, trying to free herself from his grip (with me panicking right along with her, wondering if this was a rape), until he stroked her forehead, murmuring something in a language that sounded Scandinavian. She relaxed completely then, her expression blissful as he stroked her between her legs. I have no idea what he said to her, but from that point on, she wasn't just willing, but enthusiastic.

Holding her tucked against him, spoon style, he squeezed the tip of his cock, producing a clear syrup that I thought, in my ignorance, must be semen, and spread it over the shaft. Now, of course, I realize he was lubricating it with pre-come. Rising up on an elbow, he took hold of his cock and tucked the head inside her, then closed his hand around her hip and pushed it all the way in. His expression, as he filled her, was utterly rapturous. He let out a groan that seemed to reverberate in my very womb.

He screwed her with long, steady strokes while reaching around to finger her clit. She was absolutely transported, moaning and clutching at the sheets. From where I stood, I had a pretty good view of the operative organs, and I found the sight of his hard, slick cock reaming her like a piston unbelievably arousing. I think I was breathing as hard as the two of them, and I was so wet that it was actually trickling a little down my inner thighs.

Helen came twice. As her second climax

approached, Elic raised himself up on an arm, I think to help him deepen his penetration. His entire body heaved with each sharp thrust, every muscle bulging and flexing. He stilled for a moment, then let out a series of ecstatic groans, hips pulsing. I could see his balls pumping as they emptied—fascinating! And incredibly exciting. The orgasm went on a good deal longer than I now know to be the norm. Toward the end, a creamy fluid that I realized was semen (although I recall it being thicker than normal semen) began to seep out of her.

When it was finally over, he sank back down onto the bed, breathless and spent. He lifted her great swath of gorgeous hair out of the way, tucked her up against him, and kissed the back of her neck very softly and tenderly, while whispering things I couldn't hear that made her smile. Gripping the base of his cock, he withdrew from her with apparent care. He was still semi-erect, and dripping come that looked like melted ice cream.

He sat her up to divest her of the corset and gloves, then laid her down again, suckling her breasts as he stroked his fist up and down his cock. Within seconds, he was fully erect and lifting her legs over his shoulders, this not five minutes after having withdrawn from her. Now, of course, I know this was unusual, but at the time I didn't realize that men needed a recovery period between orgasms. He fucked her a second time, again making her climax twice before he came. From all appearances, it was as powerful an orgasm as the first, though perhaps not quite as lengthy. And I didn't see any more semen, so he may have been tapped out, given how much he'd ejected the first time. A few minutes later, he guided her hand up and down his slightly waning erection to revitalize it, positioned her on her knees and elbows, and took her again.

Fine, Rèmy, don't believe me. I saw what I saw.

Or rather, I remember what I remember. Who knows if they're the same thing?

On that note, *mon chéri*, I must bid you *adieu*, because it's almost two in the morning, and I'm having a hard time keeping my eyes open. Please don't think I'm crazy for what I've just written. The only thing I'm crazy about is you.

> *Tu me manques,*
> Em

Four

EMMELINE SHRANK BACK *against the wall, trembling in awe and trepidation as Tobias's colossal man-root reared up like a proud, untamed stallion straining at its tethers.*

"Does it ... does it hurt?" she asked, staring with rapt fascination at the towering pillar of flesh.

"It aches for release, Emmeline. It aches for you."

February 9, 1922
Steamboat Springs, Colorado

Dear Rèmy,
    Your last letter was much appreciated, as always.

Loved your observations and wisecracks (so happy to have been able to provide you with "wanking material" in my absence), and I think you might be right about the power of suggestion as regards Elic. Eugène had put the idea of a dusios in my mind, so given my fatigue (it *was* the middle of the night) and the mild wooziness I'd felt since my arrival there, I imagined that the blurry shape I was seeing looked like a woman turning into a man. Makes perfect sense.

About your letter, there's something that's been niggling at me ever since I read it (and reread it about a dozen times). It has to do with this whole disclosure business as regards our playmates, if any, since we've been together. I think I was admirably forthcoming in telling you there'd been no one else, especially considering I didn't owe you that information, that I just volunteered it out of concern for your feelings. Given that, I don't for one moment think I was out of line in asking you to reciprocate in kind. For you to say that you don't owe me either fidelity or an accounting of your infidelities because we're not man and wife strikes me as surprisingly cold (really quite unlike you, Rèmy) and transparently conniving.

If you think I'm going to marry you just to find out whether you've screwed anyone else in the past year, you don't know me very well. It's not as if it's even that important to me. I've already told you—I've *always* told you—that we're both adults and may do as we please. I don't care if you've slept around. That's not the reason I'm ~~so ups~~ bringing this up. I care that you're being coy and calculating when I was so open and honest, and that you're trying to punish me when all I wanted was for you to show me the same consideration that I showed you, not because it's an obligation, but out of love.

Anyway, I just wanted to get that off my chest. I'm not dwelling on it, so if it seems like I am, I just want you to know I'm not. ~~I just can't help thinking that if you really~~ It doesn't matter. It's not important. If you don't want to tell me, don't tell me.

Anyway, on to *Emily's Adventures.*

When last we saw our plucky heroine, she was observing a marathon shagging session between Elic and Helen. I don't know how many more times they did it that night. I left in the middle of the third act, went back to my room, ran a hot bath, and gave myself three or four ferocious orgasms while recalling what I'd just seen.

I slept till ten the next morning, having been up half the night. I probably would have slept even later, but I was awakened by a knock at my bedroom door. I assumed it was Hickley wanting to say good-bye, but I was groggy and in my nightgown, and I really didn't want to speak to him again until I'd had a chance to think things through, so I didn't invite him in.

I'd been hoping the weather would have cleared so that I could drive back to Lyon, but rain was still battering the windows, so it didn't look good. Unable to get back to sleep, I dressed, grabbed *My Secret Life* and *The Autobiography of a Flea* (which I hadn't even started yet), and headed downstairs to the library to spend the day reading.

The library was at the front of the castle, with French doors leading to a ground-floor balcony overlooking the gravel driveway. The departing guests stood under black umbrellas next to a queue of waiting carriages. I recognized Hickley and stepped behind the velvet drapes, peeking through a gap between them.

He was chatting with a couple standing beneath a single umbrella, and whatever he was saying seemed to amuse them enormously. At one point, he made a circular gesture around his head, as if to suggest a large hat, then pretended to yank down on its brim as he pouted forlornly with big, cow-like eyes. His friends roared with laughter.

I felt like I'd been kicked in the stomach.

A woman in a tarty yellow-striped dress with an enormous bustle ran from the gatehouse to the protection of Hickley's umbrella, lifting her skirt with one hand and holding her hat down with the other. I recognized her as the dark-haired vamp he'd been tonguing when I interrupted his little threesome the day before, the one who'd been whipping him with the riding crop and ordering him to fuck the blonde harder. Hickley pulled her close and gave her a good, long kiss.

I shook my head, whispering, "You son of a bitch."

"Who?"

I wheeled around to discover Inigo smiling at me over the back of a leather couch in the middle of the room.

"How do you always manage to sneak up on me like that?" I asked.

"It's a skill I've cultivated in order to watch people unawares and listen in on their conversations."

"Are you serious?"

"Rarely." Shifting his gaze to the window, he said, "So, which one is the son of a bitch?"

I sighed. "Randolph Lytton, Baron of Hickley."

"Ah, Randy Randy. What an excellent judge of character you are, Miss Townsend."

I invited him to call me Emily. "I say, who is that woman under the umbrella with him?"

Squinting, he said, "That's Priscilla Brisbane," as if it were blatantly obvious.

"Who?"

"You know Randy, but you don't know his mistress? I've only just met them—they'd never visited before—but I'm told they've been together for four years, that they're never seen apart, and that he would marry her in a heartbeat if she weren't an actress with no name and no money. Have I said something funny?"

I realized I was laughing, not ha-ha laughing, but that kind of bitter, exhausted chuckling that sometimes comes out of you when you're just too far gone for tears. I told him I was just a little giddy from not having slept well.

Outside, a coachman took a lady's umbrella as he handed her up into a landau, the one that had been the scene of Claude Morel's little tryst out in the carriage house the day before. The lady was Helen, whom Elic had so thoroughly rousted in *le Boudoir des Miroirs* the night before. She was smiling, as well she might have been.

I asked Inigo if he knew who she was, and he said sure, he was always briefed on the visitors who came to Grotte Cachée. He told me her name was Helen

Forrester, and that she'd come there in the hope of getting pregnant. Her husband was evidently sterile (she was fairly sure it was he, and not she, because his first marriage had produced no offspring, either). She was desperate for a baby, but she balked at taking a lover for this purpose, not only because she loved her husband, but because she wanted her child to be of Forrester blood. She found out that her husband's estranged brother, a Don Juan named Cyrus Forrester, would be visiting Grotte Cachée, so she followed him there in the hope of convincing him to father a child on her. A lecher he may have been, and a leather fetishist as she soon discovered, but he had too much honor to cuckold his brother, estranged or no. Helen's tears and entreaties fell on deaf ears, so she was in despair of remaining childless—until she learned that a woman named Cassandra had booked an overnight stay in *le Boudoir*, and that Cyrus intended to pay her a visit. Helen somehow convinced Cassandra to let her take her place, which she did, wearing the hood so as to disguise her identity.

"She looks pretty happy," Inigo said, "so the little ruse must have worked. Here's hoping it bears fruit." He lifted a cup as if in a toast, then said, "I'm being even ruder than normal. I've brought a pot of java. Would you like some?"

"Please."

Inigo patted the couch next to him and poured me a cup, offering to spike it with brandy, like his, but I declined. As I settled down next to him, taking care to tuck my two dirty books under my skirt, I considered and rejected the notion of telling him what I'd seen in *le Boudoir* the night before. Mostly I didn't want him to know what a snoop and voyeur I was. And how could I tell him that it looked as if Elic might have switched genders, something a crazy old handyman had told me certain demons did in order to achieve a *"transfert de sperme"* between a human couple?

Instead, I inanely complimented the coffee, telling him it was the best I'd had since leaving the States. I asked him if he was from New York, because he sounded as if he was.

He said, "Not originally, but I love New York, and I have a house there. Well, we share it, but—"

"We?"

"I live here with some friends—in addition to the Archers, of course, and *le seigneur* and his son. Elic and Lili travel sometimes, but rarely to New York, so I think of the house as mine. We have another house in Paris, and that's where they usually go when they want to trade the country for the city."

"Paris is my favorite city in the world," I said. "I'd give anything to live there." I told him I knew who Elic was, but I wasn't sure about Lili.

"Long dark hair, very exotic looking. She and Elic are devoted to each other."

I wasn't sure how to respond to that.

Inigo said, "You're wondering why you've seen them with other people. It's because Elic can't . . . Well, it's complicated, but they can't make love to each other."

I didn't question that, not wanting to display my naïveté, but I must have looked puzzled, because he said,

"When I say, 'make love,' I'm talking about actual, you know…intercourse. They can do other things. Or rather, he can do things to her, but it doesn't work the other way. I'm saying too much. You're confused, and I can't… Archer's always telling me to keep my big…" He sighed and shook his head. "Sorry. I get a little too talkative sometimes."

I've wondered ever since why a man who wasn't impotent should be unable to have sex with just one specific woman. "Must they sleep with other people?" I asked. "Can't they just…do without?"

Inigo smiled and shook his head. "I'm afraid that wouldn't be possible."

I was about to question that when, in a conversational backtrack, he told me that although he kept a house in New York and sounded American, he wasn't. He said people often speculated on his origins, and that he was frequently accused of having gypsy blood, for some reason, but that he was actually born in Santorini. I said I knew all about Santorini. It was the Greek island cluster that Kit Archer had identified in his novel as being the real Atlantis. Inigo told me he'd helped Kit with his research.

Inigo said he'd been born Inignacios, which had been Latinized to Ignatius when he lived in Rome, and then to Inigo when he made his home among the Basques on the border of France and Spain. I asked where his house in New York was, and he said, "Greenwich Village—the East Village."

"Oh, my word," I said. "That's where I know you from. I saw you once. It was just in passing, but I know it was you. You were leaving Bertha Chalmers's brownstone just as I was walking up the front steps. You tipped your hat and smiled as you held the door open for me." That smile had made me weak in the knees (you had to see it to understand) but of course I didn't tell him that.

"You know Bertha?"

"I attend her literary salons. That's where I met Kit. How do you know her?"

"She spent a week or so here a while back when she was traveling through Europe. Ah, Bertha. She had it all—wit, beauty..." He looked off with this dreamily carnal smile, shaking his head a little, as if she still held him in her sexual thrall.

"When was this?" I asked. "That she stayed here?" Bertha Chalmers had to be eighty if she was a day.

"Oh. Um..." He lifted his cup, took a sip, shrugged. "It was some time ago. We've remained friends."

"Yes, but... I mean, she's—"

"Did you like the books?" he asked, nodding toward the lump under my skirt.

I've never been much of a blusher, but I could feel my cheeks growing warm as I took the books out from under my skirt.

"You know, you really don't have to hide that kind of thing around here." Pointing to *My Secret Life,* he said, "What do you think of that one?"

"Not much. I was told it would help me to understand the sexual inclinations of men, but..."

"Of men who ought to be locked up, maybe. Who told you that?"

"Lord Hickley."

"Of course. They're cut from the same mold, he and old Walt. How do you know Hickley, anyway?"

"He's asked me to marry him."

Inigo winced, no doubt recalling his revelation about Hickley's mistress.

"I'm not going to," I said.

He turned that smile on. "Oh, I do love brainy women."

Slumping down, I said, "I'm going to end up a brainy old maid. I'm beginning to wonder if I wouldn't have been better off being dumb and beautiful."

"But you *are* beautiful."

I shook my head. "If I had a figure, perhaps, and paler skin, thicker hair..."

"The current vogue is for big, soft, pigeon-breasted females, but it won't last. It never does." He launched into an amusing but surprisingly learned discourse on the various trends in female beauty in different eras and cultures. It was the first time I'd been introduced to that concept.

I said, "That's all very fascinating, but unfortunately for me, I'm living in the Western world at the turn of the twentieth century, and every man I meet thinks I'm skinny and plain."

Moving a little closer to me, Inigo said, "I think you're beautiful."

"You just feel sorry for me."

"If I felt sorry for you, would I be dying to kiss you?"

"You don't want to kiss me."

About a second later, I was in his arms, getting the

kiss to end all kisses. His mouth was so amazingly warm, and he really knew what he was doing with his lips and tongue (just a little tongue, a soft lick along the inner part of my upper lip, not enough to scare me, just enough to stop my heart). I don't know how long it went on, but before it was over, I heard a pounding in my ears, and I swear to God the room was spinning. I know I ended up lying on the couch with him half on top of me and no recollection as to how we ended up that way.

"Can I touch you?" he asked, a little breathlessly.

"Where?"

That melting smile. "It would take less time to list the places I *don't* want to touch you."

I returned the smile. "Where *don't* you want to touch me?"

"Nowhere."

I chuckled, biting my lip. Through my sensible skirt and petticoat, I could feel his erection pressing against my thigh. It felt like an oak branch. This was all happening so fast, and I wasn't at all sure I was ready for it.

"I've been thinking about making love to you ever since I first saw you," he murmured, moving against me in a frankly sexual way as he gathered up my skirt. "In my mind, I've had you standing, sitting, from behind, bent over the—"

"I'm a virgin."

He stopped moving. "Hmm."

"You're disappointed."

"No." He braced himself on his elbows to look at me. "Yes."

"Because what you'd hoped would be a nice, quick, friendly fuck"—the first time I ever used that word—"has suddenly gotten all complicated and—"

"I like sex when it's complicated," he said. "I like it when it's simple. I like it when it's sweet, I like it when it's dirty, I like it fast, I like it slow... What I don't like is when the woman I'm making love to weeps with pain, and if your first time was with me..." He shook his head.

"Isn't it *always* painful?"

He flipped open his trouser buttons and withdrew a good eleven or twelve inches of thick, hard cock.

I stared at it. My sexual inexperience notwithstanding, I knew I was in the presence of something exquisitely abnormal. Looking back, even the veins snaking beneath the surface of the shiny, taut skin were unusually fat. The head itself was like a peach, but with a damp little slit at the top. I shrank back from it even as I ached to touch it.

Sitting up to re-button his trousers, he said, "I haven't taken a virginity in... Well, let's just say you wouldn't believe how long it's been. I gravitate toward experienced women. I'm less likely to hurt them, and they're generally comfortable enough with the situation to let me know how they're feeling, so I can... slow down, or..."

I sat up, too, tidying my hair and blouse. "It's just as well. I mean, I didn't really want to. I hardly know you. And I can't think it would have been very good for you. I mean, I know nothing—less than nothing. I didn't realize how uninformed I was before I came here, but now... I wouldn't know where to begin."

"You don't have to remain uninformed if you don't want to," he said. "There's more to making love than just...opening your legs for a man. There are things I can show you, teach you..."

"Like sex school?" I stood up, smoothing my rumpled skirt. "That isn't how people are supposed to learn these things."

Rising off the couch, he said, "There is no right or wrong way to learn these things, Emily. Why not let me—"

"No. Really." I backed away as he reached out to me. "I feel self-conscious enough already."

"There's no shame in innocence. But if you do want to learn—"

"I'm sorry, Inigo," I said as I crossed to the door. "I know you're just trying to help, but I really don't think—" I gasped as I nearly collided with a dark gray cat that was heading into the library as I was heading out of it.

The cat arched its back and hissed at me.

"Relax, Darius," Inigo told it. "She's not going to touch you."

The cat darted into the library and onto a leather club chair facing the couch.

"I'll be leaving as soon as the rain stops," I told Inigo, "so I'll say good-bye now."

I left and returned to my room, where I sat on the edge of the bed and tried not to cry. I'd never felt so confused and unsure of myself. My gaze lit on my ruined black picture hat, which I'd propped on a bedpost to dry. In my mind, I saw Hickley aping me for the amusement of his friends and mistress—the ridiculous, waterlogged hat, the desolate pout and big, pitiful eyes.

The tiresome, gullible American prig: That was my role in this little drama, the one Hickley had cast me in, and which I'd played to perfection. Of course, I was just a minor secondary character in his world, a stereotype with no need for a character arc. I had arrived on the scene ignorant and overwhelmed, and I would leave the same way. So it had been decreed by Lord Hickley.

But as I well knew from my fiction writing, characters sometimes developed a will of their own, taking the story in a direction its author had never intended. I said, "Go to hell, Randy Randy." And then I got up and went back downstairs, hoping Inigo was still in the library.

He was. He looked up from his magazine when I came to stand in the doorway, and smiled.

I said, "I, um, I was thinking perhaps I was a bit hasty…"

Inigo stood up. So did another man I hadn't seen, because he'd been sitting in the club chair, the one the cat had jumped onto. He was even darker than Inigo, with a hint of a beard.

"Miss Emily Townsend," Inigo said. "May I present my friend, Darius."

"I'm pleased to meet you." I went to shake hands with him, but he bowed instead. I would have thought there was something wrong with his right hand, but he was holding a book with it.

"My pleasure, Miss Townsend." His voice was very deep, with a vague accent I couldn't quite place.

I said, "Forgive me, but isn't the cat called Darius, too?"

"He is," Darius said. "I can't decide whether it is he or I who should take offense."

Inigo took my hand, chafing it slightly in a reassuring way. Gesturing toward the door, he said, "Why don't we take a walk?"

It was a short walk that ended in his suite of rooms in the southwest tower. The Arts and Crafts style furnishings were remarkably modern even by today's standards, and imparted a warm and masculine look to the apartment. The walls were hung with original artwork by the likes of Aubrey Beardsley, Gustav Klimt, and a who's who of Pre-Raphaelites and impressionists.

Inigo offered me some cognac, and when I said yes, not even caring that it wasn't yet noon, he ushered me into his bedroom, where the liquor cabinet was. He poured us each a generous serving in delicate lead crystal snifters that rang when we touched them together.

I tossed mine back, wanting to be as relaxed as possible for whatever lay in store, but when he asked if he could take my clothes off, I felt a surge of panic. He must have seen it on my face, because he smiled and said, "Do you mind if I take mine off?"

He stripped down very efficiently, then lifted his snifter and sipped it casually, as if he weren't standing there stark naked. I tried not to stare.

"You can look," he said. "That's more or less the point."

I did look. His penis in its flaccid state was a weighty eight or nine inches long. I wanted to touch it, but I didn't have the nerve, so I was grateful when Inigo took my free hand and cupped it lightly around the shaft. I was surprised by how hot it felt, and how soft— although it didn't stay that way for long. It began to grow heavier in my hand, and longer and thicker as well. I was gripping that snifter so hard, it's a wonder I didn't snap the stem.

I asked him the most inane questions (including, I admit, whether it hurt when he got hard), all of which he answered graciously and with preternatural patience. He showed me how men liked to be touched, and explained about the different kinds of strokes and caresses. It excited me enormously when I felt the tension increase in his body and heard his voice become huskier, and realized how aroused he was becoming. That his erection could rise as high as it did, given its weight, struck me as a miracle of hydraulic engineering. He told me the little drop of clear fluid oozing out of the tip was pre-ejaculate, and that it was meant to ease the passage of the penis into the vagina, but that he usually needed an additional lubricant, like oil.

Eventually he got me on the bed with him and finessed me out of my blouse, skirt, and corset, although I was still more than covered by the absurd array of undergarments we wore back then. Having my breasts caressed was incredible, especially when he unbuttoned my chemise and touched my bare flesh. The things he did to my nipples, first with his hands and then his mouth, stole the breath from my lungs.

When he reached under my petticoats and encountered my drawers, he stripped them off, grumbling that they were pointless for women, and that he "went into mourning when they started to catch on."

I said, "Women have been wearing them for the better part of a century," but then he started fondling me, and I lost my train of thought. I came hard, and then he got on top of me with my petticoats pushed up and thrust against me, that huge cock sliding up and down my slit until we were both thrashing and moaning and clutching at each other. He hunched over and let out a long, shuddery groan. I felt hot fluid shoot onto my stomach in a series of pulses, and it propelled me into another spectacular climax.

After that, I let him completely undress me so that we could take a bath together. He read aloud to me from *The Autobiography of a Flea*, then knelt in the water and let me pull him off so that I could see him ejaculate, because I was so curious about the discharge of semen. I was surprised at how much there was, and how far it shot across the tub. It wasn't as creamy as Elic's, though— more like ordinary semen.

We took our time washing each other with a soapy sea sponge. Inigo shampooed my hair, but wouldn't let me return the favor, saying he didn't like to have his scalp touched. I remember that, because it was so unusual for him to ask not to be touched somewhere. Inigo loved being stroked and rubbed and licked and kissed and fucked and stroked some more. I mean, everybody loves it, of course, but Inigo lived for it. Physical pleasure was everything to him. Once he'd broken the ice with me, he was like a cat, always rubbing up against me, begging to be petted. He was horny pretty much twenty-four hours a day. Unlike Elic, he did need some downtime between orgasms, but not much.

He talked me into moving into his apartment for the remainder of my stay ("It's not as if anyone here will look askance"), and by the next morning, I was conversant in the joys of oral lovemaking, both giving and receiving, in every imaginable position.

The next day, Friday, we awoke to a bright, clear, beautiful summer morning. I could have driven back to Lyon, but Inigo insisted I stay until Sunday (the day I'd told Biddie would be the latest I would return) in order to "flesh out" my instruction in the various forms of sexual congress.

We spent most of that day in the bathhouse, a white marble structure that looked rather like a smaller version of our Newport summer house, albeit scoured with age. It was, after all, almost two thousand years old. Inside, it was a classical bathhouse except for the back wall, which was of moss-draped rock with a low opening that led into the *"grotte cachée."* Beneath a large skylight was a sunken pool about fifteen feet square and three or four feet deep, rimmed with an underwater marble bench. The water for this pool, which was exceptionally temperate and soothing, came from a stream gurgling out of the cave.

At each corner of the pool stood a column to which was attached a life-size sculpture of a satyr and a nymph. The satyr, who had short, curly hair, sported stubby little horns that were more like bumps growing out of his scalp, slightly pointed ears, and a tail that was like a whip with a tuft of hair at the end. I remarked that the satyr bore a striking resemblance to Inigo. This, he said, was because he was a classic Greek specimen.

"If you ever visit Athens," he told me, "you'll see my face everywhere you look." I've since been to Athens. That was not the case.

I wanted to try every position illustrated by the statues, so that was what we did. First, I knelt to fellate him, then he lifted me up onto his shoulders facing him, with my back leaning against one of the columns, so that he could return the favor. He held me against the wall and thrust against me until we both came, and then after we took a swim, he bent me over with my arms wrapped around a column and rubbed himself against my ass while reaching around to caress me. I told him I wished we could make love for real. He told me I was very snug inside, so much so that if he tried to enter me, he was afraid he might actually hurt me.

That night, in bed, he asked me to masturbate while he watched, saying nothing was quite as captivating to him as seeing a woman "make love to herself." I couldn't bring myself to do it, so he fetched some wide red grosgrain ribbons from his nightstand drawer (he had quite an intriguing little collection of playthings in that drawer) and tied my legs and left arm to the bedposts while leaving my right arm free. He told me he wouldn't untie me until I'd made myself come. I still refused, so he read aloud from one of his favorite salacious novels, *The Lustful Turk*, to get me in the mood. After an hour or so of that, I finally broke down and started tentatively stroking myself. To make sure I didn't fake an orgasm just to get the whole thing over with, he slid a couple of fingers inside me, explaining that when I climaxed, he would feel the spasms. He moved the fingers around slowly as I fondled myself, and the effect was amazing. I knew how it felt to have my clitoris stimulated, but to feel that with a full pussy while I was tied down, well it completely undid me. I didn't just come, I exploded.

The next day, Saturday, I awoke as the sun was rising and lay there in bed for a while just looking at Inigo sleeping and marveling at how all of this had come about. He was lying on his stomach with his face turned toward me, and I was struck by how terribly young he looked in the pinkish dawn light. It had been a warm night, prompting him to kick the covers off, so I sat up to admire his body, taking a mental photograph of it to savor after I left. It had never occurred to me before that a man might be said to have a beautiful rear end, but Inigo's was positively stunning—small, muscular, and with a graceful shape that put me in mind, once again, of those statues in the bathhouse. Just above the crease, in the area of the tailbone, I saw what looked to be a vertical scar about two inches long, very thin and neat, and so faint that I never would have noticed it had I not been inspecting his body so thoroughly. I leaned in closer to get a better view.

"It's from an operation."

I jumped, pressing a hand over my kicking heart. "What...um, what kind of operation?"

"I don't remember," he said groggily as he rolled over. "I was asleep at the time. God bless chloroform." He drew me into his arms, nudging me with his morning hard-on, and that was the end of that conversation.

After breakfast, Inigo took me on a walking tour of the grounds. We strolled along footpaths in the thick, sprawling woods, explored the cave (during which I became so light-headed that we had to turn back), and spent most of the afternoon in the bathhouse. He laid me on the edge of the pool so as to pleasure me with his mouth, then sat me on the bench and took me between my breasts.

Afterward, I burst into tears. He scooped me up and held me for a long time, stroking my hair, kissing my forehead, and murmuring comforting things. He asked if I was upset because we would have to part the next day. I told him no, that I adored him, but that I'd never viewed our liaison as the beginning of something, but rather as an enchanted interlude. What saddened me was that I would have to leave there without ever having truly made love to him. He tried to convince me that it was actually a blessing, because it was something I could save for when I eventually fell in love, but I was having none of that. I told him I was ready for it now, more than ready, that it was the natural culmination of everything we'd shared for the past three days, that it felt as if there was a void inside me that needed to be filled.

A little while later, Elic and Lili entered the bathhouse holding hands. I'd gotten to know them both over the past couple of days, but every time I saw them, I was struck anew by their remarkable beauty. I've already described Elic. Lili had heavy-lidded eyes, high cheekbones, and hair like a sheaf of black silk. That afternoon she wore, as usual, an elegantly simple garment of gold-embroidered silk that tied at one shoulder like a sarong. She called it a *lubushu*, and said it was what women wore in her homeland. I asked where that was, and she said, "The Fertile Crescent"; I couldn't get any more out of her. The *lubushu* fell to just above her feet, revealing a hammered gold anklet adorned with a disc of blue stone that looked like lapis lazuli.

As they greeted us, I sat in the water with my arms wrapped around myself to cover my nudity. But then they both nonchalantly disrobed and joined us in the pool, and before long my pointless modesty was a thing of the past.

Noticing my puffy eyes, Lili asked me what was wrong. I gave some mealymouthed response I can't remember now, but I could tell from her expression that she wasn't buying it. Later, as we were all walking back to the château together, the men a few yards behind Lili and me on the path, I heard their conversation drop to a near whisper. I suspected they were talking about me, and as it turned out, they were.

Inigo read to me as we lay curled up in bed that evening—not a bawdy novel, as usual, but the erotic poetry of Catullus, which had been sadly excluded from the classics curriculum at Miss Cox's. He closed the book, kissed me, and said quietly, "Elic wants to make love to you."

I was speechless, and you know, dear Rèmy, how rare an affliction that is for me.

He said, "I mean, really make love—you know."

"But Lili…" I shook my head, dumbfounded that we were even having this conversation.

"You know she and Elic sleep with other people."

"Yes, but seeing them together...it's so obvious how much they love each other. They're always touching, embracing, sharing little looks. And I like Lili. She's been so friendly to me, so warm. I feel as if I were betraying—"

"She suggested it."

I sat up. "How...how did she know...?"

Rising onto an elbow, he said, "I might have said something, when she asked why you were so—"

"This is mad," I said.

"This is Grotte Cachée." He took my hand, kissed my fingers. "Elic says you're exquisite, that you 'resonate with sublimated passion.' He's very good at initiating virgins, and he loves doing it."

"But I've only ever...done anything like that with you. I've only just met him. I've never even been alone with him, never even touched him." Ah, but I had watched him in *le Boudoir* that night with Helen. Every time I recalled what I'd seen, I grew wet and breathless.

"I would be with you," Inigo said.

"You...you would?"

"Of course," he said, sitting up. "I'm not trying to hand you off, Em, I'm just trying to make you happy. I would love to share your first time with you—unless you'd rather I weren't there. It's up to—"

"Of course I want you there."

He smiled. "Shall I invite him over?"

"Now?"

He stroked my face, saying softly, "This is your last night here, sweetheart."

I hugged him tight while I thought about it. Finally

I nodded against his shoulder. He kissed my head and got up to call Elic, who lived in another tower, from the telephone in his front hall.

When Inigo came back into the bedroom and saw that I'd put on my nightgown, I said, "Don't laugh."

"I'm not laughing." He wasn't. He wasn't even smiling.

Plucking at the skirt of the nightgown, I said, "I know there's no point to this, because he's already seen me naked, but it just...it makes me feel a little more..."

"Of course it does. Here," he said, pulling on a pair of drawers, "so you're not the only one."

He blew out all but one candle and mounted the pillows against the headboard. We got under the sheet (it was too warm a night for blankets) and reclined against the pillows with our arms around each other, kissing, until a knock came at the door of the apartment.

"Entrée," Inigo called.

When Elic walked into the bedroom, I couldn't even look directly at him at first. "Is that a new Renoir hanging over the mantel?" he asked as he sat on the edge of the bed. He was wearing an untucked shirt with dark trousers, and his feet were bare.

Inigo nodded. "I picked it up in Paris last month. Isn't it beautiful?"

Elic said, "It is, actually, and I've never been too keen on still lifes. What do you think of it, Emily?"

"I love it," I said. "It's exquisite, so lush and colorful." I started jabbering the way I do when I'm nervous. "I can't stop gazing at it, but then, parrot tulips have been my favorite flower ever since I was a little girl.

I love those twisted, feathery petals." (Yes, Rèmy, my much-loved Renoir came from Inigo.) I told them how Nana used to have vases of them in her house every spring, but my mother thought they were "too showy and ostentatious."

The conversation turned from bourgeois sensibilities to education to women's suffrage. Their effort to relax me with small talk was touching, and as I played along, it actually seemed to be working. By the time Elic reached out to stroke my hair, saying it reminded him of Fortuny's paintings of odalisques, I had all but forgotten the benign ruse.

"Your hair is Fortuny," he said softly, "but your skin is Ingres." He stroked my face and throat until my eyes drifted closed. I felt the back of his hand trail lightly down my chest and over a linen-clad breast as Inigo caressed the other one. Lips touched mine. I opened my eyes to find that it was Elic, not Inigo, who was kissing me.

"Is this all right?" Elic asked softly, earnestly.

I nodded.

He took off his trousers, but not his drawers or his shirt, probably because he sensed, from my nightgown, that I needed that thin layer of linen between us. He got under the covers and kissed one cheek while Inigo kissed the other. I smiled at the prospect of being made love to by two beautiful, sexy men who also happened to be all-around swell guys, almost too swell to be true. They both stroked and fondled me, both kissed me and rubbed against me and whispered the things every woman wants to hear. At length, someone slid a finger in me and found me slick and ready.

As Elic reached under his shirt to unbutton his drawers, I said, "I, um, wouldn't want to end up in trouble."

"You have nothing to fear in that regard," Elic said. "I'm sterile. But if it will ease your mind, I'll wear a condom."

I turned the condom down, not even thinking about syphilis or gonorrhea, that's how naïve I was. Luckily, I didn't catch anything from him, which is actually a wonder, given how many women he must have been with.

Inigo held me tucked into his embrace as Elic knelt between my legs, tilting my hips up onto his thighs. What with my voluminous nightgown and his shirt, I couldn't see what he was doing, but I could feel his fingers gently parting me, and then the head of his cock pressing in.

"Take care, brother," Inigo told Elic. "She's small."

Elic flexed and stretched me open. I flinched.

"Easy," Inigo murmured. I didn't know whether he was talking to Elic or to me.

Elic entered me by degrees, easing his cock back and forth little by little as my body conformed to it. At one point, he gripped my hips and gave a short, hard thrust, and I felt something give inside—my hymen, of course.

Stilling for a moment, Elic asked if I was all right. I told him I was wonderful, and both men chuckled. Elic continued pushing into me. There was a sort of burning ache, but it was overwhelmed by the novel sense of being penetrated by something that felt, at that moment, like a column of marble.

When he was buried completely inside me, he kissed me and told me how tight I was, and how incredible it felt. "It feels *too* good," he said. "If I get carried away and start hurting you, you've got to let me know."

I told him I would, and then I pulled up my nightgown and lifted his shirt a little so that I could see him inside me. It was a fascinating sight, and deeply arousing. Obviously sensing my curiosity, Inigo took my hand and placed it where my body and Elic's were connected. He really did feel hard as marble, and it amazed me that my body could accommodate him.

Elic made a deep purring sound as my fingertips brushed his cock. He started thrusting again, slowly but purposefully, his languorous gaze on my breasts as Inigo gently kneaded them, squeezing and rubbing my nipples through my gown. When he lowered his hand to stroke my clit, I moaned and grabbed Elic's shoulders, arching my hips. I met Elic's thrusts, which grew swifter and deeper as his pleasure mounted.

"Does this hurt?" he asked in a husky, breathless voice.

"No."

I could feel Inigo's erection through his drawers, so I reached beneath the sheet to unbutton them. He kissed me gratefully and rubbed against my sweat-slicked thigh while continuing his intimate caress. The three of us moved together in the same rhythm, panting and shuddering. A drop of sweat fell onto my forehead from Elic's face.

Inigo came first, pressing hard against me as a growl

of satisfaction rumbled from his throat. Every hot jet of come against my thigh drove me closer to the edge, so that as his climax was waning, mine was peaking. Elic reared over me with a groan, his face darkly flushed, a vein bulging on his forehead, hips jerking. I felt a pumping sensation inside me that set off a second orgasm on the heels of the first.

We lay there for a minute in a sweaty, sticky, breathless heap, and then both men whispered, simultaneously, "Wow."

The final shoot-'em-out with Hickley took place the next morning, when he returned to the château only to find me in Inigo's apartment in my dressing gown, packing my things. He really cast a kitten, called me about fifty different synonyms for slut. "You are an engaged woman, for pity's sake!"

I told him that I was, in fact, a free woman, having had the good sense not to take back his ring, and that I furthermore intended to remain a free woman for the rest of my days on earth.

He screamed (spittle flying, very attractive) that he'd ruin me, that he'd make sure everyone in New York found out about my little romp with Inigo. "You'll never receive another marriage proposal, not from anyone who matters."

I told him I'd learned some very useful and interesting things recently, the most important of which was that life was too short to end up a bird in a golden cage. "I can enjoy life very well on my own, thank you, certainly better than I could enjoy it as your wife—or as anyone's wife, for that matter."

I told him to go ahead and spew his venom in New York, that I was thinking about settling down in Paris, and that Parisians wouldn't shun me for one little affair. "In a choice between being bound in matrimony or being ruined and therefore free to do as I wish, I happily choose ruination."

And that, dear Rèmy, is the story of how yours truly came to bid *adieu* to her innocence and her tiresome fiancé, and good riddance to both. (I'll bet there aren't many women who've come not once, but twice while losing their virginity.)

By the way, Nils lost his two days ago, courtesy of my determined tart of a niece, who finally wore him down. She told me it was worth the wait, that he was a "roaring, rutting beast," and that it was "the bounce to end all bounces."

That's all for now, *mon coeur*. Please do consider coming clean about any little trysts you may have engaged in this past year. By "coming clean," I don't mean to imply that it will be a confession of guilt, because, of course, there would be nothing to feel guilty about. I just think I have the right to know. I mean, *I* 'fessed up. Not that there was anything to confess. Yes, there's that word again, but I don't mean it the way it sounds, I swear, and I won't give you a hard time if you tell me there have been other women, or should I say *when* you tell me, because I'm beginning to think there must have been other women, or you would have told me there hadn't been. Why else would you keep mum? I *would* like to know if any of them have been friends of ours, because I think I have the right to know if I've been betrayed by my own friend. And, of course, I hope you have the good sense to use rubbers, because bringing VD home to me would NOT be all right, nor would I take kindly to the notion of your fathering a child on someone else, especially since you might end up being strong-armed into marriage. You do realize there are women who trap men that way. An open relationship like ours can be very complicated, I don't know if ~~we~~ you've really considered all the possible repercussions.

I love you so very much, Rèmy. You're everything to me.

Je pense tout le temps à toi,
Em

Five

YOU ARE A *betrothed woman, for pity's sake!"* screamed Lord Hardwyck as he climbed the tower stairs toward Emmeline, spittle flying, hands balled into fists. "How dare you consort with that bloody gypsy like some common dollymop."

"He's Atlantian!" she shot back, looking down on him from the landing with arms akimbo and chin thrust high. "And I didn't consort with him. I fucked him. I fucked *him*, Archie. And I loved it!"

"Whore!" he spat out as he came to loom over her, face purple, eyes wild with rage. "Strumpet!"

"Because I have desires that I'm not afraid to satisfy? What's good for the gander is good for the goose, I say."

"You've made a fool out of me," Archie growled as he wrapped his hands around Emmeline's throat and squeezed.

"You'll pay for that, you little trull. I'm Archibald Dickings, Baron of Hardwyck and the future Earl of Upswinge. Who are you? You're nobody. Nobody, *I tell you!"*

On the verge of unconsciousness, as she feebly clawed at Archie's hands, Emmeline heard Tobias calling from below, "Emmeline? Darling, is that you?"

"The gypsy." Archie, *his face twisted in fury, turned toward his rival's voice, loosening his grip just enough for Emmeline to push him away. He stumbled backward, tumbling down the winding stone stairwell amid a battery of sickening crunches and screams as Tobias flattened himself against the wall.*

Looking down toward where Archie had landed with a heavy splat, Tobias winced. "Don't look, my dear," he said, holding up a hand to halt Emmeline as she started down the stairs. "Not till they get it all scraped up and mopped."

"Is he...?"

Still gazing down at what remained of Archie, Tobias nodded and said with a sigh, "Why does everyone always think I'm a gypsy?"

❦

February 14, 1922
Steamboat Springs, Colorado

My beloved Rèmy,

Happy Valentine's Day, *mon lapin,* or should I say Happy Belated Valentine's Day, because you won't be reading this for a few days.

Well, it's a happy day for me, that's for damn sure.

Guess what? Dr. Horney cut the casts off! I know it's a terrible cliché, but I feel as if I'm walking on air.

This will be a shorter than usual letter, because Kitty and I are spending the day packing, with the help of Nils. He finally worked up the stones to ask out that girl from church, by the way. I credit his newly acquired guts with his newly chucked virginity. Tomorrow we'll set off for the trip by rail to New York. First stop: Cunard. As soon as I've booked passage, I'll cable and let you know what ship I'll be on and when it's due to arrive. But remember, don't meet me if you don't want to be charged with committing whoopee in public, because I meant what I said about jumping you the moment I see you again. Ride 'em, cowgirl!

There's so much to respond to in your last letter. First, about the fellatio in the landau scene. Clever you, asking me why, if it was so "perplexing" and "pedestrian" of you to object to a male-male cocksucking scene, I went and turned it into a male-female scene in the book. The reason had to do with all those bawdy novels I'd read at Grotte Cachée, and the fact that although there were loads of scenes featuring two women, there were very few with two men. Since my aim was to get *Emmeline's Emancipation* published, I didn't want to put anything in there that would repulse male readers. So, you're right in saying that I knew perfectly well why you responded as you did to that scene, and that I was being disingenuous by challenging you. I can be a real pill sometimes, and I apologize.

Apology number two: so sorry to have committed

the grievous sin of "rolling the credits" at the end of my little château narrative without "wrapping up the final act." (Spoken like a true filmmaker.)

I suppose the true dénouement was, as you say, my decision to write *Emmeline's Emancipation*. The idea actually came to me after Aunt Pembridge and I had set sail for New York. As you've already figured out, Inigo gave me the Renoir parrot tulip painting as a parting gift when we said good-bye, which was actually harder than I'd thought it would be—for him, too, I think.

(In answer to your question, no, I never returned to Grotte Cachée, and no, I don't believe that it was an enchanted place populated by sexual demons—but I don't exactly *not* believe it, either. What happened to me there was like one of those strange and lovely dreams from which you awaken feeling as if the world has become a better, clearer, more perfect place than it had been the night before. You can't relive a dream like that. All you can do is tuck it away in a special place in your memory, and move on.)

In any event, I hung the painting in my stateroom, where it was a constant reminder of Grotte Cachée and everything that had happened there. I thought about writing down my experiences, and then I thought, *Why not turn them into a novel?* There was really only one kind of novel it could be, of course, and I would have to publish it anonymously, but why not? I couldn't be any worse at writing pornography than "Walter." I also thought it might be fun to write a book like that from a woman's point of view. As you know, I'd been having trouble getting a novel started, but once I turned to smut, it really freed up the old muse. The book was half-finished by the time I disembarked in New York.

Now, last but not least, about this whole disclosure business: Whereas I appreciate knowing that you haven't slept with anyone else (and thank you for telling me that), I want you to know that I'm not as easily manipulated as you seem to think. When you say you'll probably start sleeping with other women now that you realize how serious I am about free love, and that "monogamy really is pretty meaningless outside of matrimony," all you're doing is trying to scare me into marrying you. Not that I'm frightened by the prospect of you sleeping with other women, as you seem to think. What frightens me is getting locked into a marriage that limits my freedom and stifles my soul. I know you're not Hickley. You don't have to tell me that again. But you can understand how a man like that could turn a woman off to the entire institution of marriage, can't you?

At this point, *chéri,* we really need to discuss this face-to-face. I'll be home in less than two weeks. In the meantime, why don't you hold off on this new resolve of yours to sleep around until we can come to some sort of meeting of the minds? Not that I'm trying to tell you what you can and can't do, I just think it would make for a more productive conversation if we kept things as they are until then. And after all, what's the hurry? You've remained faithful to me this long. I hate that word— "faithful"—in this context, with its implication that monogamy is somehow theologically correct, but you know what I mean. Why rush into something that will only ~~hur~~ complicate things at this stage of the game?

Must run. Nils is getting ready to go into town, and I need him to mail this letter for me.

> Until we see each other again (Yee-haw!),
> *Je t'aime*,
> Em

From the *New York Times:*

EMILY TOWNSEND BINET KILLED IN INDO-CHINA

Famed Author-Reporter Dies
in Rebel Attack on Dienbienphu

By The Associated Press

HANOI, Vietnam, March 15, 1954—Pulitzer prize–winning novelist and war correspondent Emily Townsend Binet was struck by artillery fire at the French outpost of Dienbienphu yesterday and killed instantly.

She was 76 years old.

Mrs. Binet was on assignment from *Le Monde,* CBS News, and this newspaper to report on the progress of the Communist-led Vietminh toward Laos. It was to curtail that progress that the French established the air-supplied outpost of Dienbienphu last November.

Late yesterday afternoon, after two days of sporadic harassment by artillery and mortar fire, the Vietminh escalated the attack, pounding the outpost with fire from 105-mm and 75-mm guns hidden in the surrounding wooded hills. It was during this barrage that Mrs. Binet was killed.

Colonel Christian de Castries, who commands Dienbienphu's force of foreign legionnaires, Moroccans, and French and Vietnamese paratroopers, describes Mrs. Binet, who wore fatigues in the field, as "brilliant and charming," with "an *outré* sense of humor that endeared her to the men."

An expatriate American individualist who had made her home in Paris for over half a century, Mrs. Binet was best known for her novels, which have been praised for their psychological sophistication and subtle skewering of the manners and mores of the upper classes. The most famous of these is *A Rarefied Air,* for which she won the Pulitzer Prize for fiction in 1949.

It was her second Pulitzer, the first having been awarded to her a decade earlier for her reports on the Spanish Civil War, during which she drove an ambulance with the Abraham Lincoln Brigade. Her first wartime reports were published during World War I, while she nursed wounded men in a frontline French hospital. She reported on World War II also, while aiding the French resistance. Between wars, she published, in addition to her novels, myriad accounts of her adventures and exploits all over the world.

Mrs. Binet is survived by her beloved husband of 32 years, French film director Rèmy Binet, her stepchildren,

Jules Binet and Inès Langelier, both of Paris, five step-grandchildren, and her niece, Kitty Cavanaugh of Boston, Massachusetts, and Arlington, Virginia.

Mrs. Binet resided with her husband in a town house in the beautiful and historic Marais district of Paris. Last night, as news of her death reached the adopted city she loved so much, the Parisians who loved her back began to leave flowers, notes, and candles on her doorstep.

This morning there appeared, in addition to these tokens of affection, a veritable mountain of multicolored parrot tulips tied with a wide red grosgrain ribbon, but there was no card to identify who they came from.

Slave Week

Take me to you, imprison me, for I, except you enthrall me,
shall never be free, nor ever chaste, except you ravish me.

John Donne

"The Wandering Outlaw"

For he through Sin's long labyrinth had run,
Nor made atonement when he did amiss,
Had sigh'd to many though he loved but one,
And that loved one, alas! could n'er be his.

From Canto I of Childe Harold's Pilgrimage
by Lord Byron, 1812

One

London
June 19, 1817

"HAVE YOU ANY objection to being raped?" inquired the silver-haired, nattily attired Sir Charles Upcott as he dipped his quill in a cut-glass inkwell.

Caroline Keating stared at Sir Charles, barrister and baronet, across the marble and ormolu desk that was the focal point of his imposing Regent Street office. Taken aback by the query—indeed, deeply dismayed by it—she said, "Is it not in the nature of...such an act for the lady to object?"

Sir Charles glanced at her over the top of his spectacles and wrote something on a sheet of foolscap. "Should you be chosen to go on the block, the gentleman who purchases you—your master—may subject you to any number of secret proclivities that he would be loath to reveal to his wife or mistress. He may have wondered, for example, how it would feel to force himself on an unwilling female—something no civilized man would do in the normal course of events, even to a lady of limited virtue. But even civilized men have their dark fancies. As I explained at the outset, Miss Keating, your master may enjoy you in any manner he sees fit during the seven days in which you are his property, short of causing injury so severe as to require the attention of a physician— although there will, of course, be a physician on hand at all times."

"But if I am, indeed, forbidden to resist my...the man who...buys me, how *could* he force himself on me? He would have no cause to do so—indeed, no opportunity—were I to submit willingly every time...he requires it."

Without looking up from his note-taking, Sir Charles said, "He may order you to resist. Or he may employ such brutishness in the act, or encourage it on the part of others, that you will naturally resist."

"Others?" Caroline asked in a thin voice.

"He will be at liberty to lend you out, as it were, to another gentleman at the château, or to several at once if the fancy strikes him. A slave must be prepared for any contingency."

"But did not you say that I would be forbidden to...give myself to any man but my master during the week of my servitude?"

Looking up with a sigh, Sir Charles said, "Unless it is at the *behest* of your master. Should he command it, you must do it, unquestioningly and without reluctance. It is really a very elegantly simple arrangement."

"But why would he encourage someone else to...?"

"Usually it is so that he can watch."

Watch? Caroline blinked at the barrister. And violent ravishment...by more than one man! Good Lord, what else did she not know about the "secret proclivities" of ostensibly civilized gentlemen?

Sir Charles removed his spectacles and sat back in his chair with a squeak of leather, studying her with quiet speculation. No doubt he was pondering the wisdom of selecting such a naïve creature as she to go under the hammer two weeks hence at some mysterious, isolated château in France.

"Miss Keating," he said, "I am required by the party I represent in this matter to ask you these questions in order to ensure your aptitude for sexual enslavement. I must warn you, however, that if you offer even one negative response, you will not be chosen—and as I'm sure Lord Rexton explained when he recruited you last night, there is a great deal of money at stake, thousands of pounds."

Caroline turned to gaze through a window curtained in sun-hazed silk billowing on a warm breeze. This time yesterday morning, she'd been standing in a crush of onlookers on the north bank of the Thames watching the opening ceremony of Waterloo Bridge and reflecting that she didn't even have the halfpenny they were charging for a toll.

Sir Charles allowed her a few moments to contemplate the magnitude of her plight, then put his spectacles back on. "As to the question of rape?"

"All right," she said on a sigh, recalling the deal she'd struck yesterday afternoon with Bram Hugget, the street sweeper who'd been begging for a kiss for weeks.

"Just one," she'd said, "but it will cost you a halfpenny."

He'd scratched his stubbly boulder of a jaw. "Only if I get to feel them diddies, too."

She'd clenched her teeth against the urge to weep and scream. "Over my clothes, not under. You've a minute to be done with it."

"Miss Keating?"

She looked toward Sir Charles, regarding her expectantly, his quill poised over the inkwell.

"Fellatio?" he said.

She frowned in bewilderment.

"Oral copulation. Are you willing to perform it?"

"Oral? Do you mean kissing?"

Sir Charles withdrew from a drawer a leather folio, which he untied and opened, revealing a stack of pictures. He sorted through them, chose one, and handed it across the desk to Caroline.

It was a tinted engraving executed in loose, jaunty pen-strokes of a man, fully clothed, and two plump, naked women. The man lay on a bed with his feet on the floor and his breeches wide open, kneading the breasts of a woman who was squatting on his face. The other woman knelt between his outspread legs, sucking on his erect organ as she fondled both him and herself.

Caroline stared in unblinking shock.

"Lord Rexton gave me to believe that you were a lady of some experience in these matters," said Sir Charles. "When he recruited you yesterday, did you not tell him that you'd been ruined through a liaison with a soldier?"

Finding her voice, she said, "It was a very brief liaison."

"How brief?"

"One night."

"How long ago?"

"Somewhat over two years."

Frowning, he dipped his quill and noted this information. *Thousands of pounds.*

"My ... my experience is limited," she said, sitting forward, "but I assure you, Sir Charles, that I will not balk at—"

"Yes or no to performing fellatio, Miss Keating?"

She swallowed hard as she returned the picture to the barrister. "Yes."

"Are you willing to have relations in the Greek manner?"

"I'm sorry, sir. I do not know what that is."

With an expression of weary forbearance, Sir Charles chose another engraving from the stack and handed it to her.

A man and a woman, both naked, were coupling on an elaborately draped bed, she with her bottom raised high, he taking her from behind. Caroline had to study the picture for a moment before she realized that he was penetrating her in an aperture other than that intended by nature.

"Oh," she said quietly.

Sir Charles regarded her expectantly over his spectacles.

"Is it painful?" she asked.

"That depends largely on whether the gentleman wishes it to be so. Yes or no?"

She handed the picture back, nodding listlessly.

"Are you willing to suffer such physical punishments as spanking, birching, and caning?"

She hesitated, wondering with a surge of dread what punishment had to do with copulation. "Why ... why would a man want to do such things?"

"Because it arouses him. There are some—many, in fact—who find carnal pleasure in inflicting such punishments." He produced another engraving, this one depicting a terrified-looking young woman lying facedown astride a narrow bench, her petticoats canted up to reveal a bare posterior ribboned with welts. To the side of her stood a dapper, maliciously grinning gentleman stroking his exposed erection with one hand as he raised a length of bamboo with the other.

Caroline's stomach clenched as she fought the urge to bolt up out of the chair and flee the room.

"Well?" prompted Sir Charles.

She thrust the picture back at him, bombarded by the memory of all those beatings her father had dealt to her and her brothers, hundreds of them over the years, for infractions as trivial as forgetting a line of a psalm or erring in a mathematical calculation. Hanging in the little schoolroom on the third floor of the castle-like rectory in which she'd been reared were a broad leather strap, a bamboo cane, and a perforated wooden paddle, all well worn. She couldn't remember a time when she wasn't mottled with bruises from his sudden, impulsive batterings, mostly on her back, sometimes her chest or legs—but never on the face or arms, where they might have been visible to the Reverend Mr. Keating's parishioners. He was cruel and pitiless and probably half-mad—from the French disease, her brothers whispered, acquired during his reckless youth—but he was far from stupid. Caroline had promised herself, when Aubrey rescued her from the dismal gaol that was her family home, that no man would ever strike her again.

"Miss Keating? Yes or no?"

The air left her lungs on a whispered, "Yes."

"I beg your—"

"*Yes,*" she said, feeling perilously close to tears. "Yes. Yes. Yes to all of it."

"Still, I am required to elicit clear and unequivocal consent to each particular act, lest you protest later that you weren't adequately warned as to what might be done to you. You are willing to be bound, gagged, blindfolded?"

"Yes."

"Are you willing to perform sexual acts before an audience?"

"Yes."

"Are you willing to engage in sexual activity with another female?"

Dear God. "Yes."

"Do you achieve orgasm, Miss Keating?"

Heat swept in a wave from her throat up to her hairline.

"I shall take that for an affirmative," said the barrister as his pen scratched over the foolscap. "You enjoy sexual relations, then?"

"I . . . I did so on the one occasion when I engaged in them."

"Your age?"

"Twenty."

"Height?"

"Five feet, six inches."

"Weight?"

"I couldn't say with certainty anymore."

"Eight stone at the most," he muttered as he wrote. "Complexion pallid but unblemished. Hair golden blond."

"I was wondering, about my hair . . ."

"Mm?"

"I thought I might henna it, if that would be permissible."

"In order to help disguise your appearance? Some of the ladies do change their hair color and employ cosmetics for that purpose. I must say, it would be a shame in your case, but you are within your rights to do so if you wish."

"Thank you."

Setting his pen aside, Sir Charles slid off his spectacles and scrutinized her thoughtfully.

"Will I do?" she asked in as even a voice as she could muster.

"It is a pity you've been deflowered, Miss Keating. An intact maidenhead is highly prized in a slave. Virgins tend to command the highest prices, debauchees nearly so—the innocent on the one hand and the unabashedly wanton on the other. You, unfortunately, are neither. But then, great beauty is also a factor of some consequence, which will serve to your advantage. And you are, if not entirely untarnished, nearly so, with a guileless manner of the type that certain gentlemen find irresistible."

He closed the folio of lewd pictures and returned it to the drawer, then took out what looked like a visiting card and handed it to her. Engraved on heavy cream stock were the name and address of a Dr. Humphrey Coates.

Sir Charles said, "You will report to Dr. Coates tomorrow afternoon at five o'clock for a physical examination. This is to ensure that you are of an adequate constitution to endure the rigors of Slave Week and to pronounce you free of disfigurement and disease. Incidentally, the gentlemen who attend Slave Week are also required to submit to an examination by Dr. Coates in order to ensure that they do not suffer from any maladies of a private nature that they might pass on to their slaves. Assuming you pass inspection, Dr. Coates will provide you with a means to prevent you from getting with child, and I will arrange for you to—"

"That's possible?" An unwed pregnancy had been one of the perils that Caroline had lain awake all night fretting about. "To ... have relations without conceiving?"

"There are two devices that serve this purpose, a sheath of sheep-gut for the gentleman and a vinegar-soaked sponge for the lady. As it wouldn't do to inconvenience your master, you will be given a sponge, which you will be required to wear internally at all times, removing it only to clean and refresh with vinegar during your morning bath. Should you neglect this precaution and find yourself afterward in a delicate condition, it will be on your head entirely. By the terms of your contract, you will be forbidden to communicate with your master or to name him as the father."

"Contract?"

"As I *had* been explaining," he continued wearily, "pending a positive report as to your physical condition by Dr. Coates, I am willing to approve you to go on the block. In that eventuality, you will return here to execute a binding legal contract setting forth the rules by which you must abide during your week of enslavement. Primary among them is the requirement of utter and absolute obedience to your master, to whose every command you must submit without hesitation or protest of any kind. Should you fail in this even once, you will be sent home with nothing but your traveling expenses." Sir Charles recited this information in a disinterested drone, as if he'd done so scores of times, which she supposed he had.

He said, "Your master will be free to enjoy you in any manner he sees fit, so long as he abides by the rules of behavior stipulated in his contract. Should he fail in this, you will be taken from him and re-auctioned to another gentleman, in which case you will receive both purchase prices. Should you sustain an injury at the hand of your master, and if Dr. Coates determines it to be adequately severe, you will be released from servitude, but your master will still be required to pay you the agreed-upon sum in its entirety. Should you be uninjured and request release from your contract at any point before the end of the week, or if you violate the rules of your enslavement, you will be sent back to London immediately at no expense to yourself. However, in that eventuality, you will be deemed to be in violation of your contract, and your master's financial obligations thereunder will be null and void. Do you understand what I have just explained?"

"I do."

"In addition," he continued, "you are obligated to secrecy about the location of the château to which you will be taken, as well as the identities of the participants, master and slave alike. You will hear the gentlemen addressed by name, but you must never do so yourself, and you must dismiss those names from your memory upon your departure from the château. Should you, at some future point, find yourself in the company of someone whom you recognize from Slave Week, you are to conduct yourself as though you'd never met. The contract that the gentlemen sign stipulates the same requirement. The punishment for violating this crucial confidentiality, for the gentlemen as well as for the slaves, is complete social ruin."

Caroline said, "How can you...?"

"Certain exceptionally grievous sins, should they become public knowledge, will make a pariah of even the most revered member of the ton. Such sins will be invented, if necessary."

Sir Charles gave her two other cards, one for a dressmaker who would supply her with frocks and underpinnings sewn to their particular requirements. "The other card is for a master swordsmith who does very special work for us. He will measure you for a collar, a pair of wrist cuffs, and a pair of ankle cuffs. These he fashions of gilded steel, with rings for the attachment of chains and leashes."

Caroline stared at Sir Charles.

He held her gaze steadily until she looked away, letting out a tremulous breath.

"The collar and cuffs are to remain on for the entire week," he said, "even when you bathe, which you will do every morning in water scented with fragrant oils, which a chambermaid will prepare."

Well, that was something, Caroline thought. She hadn't had a proper bath in far too long, and she'd missed it. When she was younger, she could lie in a warm tub with her thoughts drifting for an hour or more.

"You will be contacted regarding transportation arrangements to Calais and from there to the château." Recharging his quill with ink, he said, "Where do you live, Miss Keating?"

"St. Giles," she said, noting how his eyebrows quirked at the mention of the notorious slum. "I share a bed in a lodging house on Denmark Street and Charing Cross Road. But . . ."

"Yes?"

"When I left yesterday evening, I told Mrs. Milledge, my landlady, that I wouldn't be returning, and I . . . I don't know if she'll let me back in, because it's tuppence a night, and I haven't been able to pay it for some time."

With a little grunt of acknowledgment, Sir Charles wrote a note on a sheet of writing paper, folded it up around a five pound piece, and sealed it with wax. "Give this to Mr. Peckham at the St. James's Royal Hotel on St. James's Street. The payment covers your bed and board for two weeks. See that you eat your fill, and then some—your thinness detracts from your beauty. Eat beef and mutton washed down with plenty of good, rich burgundy. It will put some much-needed color on your cheeks."

She took the note, heavy with the weight of the hefty gold coin. It was more money than she'd had in her hands—more than she'd *seen*—in a very long time. "Thank you, sir," she said. "You are most generous."

"It is not generosity so much as an investment in future profits. My firm will retain a five percent commission on your sale price, as will Riddell's Auction House, which oversees the event. The more you sell for, the more we make, and I daresay your value will be higher if you are rested and in fine fettle when you go on the block. I need hardly remind you that your attractiveness as a slave will determine how much money you leave with at the end of the week."

One week of appalling degradation. If she could stomach it, she would be free forever from the ever-worsening squalor and hunger and hopelessness in which she'd been mired these two years past. She could buy a little cottage in some village in the Cotswolds where no one had ever heard of Caroline Keating and her tattered reputation. Perhaps she could even open the school for girls that had been her dream since childhood.

"If you've no further questions..." Sir Charles scooted his chair back.

"The money," she said, sitting forward. "You said thousands. Lord Rexton did, too. Is that true? Is that how much a slave can expect to... sell for?"

"Two thousand at a minimum," he said, "and possibly quite a bit more. The highest price in the centuries-old history of Slave Week went to a young lady last year, an astonishing beauty, the virginal younger daughter of a duke. She cost her master twenty-three thousand guineas."

"Good Lord."

"Once the winning bid has been accepted, the gentleman is required to sign a note of indebtedness for that amount, minus the ten percent commission, to the lady whose services he has purchased, which note is held in escrow by Lord Rexton."

"He will be there?"

"As a representative of Burnham, Childe and Upcott, yes. Our client, I shall call him Seigneur X, retains us to handle the legal and pecuniary aspects of Slave Week—and to recruit young ladies here in Britain. The foreign ladies are recruited by Seigneur X's administrator, a Mr. Archer. The gentlemen are chosen by Riddell's, but only issued formal invitations after I have personally ensured their financial solvency. Of course, it goes without saying that some are in a position to bid a good deal more than others. At the end of the week, if all has gone well and the lady has upheld her end of the contract, the note and the funds it represents will be handed over to her. You see?"

He pressed his lips together in what she took to be his idea of a smile. "Elegantly simple, the entire affair."

Two

Grotte Cachée
Two Weeks Later

"THERE'S THE QUEER fish that bought me last year," whispered the slave called Violet as she stole a peek through the curtained service door into the great hall of Château de la Grotte Cachée, resonating with a tapestry of male voices. "Didn't lay a hand on me the whole week, just made me walk about in men's tall boots while he rubbed himself off. Well, sometimes I had to let him rub himself on the boots. I made twelve thousand guineas that way."

"Which one? What does he look like?" Caroline jostled for position among the slaves crowded into the dark screens passage between the buttery and the pantry until she was near enough to the curtain to pull back an edge and look through. She would much rather prance about in boots than do some of the other things recounted by the slaves who'd served last year. The stories she'd heard since her arrival at Grotte Cachée the day before had exceeded her worst imaginings.

Caroline peered into the lamplit great hall, in which about two dozen men milled about waiting for the Inspection of the Slaves that would serve as prelude to the auction. She couldn't see much through the narrow gap between curtain and door-jamb, just a thin slice of the vast, sumptuous room and its occupants, all identically attired in full-dress cutaways and knee breeches, their necks buried from the chin down in mounds of elaborately knotted white silk. Several had their noses in a little pamphlet called *A Floral Compendium,* the cover of which was illustrated with an etching of an orchid growing through a link in a chain; the blossom bore a remarkable resemblance to the feminine nether parts. Within its pages were descriptions of the sixteen beautiful young women who would be offering themselves for sale that evening. Attached to each booklet by a ribbon was a little polished ebony pencil for taking notes.

"Mr. Boots is the strutting rooster with the monocle," said Violet, whose real name was Elizabeth. She spoke, as did about half of the slaves, in the patrician tones of the British upper classes. The rest had foreign accents and sometimes foreign looks. There was Tulip, a delicate beauty with Oriental features who barely spoke English; Columbine, the caramel-skinned illegitimate daughter of a wealthy sugar grower from somewhere in the West Indies; and Lili, who was Persian by Caroline's best guess, with exotic eyes and a torrent of lustrous, well-brushed black hair. Like several of the others, Lili was a veteran slave, having put herself on the block the previous summer. Slave Week had been suspended for twenty years before that, owing to the warfare Napoleon had waged against Britain and her allies.

Some of the slaves were clearly friends away from this place. There were two American heiresses called Aster and Iris, both vibrant redheads, who had been best friends at a girls' academy in New York City. Novice slaves, they appeared to view the experience as an uproarious lark, which they had arranged by convincing each girl's mother that her daughter was on holiday with the other's family. Two of the veteran slaves, the voluptuous Laurel and the boyish Jessamine, who wore her hair close-cropped in the smart new Grecian style, had formed a bond during last year's Slave Week, and remained close friends upon their return to their native London. And Lili, although a veteran, enjoyed a warm friendship with one of the novices, a six-foot-tall blond beauty called Elle.

Foreign or not, one could tell by the slaves' comportment and speech that they were all of gentle blood. Some, like Caroline, were wellborn young ladies in embarrassed circumstances, others adventuresses in pursuit of the ultimate sexual thrill.

The slaves—curious how Caroline had come to regard them as such—had all been given assumed names in an effort to help disguise their true identities; Caroline's was "Rose." In addition, several of them had made an effort to alter their appearance, as had Caroline. Her hair, now a burnished russet, was arranged in a modish Grecian topknot with curls framing her face and tumbling down her nape. Her eyes were limned with kohl, her brows darkened, her cheeks and lips boldly rouged. The effect was remarkable; her own brothers wouldn't have recognized her.

Like her fellow slaves, Caroline wore around her neck a wide, gold-plated band with steel rings and clips hanging off it, which had been locked onto her upon her arrival here; a leash of braided black leather almost five feet long dangled from a ring in front. Smaller versions of the collar adorned her wrists and ankles, the wrist cuffs having been clipped together this evening so that her hands were essentially manacled in front of her. She was attired identically to the other slaves in an "Inspection gown" of ivory silk chiffon gathered with a satin ribbon just under the bosom, and a pair of dainty gold brocade slippers. Beneath the filmy gown she wore nothing, as required, a fact readily apparent from the sheerness of the silk and the way it clung to her feminine contours. Her de facto nakedness, and the fact that she was about to be scrutinized and fondled by strange men, should have paralyzed her with shame, but there was comfort in numbers. With fifteen others in the same boat, she felt less exposed than if she were getting ready to walk out there all alone.

"Oh, my word, it's Brummel," said Violet as she covertly surveyed the great hall. "I haven't seen him since he left England."

"*Beau* Brummel?" Caroline said.

Violet nodded. "A few years ago, he insulted Prinny and had to... Oh, bloody hell," she muttered. "The Flogster's here."

There were groans from the other slaves who'd been there last year, followed by a sharp "Hush!" from Mr. Llewellyn, a dandyish young employee of Riddell's Auction House—a *bardache*, Caroline suspected—whose responsibility it was to run herd on them. Gesturing with the long, slender coach whip he was never without, although Caroline had yet to see him strike anyone with it, he said, "Lower your voices or I shall be forced to order you not to speak at all. And remember, not a peep during Inspection, unless one of the gentlemen asks you a direct question."

"What's a flogster?" Caroline asked apprehensively.

"Someone you don't want for a master," said Elle. "The Marquess of Dunhurst, rich as Croesus and nasty as the Devil."

"How do you know that?" asked a buxom girl with black-dyed hair who'd been dubbed Jonquil. "You weren't here last year."

"I warned her about him," said Lili, catching Elle's eye for a fleeting moment, as they often did.

"Even the other gentlemen call him the Flogster," Violet said. "He's the bulldog standing with the group of men by the hearth—the one carrying the walking stick that has the ivory cockhead for a knob."

"The *what*?" Caroline let out an incredulous little gust of laughter. "You can't be serious."

"He carries it everywhere, even in polite company," Jonquil said. "At a glance, it looks rather like a mushroom. But if you look closely, you can see the little bishop's eye, and then you realize it's none other than the old bald rat itself. We call it Dunhurst's dilly-whacker."

Violet said, "He came here last year with a whole trunk full of manacles and whips and paddles, all different kinds. The girl that got stuck with him was called Dahlia. A pretty little blonde, Finnish, I think. Poor thing barely spoke English, but she told us the bastard never even tried to bed her, all he wanted was to cause her pain. She always had tearstains on her face and whip marks all over her. She moved like an old woman—you could tell she was in constant pain."

Caroline said, "I thought the masters weren't allowed to hurt us."

"Only superficially," said Jonquil. "That's the rule, anyway, but Dahlia claimed that Dunhurst had violated it. She went to Dr. Coates covered in bruises one morning, said he'd beaten her savagely with a black stick, which would have meant she could leave but still get the money. Dunhurst denied it, said she'd taken a tumble down some stairs and that he didn't own a black stick. His chamber was thoroughly searched, but nothing of the sort turned up. Mr. Riddell dismissed Dahlia for being disobedient and a liar. After days of abuse, she had to leave here empty-handed—and Dunhurst got to have his fun without paying."

Violet said, "The outlook is not entirely grim, ladies. Remember that handsome young blood from last year with the black, curly hair? And that *smile*?"

"Inigo," Jonquil said excitedly. "*He's* here?"

"He's got a bloody club between his legs," Violet told Caroline. "The girl he bought could barely walk by the time she left here, but she said it was worth it."

"Is his friend with him?" Jonquil asked. "The blond one with those dazzling blue eyes? They called him Elic."

Lili and Elle exchanged another look for some reason, this one slightly amused.

Craning her head to see through the narrow opening, Violet said, "I don't see Elic, but Lord Cutbridge is here."

"Is he?" said Poppy from somewhere behind Caroline. "He was my master last year. A real gentleman, that one, but a rutting stallion in bed. I never met a man who loved bedsport as much as Cutbridge—and he always saw to my pleasure. It got to where I'd come if he just gave me *that look*. I wish they could all be like him."

"A *gentleman*?" scoffed Narcissa, the beautiful but appropriately named young widow of an earl. "He's a one-eyed tanner's son."

Elle spoke up. "I understand your Prince Regent thought enough of that tanner's son to make him baron after the Battle of Vitoria, which was where he lost that eye, no? I should hardly think there's any shame in earning one's title through heroism—quite the contrary."

Violet, still peering through the curtain, said, "Things really are looking up. Rexton's here."

Her observation was greeted with sighs and one or two carnal little growls.

Scanning the great hall as best she could, Caroline spotted David Childe, Lord Rexton, lounging on a purple velvet settee with his long legs crossed, a snifter cupped lightly in one hand, cigar in the other. His thatch of dark, wavy hair was a bit more neatly combed than the last time she'd seen him, but his expression of languid indifference was the same. He sat all alone, his only company the lacquered writing box on the seat next to him.

"Who is this Rexton?" asked Angelique, who was French and a novice slave, like Caroline.

"He's a viscount," said Violet. "And a barrister, though you'd never guess it to look at him. He's only here to handle the money and the contracts—more's the pity. I wouldn't mind being *his* slave."

"He's a cock of the game, and no denying it," Narcissa said. "He's also as cold-blooded a viper as ever lived."

"You're just saying that because he cut you loose before you were ready to go," Jonquil said.

"She was his lover last year, but it only lasted a few weeks,"

Violet whispered to Caroline. "He's better off without her. She's got opinions on everything and everyone, and you can't shut her up once she starts airing them—a tiresome little magpie if ever there was one."

Angelique asked the question that had been on Caroline's mind ever since she'd met Rexton. "Why would a viscount become a barrister?"

"No one knows," Violet said. "He's a partner in Burnham, Childe and Upcott, but he doesn't really practice law, from what I've been told. He mostly lures rich clients to the firm— and girls like us to Grotte Cachée. Most of us English girls were recruited by him. Silver-tongued devil. He could talk a cloistered nun into putting herself on the block."

Rexton, you blackguard, Caroline thought as she watched him raise his snifter to his mouth. *You jaded, conscienceless rakehell.*

She thought back to that night two weeks ago when he'd snagged her in his talons, preying on her anguish and her desperation—a desperation that had driven her, that afternoon, to let Bram Hugget worm his big tongue into her mouth and maul her breasts for the halfpence it would cost her to die.

❧

"A ha'penny to cross our fine new bridge, miss." The bells of St. Paul's Cathedral had started chiming midnight as Caroline handed her hard-won halfpenny to the rotund little toll-man.

"A bit late for a lady to be out and about without an escort," he said as he tucked her toll into the big coin pocket tied like an apron over his round stomach. "Mind you keep your wits about you, crossing the bridge. They ain't got the gas lamps working yet, and it's a dark night, what with all them clouds and not much moon. Don't tarry. The way this wind's picking up, I reckon there's a storm on the way."

Touching the brim of his leather cap, he gestured her toward the footpath along the east side of the bridge, and the iron turnstile that served as a barrier to it, which clicked heavily as she pushed through it.

Waterloo Bridge, a quarter-mile of flat roadway supported by nine granite arches, had been officially inaugurated that day—the second anniversary of the one-day battle for which it was named—with a military cavalcade and a procession that included the Prince Regent, the Lord Mayor, and the Dukes of York and Wellington. The bridge was bedecked with pennants for the occasion, the sun-spangled river thick with pleasure boats and barges. Spectators from all walks of life crowded onto riverbanks, terraces, and rooftops to view the ceremony. It was the most extravagant event that Caroline had ever witnessed.

The prince's embarkation upon the royal barge was marked by volleys of artillery so concussive that Caroline, standing all too close to the twenty howitzers, had to cover her ears. Still, the detonations made her heart kick, her teeth clatter. Worse, they reminded her of Aubrey, smashed to bits by an iron ball two years ago that day.

Huddled amid roaring strangers with her eyes squeezed shut and her hands clamped over her ears, thinking about her beloved Aubrey and her wretched existence since she'd lost him, Caroline had an epiphany. She realized, with sudden, ringing clarity, why she'd been drawn to this bridge on this day, and what she was meant to do. A strange warmth and serenity enveloped her, as if Aubrey himself were wrapping her in a blanket and whispering in her ear, "Tonight. Do it tonight, my love, and then you will be with me always." Never had she felt so calmly resolute.

She felt that resolve still as she made her way along the footbridge, one hand skimming the stone balustrade to help guide her in the dark, the other clutching her wind-battered bonnet. About halfway down the bridge, she stopped and gripped the balustrade with both hands, grateful that they hadn't gotten the lamps working yet, lest she be seen by the toll-men at either end. So impenetrable was the gloom that the only buildings she could make out were the majestic Somerset House near the bridge's north end, from whence she'd come, and beyond it, the dome of St. Paul's. Her gaze on that most venerable and resplendent of God's houses, she whispered, "Forgive me."

Caroline climbed with some difficulty atop the balustrade and stood there, her skirts snapping and billowing. She breathed in the river's familiar murky smell, heard it slap-slap-slapping against the granite piers—but all she could see of it was a fathomless black abyss.

Untying her bonnet, she let the wind wrest it from her hands. It soared into the night, ribbons flapping.

A gust of wind buffeted her, almost lifting her off her feet. She waved her arms frantically to regain her footing, heart seizing in her chest.

Poised in a wavering half-crouch with both arms extended for balance, lungs heaving, Caroline stared down into the inky oblivion of the Thames. Gone was her placid resolve, replaced by roiling terror. Would she be filled with such dread if she were truly meant to do this? Perhaps—

Another gust toppled her forward, the timeworn soles of her slippers sliding and skittering on the railing. *God, no—*

She grabbed wildly at nothing as the world careened. A wall of water, cold and hard, bashed the breath out of her.

She thrashed as she sank, legs pumping against her water-logged skirts, lungs swelling. *Oh, Jesus, I'm sorry. God, I'm sorry, I'm sorry.*

She flailed her arms, straining upward, clutching at the blackness above. *Please, please.*

Her lungs burned as she fought the urge to inhale. She clawed and kicked and prayed, and then something nudged her, something hard. It prodded her, poked her in the chest, the stomach.

A gruff male voice, muffled by the water overhead, hollered, "Take it! Grab hold!"

Caroline gripped it with both hands, finding it flat, with smooth, tapered edges—an oar. She felt along the blade until it narrowed into the throat, and this she closed both fists around.

"Hold on," the voice called.

Caroline felt herself being pulled upward along with the oar. As her head breached the water, she dragged in a spasmodic breath through the hair plastered over her face, and then another, and another, coughing and sputtering. Hands tugged at her, seizing her under the arms to haul her up over the side of a small rowboat. "Easy, Jack," a voice grunted as the boat rocked and pitched. "We flip this thing, we'll all end up in the drink."

They managed to drag her aboard without tipping over. She collapsed, drenched and shaking and no doubt well-bruised from her rescue, but infinitely grateful for it.

"Thank you," she rasped. "Oh, my God. Thank you."

There were two men in the boat, both bearish and humbly dressed. One set about rowing them to the north bank, while the other, the one called Jack, sat Caroline up and raked the hair off her face. "Threw yourself off our fancy new bridge, did you?"

Caroline dropped her head in her hands and nodded.

"Now, why would a pretty little wench like you want to be doing a thing like that?"

She shook her head wearily.

"Self-murder ain't the answer to a life of sin," he said.

She looked up.

"You ain't the first sporting girl that's ever flung herself into the Thames when she couldn't take the life no more." Before she could correct his assumption, he said, "You know we're going to have to take you in, don't you?"

"Take me in?"

"Me and Hugh are river watchmen. We seen a straw bonnet come flying off the bridge, so we headed that way and heard you scream when you jumped. There's laws against killing yourself, you know. You get caught trying to do it, you got to be dealt with."

"I . . . I didn't really mean to." Caroline didn't remember screaming, but her throat felt as if it had been scoured raw. "That is, I meant to, but I changed my mind."

"Folks generally do, once they hit the water," Jack said. "Where do you live?"

"Nowhere anymore. I have no home. I have nothing."

"Right, then. We're going to take you to the Newcastle Street watch house, then you'll go before the magistrate in the morning."

Docking the boat along the embankment northeast of the bridge, the watchmen guided Caroline, wet and shivering, up a narrow flight of steps to Wellington Street. With Jack gripping one of her arms and Hugh the other, as if they thought she had enough energy left to make a break for it, they walked her along the Strand past the Somerset House, turning left on Newcastle. Her hair was a matted tangle; her sodden skirts, stretched out from the water, dragged heavily along the ground.

Leaning against a building up ahead was the tall figure of a man tilting a flask to his mouth, a cocked hat tucked under his arm. From somewhere came a woman's breathless laughter.

"You there!" called Jack. "You know you can't be drinking out on the street like that, I don't care what time of night it is."

With unhurried nonchalance, the man pushed off the wall and strolled under a streetlamp. He was perhaps thirty, with slightly mussed dark hair, well dressed but for his untied cravat and open collar.

"Lord Rexton. Beg your pardon, your lordship," Jack said with a little duck of his head as they approached. "Didn't realize it was you."

"Just waiting on my friend," Rexton said in a deep voice woolly with drink.

The unseen woman laughed again, saying, "Lookit that fine upstanding prick. Fill my naggie. Fill it deep."

"Lift your arse, Molly," came a male voice. "Good girl," he said with a grunt of effort. "Ah, yes."

Caroline and the two watchmen looked into an adjacent alleyway, quite long and narrow, which connected Newcastle to the next street over. Toward the middle, barely visible in the dim passage, could be seen a man and a woman. The frowzy redhead stood bent over with legs widespread, one hand braced on the brick wall while the other held the skirts of her bright green frock bunched at her waist. Her bodice was unfastened at the top, allowing her enormous breasts to hang free. The man, hatless but as finely attired as Rexton, stood behind her gripping her meaty rear end as his hips churned, her breasts swaying with every thrust.

Caroline averted her gaze from the sight, only to find Lord Rexton giving her a lingering appraisal from head to toe, taking in her snarled hair and shabby, sodden frock with a vaguely amused expression. "Dredged up a little river rat, did you, boys?" He took a long swallow from his silver flask. "What did she do? Get soused and fall off a pier?"

"Tried to drown herself," Jack said.

His lordship's gaze met Caroline's; the smirk faded.

"Harder," demanded Molly. "Fuck me deep. Squeeze my tits."

"She's the sixty-fourth chit to jump off a bridge this year," Jack said, "but first one to get fished out alive."

"What are your plans for her?" his lordship asked the watchmen.

"She'll spend the night in the cage," Jack replied, "then we'll bring her before the magistrate in the morning. Seeing as she tried to do away with herself, he'll have her confined to a madhouse."

"*What?*" Caroline's trembling, which had begun to ease, renewed itself. She'd assumed that her foolhardy act would earn her a brief sentence in the house of correction—an unpleasant prospect, to be sure, but one she could have endured. Madhouses were a different matter entirely. The man in the alley started groaning in time with his quickening thrusts.

"Aye, sir, that's the way," praised the whore. "Deep and fast. Let's feel you spurt. Come on. Come on."

"Most of the lunatic paupers," Jack continued, "he sends 'em to Bethnal Green Asylum, else White's if there ain't no room at Bethnal."

"No," said Caroline, who'd heard stories about both asylums that had sickened and horrified her. "No, please. Let me go," she pleaded, trying to wrestle out of their grip. "I...I'm sorry I jumped from that bridge. I won't do it again, I swear."

"We ain't fixing to give you the chance," Jack said. "Come on, Hugh. Let's get this one in the cage before she starts biting and clawing. I've still got the scars from that whore we pinched last week."

"I didn't mean to do it," she said desperately as they dragged her down the street, she struggling violently against their ever tightening grip. "I can't be condemned to an asylum. It's not right, not without giving me a chance to prove my sanity. There must be some legal recourse available to people in this situation. Won't you please just—"

"Wait," ordered Lord Rexton as he strode toward them, stowing his flask in his coat and replacing his hat on his head. Coming to stand before Caroline, he tilted up her chin and pushed her hair out of her eyes. Sounding a bit more sober than he had a moment ago, he said, "It is a rare river rat who speaks the King's English. What is your name?"

In a feeble voice, she said, "Caroline Keating, my lord."

"Are you any relation to Reginald Keating, Baron of Welbury?"

"He is my uncle, my father's brother."

"And your father is . . . ?"

"Obediah Keating, Rector of Welbury Parish. But . . ."

"Yes?"

"I am disowned."

"Have you a husband?"

"No, my lord."

He studied her face for a long moment, then released her chin and said, "Under current British law, Miss Keating, anyone who attempts suicide is automatically deemed non compos mentis—insane. You can, indeed, be confined in a madhouse for having jumped off that bridge, and the magistrate can send you there without any further legal proceedings."

"Are you quite sure?"

"Believe it or not, I am a barrister—by training, if not by inclination." Withdrawing a kid purse from inside his coat, he said to the watchmen, "Gentlemen, I suspect Miss Keating has learned her lesson well enough to avoid any midnight dips in the future."

"We can't just let her walk away," Jack said.

"Fortunately for you, I am willing to take her off your hands." He plucked two gleaming half sovereigns from the purse and handed them to the gaping watchmen. "For your troubles."

They looked at each other a moment, and then, having come to a silent consensus, they stuffed the coins in their pockets and released Caroline's arms.

"Miss Keating," said Rexton, "if you will come with me, I

believe there is a coach stand on the Strand in front of the Somerset House."

"My lord," Caroline said, "I . . . I can't go with you. I don't even know you."

"David Childe, Viscount Rexton, at your service." He lifted his hat and executed a bow that had a slightly mocking edge to it.

"Where do you mean to take me?" she asked. For all she knew, he might intend to sell her to an Ottoman sheik, having first assured himself that she had no family, at least none that would miss her.

"We are going to my home," he said.

"Your *home*? I . . . I can't . . ."

"It is that or the madhouse, Miss Keating. The choice is entirely yours."

Three

"GROSVENOR SQUARE," REXTON told the coach- man as he handed Caroline into the hackney they'd found waiting in front of the Somerset House. "You're shaking like a rabbit, Miss Keating."

"I'm cold," she said as she sat on the front-facing seat, wrapping her arms around herself. "My clothes are soaked through."

"It has naught to do with me, then?" He settled in opposite her, setting his hat on the seat next to him as the shabby old carriage rattled away from the curb.

"You seem disappointed, my lord."

"Just skeptical," he said, looking both surprised and amused at the cheekiness of her response. He shucked off his coat, beneath which he wore an ivory waistcoat over a shirt with billowing sleeves. "Lean forward."

When she hesitated, he pulled her toward him and draped the coat over her shoulders. It felt huge and heavy and smelled of clean, damp wool and tobacco. Thunder grumbled in the distance.

"Thank you," she said.

"Merely trying to prevent you catching a chill, Miss Keating. Wouldn't want you falling ill before we've gotten the chance to know each other." He propped one long leg on the seat next to her, assessing her with insolent directness.

Lightning fluttered across his face, casting his eyes into deep shadow.

Pulling the coat around her, Caroline turned to look out the window, spattered with the first few droplets of what promised to be a violent summer storm.

"Tonight only," she said without looking at him. "You've saved me from Bethnal Green, and I've nowhere else to go, but I am no whore, desperate though I may be. One night, no more."

He gave her an indolent smile. "If it is ravishment you expect, Miss Keating, I'm afraid I shall have to disappoint you. Given how much brandy I've swilled tonight, I fear such an attempt would prove rather uninspired. Instead I shall hand you over to my housekeeper, Mrs. Allwright, who will provide you with a warm bath, dry clothes, and a bedchamber that locks from within. In the morning, you will be free, should you choose it, to go on your way and never lay eyes on me again."

"Should I choose it? Why would I not?"

She recoiled with a gasp as Rexton leaned over to slide a hand beneath the coat wrapped around her. He withdrew his silver flask from a pocket in the garment's satin lining and uncapped it. Sitting back, he tilted it to his mouth and took a long swallow.

He said, "Are you with child, Miss Keating? Is that why you attempted suicide?"

"No, my lord."

"Why did you, then?"

"I don't really see that it is any of your—"

"Since I'm not making you fuck me, Miss Keating, I should think the least you could do is to humor me with a bit of conversation."

Caroline was astounded. Although she'd grown used to coarse language from living in St. Giles, she'd never thought to hear it from the mouth of an aristocrat. Too late, she realized how gratifying her expression of shock must be to Lord Rexton, who had undoubtedly used that word in the hope of eliciting such a reaction.

"Was it because you'd been disowned?" he asked.

She looked away, gritting her teeth. "No."

"Then it doubtless has to do with the transgression that prompted your reverend father to repudiate you. You've been ruined, I take it."

"Yes."

"Seduced and abandoned?"

"No, it wasn't . . . We were in love. We were betrothed, but secretly."

"Your father didn't approve?"

"Aubrey was Catholic."

"Was?"

"He was a captain in the Royal Horse Guards. They were sent to Waterloo, and he died there."

Some of Rexton's cockiness seemed to dissipate. He looked away and took another swig of brandy. "Two years ago today. I must say, you chose to mark the anniversary in rather lurid fashion."

She ignored that.

"Papa wouldn't accept you back into the bosom of the family?" he asked.

"He'd made it quite clear when Aubrey took me to London that I was dead to him. He poisoned my uncle and aunt against me as well."

"Your mother went along with this?"

"She died of childbed fever after I was born."

"You've no other family?"

"I have two older brothers, but they both joined the East India Company as soon as they came of age. They're halfway around the world. I haven't seen them in years, and I doubt they'll ever come back to England. Not to live. It would mean dealing with my father."

"So you've been living on your own in London since then? How have you supported yourself?"

"I get a little piecework now and again—embroidery and the like. But it's not steady. I've never been gifted at needlework, so I'm only called upon as a last resort, and it pays pittance even when I do get it. I've always been interested in educating young girls, so in the beginning I tried to obtain work as a governess or tutoress, but no one would have me. People actually slammed doors in my face. It was mortifying—and utterly confounding. I found out later that my father had told everyone he knew in London that I'd turned to a life of sin. Those people told other people. They probably thought I'd been . . . selling my favors."

"You never considered it?"

"Is that supposed to be a jest, Lord Rexton?"

"Not walking the streets, I mean, but getting a place in one of the better houses? Or perhaps securing yourself a gentleman friend?"

"Never. I'd rather die."

"Yes, well, it would appear that you've already explored that option, with limited success," Rexton drawled.

"It was the last option at my disposal," she said. "It would have solved all of my problems for good, but I failed even at that. Which leaves me at something of a loss, as I've exhausted every means to repair the fix I'm in."

"Well." The viscount smiled slowly. "Not quite."

⁂

The next morning, Caroline stood outside Mrs. Milledge's lodging house in the teeming squalor of the St. Giles Rookery, trying to work up the stomach to walk in and ask for her old bed back. Getting inside the ramshackle building would involve stepping over or hauling aside Reenie Fowls, who lay in a tattered heap on the front stoop with an empty gin bottle next to her. Her skirt, painted with mud from last night's rainstorm, was shoved up around her thighs, and her legs were spread wide. Caroline wondered how many men had eased their lust in her during the night without her knowing it.

"A sex slave?" Caroline had exclaimed in response to Lord Rexton's appalling proposal. "Are you mad? Do you think I'm mad?"

"In truth," he'd replied, "you strike me as refreshingly sane and logical—and with a degree of pluck one wouldn't normally

*expect from a ruined rector's daughter who's just been dredged
up out of the Thames. You are, of course, far too bound by con-
vention to greet my proposal with anything but righteous outrage, yet too savvy and spirited not to mull it over in that little
corner of your mind that realizes this may very well be your last
chance at a decent life."*

"Decent? I'm surprised you even know that word."

*"It would only be a week, after all—seven days that could
change your life—that undoubtedly* will *change your life, forever."*

"It's—it's sickening," she'd sputtered. "Utterly degrading."

"More so than the alternative?" he'd asked.

At least that alternative—half of a flea-infested bed—was
affordable now. That morning, when she'd awakened in a
guest chamber of Lord Rexton's majestic Grosvenor Square
town house, she'd found a periwinkle silk frock laid out for
her, along with underpinnings, bonnet, gloves, shoes, and a
dainty mesh reticule containing a double guinea and a calling
card for Sir Charles Upcott of Burnham, Childe & Upcott,
with an address on Regent Street. On the back of the card was
scrawled: *See Sir Charles about the matter we discussed last
night. Rexton.* Quite a presumptuous note, considering she'd
rejected his proposal out of hand, and in no uncertain terms.

Caroline had asked Mrs. Allwright to return her old frock
to her, only to be told that it had been burned per the instructions of Lord Rexton, who was still abed. The genial old
housekeeper had likewise refused to take the money back, saying she'd have the devil to pay from her employer if she allowed Caroline to leave empty-handed.

It had been a pleasant shock to wake up in that big feather
bed with lavender-scented sheets and a silken coverlet. Not for

a very long time had Caroline had a bed all to herself, and never in her life had she slept in such luxurious surroundings. She had breakfasted like a queen on ham, scones, and eggs *en coquette*. It was the first time in two years she'd eaten her fill.

"Carrie? That you?"

She turned to see Bram Hugget lumbering toward her with his broom on his shoulder, his boots coated with mud and horse droppings.

"Lookit you, all flashed up like that. I hear you told Mrs. Milledge you'd not be back. Yet here you are. Did your new sweetman toss you out after just one night?"

"I don't have a sweetman. You know that."

"Only two ways for a penniless wench like you to get fancy toggery like this," he said, stroking a hand over the lace fichu pinned around her shoulders. "On your back or on your knees." He grabbed her breast with a big dirt-caked hand and squeezed.

She pushed him away. "Get your filthy hands off me."

"Too good for me now, are you?" He wrestled her one-handed against the wall of the lodging house, slammed the broom handle across her throat to hold her in place, and groped her roughly between her legs. "You wasn't too good last night," he sneered as Caroline choked and flailed.

A pair of young ruffians sauntering down the street glanced in her direction, smirked, and continued on.

"I should of kept me ha'penny," he said as he ground his erection against her. "I should of shoved you down on your hands and knees and fucked you like the little bitch you are."

She struck out with her fists, battering his head, his face. Bram ignored the punches until one connected with the bridge of the nose. "Fucking little trull!" He pressed the broom hard against her throat. "Hussy. Whore. This is the way you like it, ain't it?" Gathering up her skirts, he said, "I bet you're dripping for it. Let's get a couple fingers up there and see."

Fingers, Caroline thought as his big crusty hand crawled up her inner thigh. *"Two fingers, one in each eye,"* Aubrey had taught her. *"As hard as you can. There's no room for delicacy if some blackguard has designs on you."*

Summoning all her strength, she raised her hand, locked two fingers, and drove them straight into Bram Hugget's eyes.

He roared and stumbled back, dropping the broom handle as he pressed his hands to his eyes. "Fuck! Shit!"

She lifted her skirts and fled north on Charing Cross Road as he bellowed and raged.

"Fucking bitch! You blinded me, you fucking strum. I'll kill you if I ever see you again!"

Then here's hoping I really have *blinded you*, thought Caroline as she waved down a hackney coach rattling toward her. She leaned on a lamppost to catch her breath as the coachman climbed down to open the passenger door.

"Where to, miss?" he asked as he held out his hand.

"Regent Street," she said breathlessly.

Four

TWO MINUTES TILL Inspection. Queue up, girls."
Pointing with his coach whip, Mr. Llewellyn said,
"Violet first, then Angelique, then Laurel, then...oh, blast."
He pulled the *Compendium* from his coat pocket and flipped
through the pages to confirm the slaves' proper order. "After
Laurel comes Narcissa, then Jessamine, Jonquil, Elle, Aster,
Iris, Columbine, Poppy, Holly, Tulip, Rose, Lili, and Saffron.
Lick your lips and rub your nips!"

Caroline felt starved for breath as she took her prescribed
place. *What am I doing? What in God's name am I doing?*

"Each slave is to take the loop at the end of her leash and
attach it to the collar of the slave in front of her, taking care to
keep her wrists above the leash," the little dandiprat continued. "Use that hook hanging off the nape. Except, of course,
for you, Violet. I'll be taking your leash to guide the procession

into the hall. Once Inspection is over, we shall leave through the other end of the hall and wait in the courtyard while each of you takes her turn on the auction dais."

"Oh, God," Caroline murmured as she struggled with her shackled hands to hook her leash to the back of Tulip's collar. "This is insane. I can't do this."

A hand, cool and soothing, stroked Caroline's shoulder from behind. "Don't be afraid," Lili whispered in her throaty, lightly accented voice. "It is not so bad. You'll see. Who knows? You might even enjoy it."

Enjoy it? Turning to look at Lili over her shoulder, Caroline said, "Do *you* enjoy it?"

"Of course. Why else would I be doing it?"

"For the money."

"I've no need of money. What I need is . . . stimulation."

This came as a surprise to Caroline, who hadn't thought of Lili as that type.

"You needn't stay, if you don't want to," Lili said. "You can leave right now and go home. Where *is* your home? London?"

"Yes. No. I . . . I have no home, no family. That's why I'm here. I'm in desperate straits. You've no idea how desperate." She shook her head helplessly. "I can't leave. I've got to stay and do this, but it's . . . I can't imagine how I'll get through it. I'm not the kind of woman who can just . . . do these things. I'm a rector's daughter, for pity's sake."

"Place your clasped hands behind your head," Mr. Llewellyn continued. "Your wrist cuffs are to be clipped to the back of your collar by the slave behind you. Angelique, you'll do Violet. Then Laurel, you'll do Angelique, and so forth. Saffron, I shall do you since you are last in line."

"Be someone else, then," Lili whispered. "Don't be

Caroline. Be Rose. Rose wouldn't be afraid. She would view this as a grand adventure. And then, in a week, it will all be over and you'll have the money."

"Aster! Iris!" Llewellyn tapped each of the girls on the shoulder with his whip. "Cease that bloody giggling. Meekness and humility, remember? You're slaves, for pity's sake."

From the other side of the curtain came the voice of Mr. Hamilton Archer, the English *administrateur* to Théophile Morel, the shadowy Seigneur de Ombres who was the lord of Grotte Cachée. Caroline liked Mr. Archer, who had greeted the slaves warmly and respectfully upon their arrival at the château. Mr. Archer welcomed the gentlemen with a brief speech before introducing Mr. Oliver Riddell of Riddell's Auction House, who announced in his distinctively resonant, stiff-jawed voice that the slaves would be making their entrance shortly.

"Chins up, eyes forward," Llewellyn ordered as he took hold of Violet's leash. "Posture upright, tits out. Keep your walk graceful and maintain a full leash length from the slave in front of you."

"Without further preliminaries, then," Mr. Riddell announced, "I present to you . . . the Inspection of the Slaves."

Llewellyn pushed the curtain aside with his whip and strode through, holding Violet's leash as if leading a pony by its reins. She straightened her back and followed him. Angelique whispered something that sounded like a prayer, and then she, too, entered the great hall, trailed by Laurel, Narcissa, Jessamine . . .

From her place toward the end of the line, Caroline could see very little of the hall, but she could hear the audience applauding the slaves as they made their appearance for the first time. It must have been quite a spectacle, a parade of lovely, wellborn young women in transparent gowns and slave collars, leashed together like animals. The tethering of their hands to the back of their collars had the effect of thrusting their breasts up and out. Through their filmy gowns could be seen their nipples and the dark shadows between their thighs.

"Be Rose," Lili whispered as Caroline, her heart pounding, followed Tulip into the cavernous, high-ceilinged hall. The long wall to the right was lined with tall leaded-glass windows open to let in the warm night air. On the left-hand wall were two doors opening onto the castle's central courtyard, the ornate main entrance and a service door near the velvet-draped dais at the far end of the hall that would serve as the auction block later that evening.

The elegantly attired men were all on their feet, save for Lord Rexton on his velvet settee. He glanced at the slaves one by one as they took their places along the window-lined wall, guided by short little taps of Mr. Llewellyn's coach whip as he patrolled the lineup.

Caroline looked straight ahead, as required, but her field of vision encompassed most of the room. She could see the viscount, his brow slightly creased, scanning the slaves a second time. His gaze bypassed Caroline, and then returned. He studied her for a moment, no doubt reflecting upon the change in her appearance. His gaze lit on her breasts and then he looked away, lifting his snifter to his mouth.

As the applause died down, the prospective buyers began conferring among themselves, pointing to this slave and that as they consulted their compendia. Most looked to be British, American, or northern European, but there were a few swarthy Mediterranean types, and one who appeared to be a mulatto.

There was even a Chinaman, rather tall for his race and exotically dashing in his European-style full-dress.

"Gentlemen, if I may have your attention for a few moments…" Mr. Riddell, standing at his podium on the dais, gave his gavel several quick raps. "I will endeavor to be as brief as possible, however it is incumbent upon me to ensure before Inspection begins that you all understand certain fundamental requirements of slave ownership. Should you take issue with any aspect of this regime, now would be the time to exempt yourself from further proceedings.

"First, please note that if you purchase a slave this evening, she is required to be collared and cuffed day and night for the entire week. Should it become necessary for reasons of health or safety to release her, you are to see Mr. Llewellyn or Dr. Coates, who has established a dispensary in the chapel withdrawing room. Both gentlemen are in possession of a key that will unlock your slave's shackles.

"Your slave will have been provided with an appropriate wardrobe, which will be delivered to your bedchamber at the conclusion of tonight's auction, along with a case containing various gear and restraints that may prove useful. Her attire, however, is entirely at your discretion. She may wear clothing provided by you, or no clothing at all, as you wish. She must sleep in the chamber assigned to you unless you choose to tie her up outside or keep her in the stable."

The stable? Caroline glanced at the other slaves to note their reaction to this, only to earn a censorious little smack on the cheek from Mr. Llewellyn's whip. "Eyes forward, Rose."

"You may leave your slave alone in your chamber only if she is securely locked inside," Mr. Riddell continued. "When she accompanies you beyond it, she must be under restraints at all times. In general, this means either leading her by the leash or tethering her to a secure object. You are to address her by the name assigned to her, even if you are aware of her real name, and you may not permit her to call you anything but 'Master.' May I remind you that a gentleman who habitually fails in these requirements risks having his slave removed from him and re-auctioned to one of the other gentlemen.

"Since the number of gentlemen present exceeds the number of ladies going on the block, some of you will unfortunately not succeed in purchasing a slave, however you are welcome to be our guests at Grotte Cachée for the remainder of Slave Week. Bear in mind that as an Unattached Gentleman, you may not touch a slave unless you request her services from her master. Should he confer such a privilege, he will prescribe the manner in which you may use her. Under no circumstances are you to avail yourself of those services without securing such permission. The same caveat applies to masters who wish to make use of another master's slave. The only exception to this rule is if the slave in question is wearing one of these."

He held up a heavy gold chain dangling a heart-shaped padlock of black enamel decorated with gilt. "This is a Master's Pendant, commonly known as the Black Heart, which each master is given, along with its key, when he takes possession of his slave. You are to wear it around your neck to signify your status as the owner of a slave. The heart itself may be removed and locked onto your slave's collar should you choose to temporarily offer her as community property. In that case, you are to tether her in a location that is accessible to all, and whoever avails himself of her must leave her where he has found her so that others may enjoy her as well. Your slave must also wear the Black Heart for participation in games or other amusements during which she may be subject to the intimate attentions of gentlemen other than yourself."

Dear God, Caroline thought. *What have I gotten myself
into?*

"With those caveats understood, you are now at liberty to
inspect the slaves at your leisure," said Riddell, adding, as the
men approached the lineup, "You may examine them as you
see fit, short of lifting their Inspection gowns or touching
them in a painful or penetrative matter. A slave may be disrobed and enjoyed only after she has been purchased, and then
only by her master or by a gentleman to whom her master has
granted this privilege."

Caroline's heart felt as if it might hammer right out of her
chest as a craggily handsome fellow with an eye patch—Lord
Cutbridge, hero of the Battle of Vitoria, no doubt—strode up
and dipped his head in greeting. It was a nicety that Caroline
would not have expected under the circumstances. He took
her by the chin, gently turning her head this way and that as
she strove to keep her gaze fixed directly in front of her.

"You have the face of a goddess," he said.

"Thank you, sir."

*"A gentleman is to be called 'sir' when you are given leave to
speak to him, never by his actual name and title,"* Mr. Llewellyn
had instructed. *"Except, of course, for the gentleman who buys
you. He, you will address as 'master.' "*

Indicating the *Compendium* in his hand, Cutbridge said,
"Is it true, as this book claims, that you take pleasure in the act
of love?"

"Er . . . yes, sir."

As if to test this claim, he stroked a fingertip back and forth along the seam of her sex through her gown, making her breath hitch.

"I do not care to share my bed with a lady who merely endures the act, or who feigns pleasure while thinking only of the money." He caressed her lightly, deftly, inciting in Caroline a reflexive hum of arousal. "One may as well make love to a piece of furniture. And there are many such women in this world, far too many. I have had my fill of them. When I am inside a woman, I want to feel her writhe and tremble as her pleasure mounts. I want to feel her sex clutch at mine as she spends."

Heat stung Caroline's cheeks as she felt herself grow damp, knowing he could feel it through the tissue-thin chiffon.

"Lovely," he said with a smile. He opened his *Compendium* to the page with ROSE printed across the top in florid lettering, and made a notation she was able to read upside down: *Stunning and responsive.*

After he left, a dignified, silver-haired man who had been awaiting his turn nearby stepped forward and proceeded to feel Caroline all over with detached thoroughness, as if she were a broodmare he was considering for purchase. He actually opened her mouth to scrutinize her teeth and gums.

He closed his hands over her breasts and squeezed them as if testing their resilience. "You've never been with child?"

"No, sir."

"And you've been taken just the once?"

"Y-yes, sir."

On her page, he wrote, *A near virgin, should be tight.*

As he walked away, she closed her eyes and took in a deep, shaky breath. From her right came a barely audible whisper. "Be Rose."

Caroline glanced surreptitiously to her right to find Lili winking at her as a bespectacled, scholarly looking fellow stood behind her, kneading her derriere with a thoughtful expression.

More men came and went. They peered at Caroline, fondled her, and questioned her about the most appalling things. Her only consolation lay in the fact that she was not alone. Every slave in the queue was enduring the same humiliating treatment, some with obvious discomfort and others, like Lili, with apparent equanimity.

Even Caroline, despite her embarrassment and apprehension, couldn't help but feel a stirring in her blood as strange hands groped and molded and explored her body. She found it oddly comforting to be manacled and tethered, and therefore utterly helpless to resist these lewd appraisals. It was as if the heavy collar and cuffs absolved her of responsibility for what was being done to her, freeing her to savor the sensations those strange hands provoked in her. At first, she was appalled at herself for taking pleasure in something so unseemly, but as she thought about it, she realized the coming week would be far more palatable if she could banish her reservations and play the role in which she had voluntarily cast herself.

Be Rose...

Rose wouldn't fret or doubt herself. She would embrace the experience with a sense of adventure, as Lili did.

More men examined her. They lifted her breasts, plucked at her nipples, slid their hands between the cheeks of her bum and the lips of her sex... and then they moved on and did the same to other slaves. One of the few who didn't manhandle her was a dashing, fair-haired fellow in an exquisitely tailored coat and full-length trousers, the latter an unorthodox choice for evening dress. She recognized him from magazine illustra-tions as the exiled Beau Brummel. He looked her over rather cursorily, complimented her eyes, and continued down the line.

Caroline was surprised to observe that occasionally a slave and a gentleman seemed to have more than a passing acquain-tance. Tulip, to her left, was approached at one point by the Chinaman, who spoke to her in his native tongue, softly and with a tone of affection. She responded in the same language, a sultry smile replacing her usual expression of quiet watch-fulness. He gave her cheek a tender caress, then took a seat and lit a cigar.

Not long afterward, as "Mr. Boots" knelt before Caroline caressing her slippered feet and murmuring "Lovely, lovely," a handsome young man came up to Lili and greeted her famil-iarly. He had a boyish smile and sported a mop of inky ringlets clubbed at the nape. Like Mr. Brummel, he wore the modish trousers in lieu of breeches. Even before Lili called him by name, Caroline knew that he had to be Inigo, of whom the veteran slaves had spoken.

Nodding across the room, Lili told him, "We have com-pany."

Caroline followed Inigo's gaze to the nearest window. There was a cat she would never have noticed on her own, its fur being nearly the same dusky gray as the deep stone sill on which it sat. Inigo winked at it, and it winked back—or ap-peared to.

"Have you ever had your cunny licked?"

Mr. Boots was gone, replaced by a big, boxy man who had the aura more of a prizefighter than of a gentleman, despite his fine clothes. In one hand he held the *Compendium*, opened to her page. The other was curled around the ivory knob of the walking stick poised next to him.

It was the Marquess of Dunhurst.

The Flogster.

He said, "I asked you a question, Rose."

"I . . . I have not, sir," she managed, her mouth so suddenly dry that she could barely get the words out.

"Do you play fumble and grope with the boys? Diddle them while they diddle you?"

"N-no, sir."

"And if I am to believe what is written here," he said, indicating the booklet in his hand, "both your mouth and your arse are in an unsullied condition."

"Y-yes, sir."

"Not so that little eel-skinner, though." Lowering his gaze to his *Compendium,* he read, " 'Deflowered two years ago, but not enjoyed since.' " He looked up. "Not a single stab in two years?"

"No, sir."

Returning to the booklet, he read, " 'A charming innocent unschooled in the arts of love, Rose was brought up in a country village, the youngest child of a churchman.' "

"Yes, sir."

"I did not ask you a question, Rose." Dunhurst pinned her with eyes like hard little black buttons. "Were you not trained to keep that pretty little mouth shut unless you were granted permission to speak?"

Caroline's voice snagged in her throat. She swallowed and said, "Yes, sir."

He made a note in the *Compendium: Resistant to training.*

"Popular sentiment notwithstanding," he said, "it has been

my experience that the daughters of the clergy are, by and large, of limited virtue and base character. As a young man, I fell prey to a vicar's daughter as faithless and wanton as any Covent Garden whore. It was a painful but enlightening lesson." Stowing the booklet inside his coat, he said, "Do you toss yourself off?"

"I . . . I am sorry, sir. I do not know what you mean by that."

"Do you finger the little ploughman, frig yourself with dildoes . . ." Grasping her nipples through her gown, he rolled and pinched them with strong, rough fingers. "Do you play with these to incite your lust?"

"I . . . I . . . no."

He glared at her.

"No, *sir*." In fact, several times after Aubrey left with his regiment, Caroline had touched herself where he had touched her when they'd made love, trying to relive the precious intimacy of their one night together—but afterward, she was always consumed with shame.

"Curious." Reading from the *Compendium*, Dunhurst said, " 'Rose takes great pleasure in the sport of Venus, and climaxes with ease.' Yet you've only been fucked the once, and I've never yet known a wench to take pleasure in having her maiden-ring torn to shreds. And you claim to have never been gammed or rubbed off, so how can you possibly know that you're orgasmic at all unless you make yourself spend?"

Caroline stared at him, plumbing her mind for a response.

In an icy-soft voice, he said, "You are a liar, Rose. Someone should take you in hand." He twisted her left nipple hard, making her cry out in pain.

"That's enough, Dunhurst." Viscount Rexton, whom

Caroline hadn't even realized was nearby, muscled the Flogster aside and positioned himself in front of Caroline.

"Just a little antepast, old man," said the marquess. "I realize I can't savor the entire meal till it's bought and paid for."

Caroline's horror must have shown on her face, because Lili caught Dunhurst's eye with a coy smile and said, "You ought to buy *me*, Lord Dunhurst. I could do with a strong whip hand. Upon my word, I have the devil of a time being good."

Dunhurst looked her up and down with a speculative glint in his eye. Caroline thought he would chastise her for speaking out of turn and addressing him by name. "Lili, is it? I shall bear that in mind."

"Move along," Rexton told Dunhurst. "You're through inspecting this one."

Rexton left on Dunhurst's heels, without having spoken to Caroline or even looked her in the eye.

Caroline whispered to Lili, "You didn't have to do that. What if he ends up buying you?"

The beautiful Persian smiled enigmatically. "I have my ways of making naughty boys behave."

❧

"Pinch your cheeks, Rose," whispered Mr. Llewellyn in the moonlit courtyard where Caroline, Lili, and Saffron were waiting outside the service door for their turns on the dais. "They're almost done with Tulip. You're next."

Caroline lifted her trembling hands—still shackled, but unhooked from her collar—to wipe her brow, beaded with sweat despite the cool night air.

Mr. Riddell's resounding voice was clearly audible through the cracked-open door. "I hear seventeen thousand five hundred guineas from Sir Edmund Byrde. Shall we advance to eighteen thousand? Do I have eighteen thousand for this exotic beauty from the mysterious East? She is talented in ways quite unknown to her sisters from the West, and of a yielding disposition. Eighteen?" After a brief pause, he said, "Eighteen thousand is bid by Monsieur Inigo. Shall we have eighteen thousand five hundred? I have eighteen thousand five hundred from Lord Madderly. Do I hear nineteen thousand? Monsieur Inigo bids nineteen thousand guineas. Who will bid nineteen five?"

There came another, longer pause. "It is little enough to pay for this Oriental enchantress." It was, in fact, more than had been paid for any slave that evening save Elle, who had been auctioned off to Lord Cutbridge for twenty-seven thousand five hundred guineas, a new Slave Week record. "Nineteen thousand. Do I hear nineteen five?"

Several seconds passed. "This is your last opportunity, gentlemen. . . . That's it, then." A crack rang out as Mr. Riddell's gavel struck the podium. "Sold for nineteen thousand guineas to Monsieur Inigo! Monsieur, you've only to see Lord Rexton to execute the necessary documents, and the bewitching Tulip will be yours."

"Get ready," Mr. Llewellyn whispered to Caroline.

"Be Rose, be Rose, be Rose," Caroline breathed.

Lili kissed her cheek. "Rose is beautiful, and she knows it. She'll love standing on that dais. You'll see."

"Our next offering," Mr. Riddell announced, "is an exquisite and sweet-natured creature certain to please the most discriminating taste. Gentlemen, I give you . . . Rose."

Mr. Llewellyn opened the door and ushered Caroline into the hall with a sweeping gesture of his coach whip. Applause greeted her as she stepped up onto the dais and took her place next to Mr. Riddell's podium.

She turned to face the audience, which was now comprised not just of the two dozen gentlemen, but of the thirteen slaves who had been auctioned off thus far, each with her leash wrapped around the fist of her new master. Some of the slaves were standing, like Elle. Others rested on their haunches, which was the position Mr. Llewellyn had taught them to adopt when their master issued the "sit" command. The other commands were "kneel," "hands and knees," "await," which meant to stand bent over with one's hands braced on the legs, and "kneel down," which meant to kneel with one's cheek resting on the floor, a posture that Caroline found mortifying. Finally there were the lying-down commands, "supine" and "prone," which were to be executed with spread legs.

Caroline's hands trembled in their manacles; heat suffused her face. If she'd felt exposed before, she felt doubly so now, standing nearly naked on this stage with so many eyes upon her. She kept her own eyes aimed straight ahead at the empty musicians' gallery across from her, but her field of vision encompassed most of the vast room. On the exterior wall, between two windows, was a tall console table at which Inigo, with Tulip at his side, stood signing papers handed to him by Lord Rexton.

"If you will consult your compendia, gentlemen," said Mr. Riddell, "you will see that our beguiling Rose has been plucked but once, and so will suit any gentleman who relishes innocence without the onus of taking a maidenhead. She is charmingly naïve, but eminently trainable, and of a complaisant temper. And I need hardly point out that her beauty is second to none. We shall open the bidding for this novice slave at the customary two thousand guineas. Thank you, sir," he said as Mr. Boots's hand shot up a fraction of a second before the others. Two thousand from Sir Thomas Quirk."

Please let Mr. Boots buy me, Caroline silently prayed. *Please...*

"Do I hear twenty-five hundred?" Mr. Riddell asked. "Twenty-five hundred is bid by il Conte Montesano. Who will bid three thousand guineas? I have three thousand from the Marquess of Dunhurst."

No, no, no, not him. Please, God, anyone but him.

"Do I have three thousand five hundred...?"

The auction proceeded swiftly, with nearly all of the dozen or so remaining men participating eagerly. Caroline's heart raced as the purchase price surpassed ten thousand guineas, then fifteen. The field of prospective buyers narrowed more slowly than she would have expected, possibly because only Lili and Saffron remained to be auctioned off after her; if one didn't want to be left without a slave, now was the time to bid.

Several men—including Mr. Boots, worse luck—dropped away at the twenty thousand mark, having obviously reached their limit of affordability. A drone of murmurs filled the hall as the bidding approached Elle's purchase price of twenty-seven thousand five hundred guineas. When the Italian count named Montesano offered twenty-eight thousand, the other men applauded the new record. "Well done, old man!" "She's worth every penny!"

Twenty-eight thousand guineas, Caroline thought dazedly. After the ten percent she would owe the auction house and law firm, that left twenty-five thousand two hundred guineas, an astonishing sum, more than enough to buy a cottage and a school—or perhaps she would have a house built to her specifications, a big one with room for classrooms and a dormitory.

Caroline's excitement dissolved when Dunhurst responded to Mr. Riddell's call for a bid of twenty-eight thousand five hundred. He slid a cold sneer toward Caroline as he raised his walking stick.

"Do I hear twenty-nine thousand?" the auctioneer inquired. "I have twenty-nine from *il conte*. Twenty-nine five hundred? Twenty-nine five from Lord Dunhurst. Who will bid thirty thousand?"

The count hesitated. He looked toward Caroline, as if to confirm that she was worth the price. She met his gaze with what she hoped was a sweetly seductive smile.

Please, oh please . . .

He raised his hand to cheers from his colleagues.

Caroline let out a pent-up breath. *Please keep bidding. Please win me. I can't go to Dunhurst.*

The bidding alternated between the two men until Dunhurst's bid of thirty-nine thousand five hundred guineas.

"Do I have an advance on the marquess's bid?" Mr. Riddell inquired of il Conte Montesano.

Montesano's expression as he regarded Caroline was pained.

"Will you bid forty thousand, sir?" Riddell asked.

Caroline silently implored him with her eyes. The count looked away with a resigned shake of the head.

Dunhurst gave Caroline a dead-eyed smile.

Five

CAROLINE FELT HER flushed cheeks go cold as the blood drained from them. Her lips grew numb.

The slaves exchanged grave looks. A gentleman standing close to the dais turned to his neighbor and said softly, "Look at her. She's gone white as bone."

"Wouldn't *you*, if you were about to be sold to the Flogster?"

"I have thirty-nine thousand five hundred guineas," Mr. Riddell announced to the group as a whole. "Do I hear forty?"

The men consulted one another in whispers, shaking their heads, and no wonder; forty thousand guineas was an astronomical sum.

"Forty thousand to master a near-virgin of incomparable beauty," Riddell said. He paused to sweep his gaze across the audience, then lifted his gavel.

Think, think, Caroline commanded herself. Should she try to last out the week, or leave now and sacrifice the money?

Her share of the purchase price would be thirty-five thousand five hundred fifty guineas. Dear God. How could she give it up? But how could she stay and let Dunhurst brutalize her as he'd brutalized Dahlia...? Caroline had promised herself, after escaping her father's clutches, that she would never again sit still for such viciousness.

"Speak now, gentlemen, for this rare opportunity is about to slip through your fingers," warned Mr. Riddell.

"Right then." He raised the gavel high overhead.

"Forty thousand."

Amid a flurry of exclamations, all heads turned toward Lord Rexton, leaning against the console table with his ankles crossed, his brandy snifter lifted as if in a toast.

Caroline gaped at Rexton, who didn't so much as glance in her direction.

Mr. Riddell lowered his gavel slowly, his brow furrowed. "My lord, do you mean to say that you wish to bid on—"

"He can't!" Dunhurst interjected. "He's here in an official capacity. It would be highly irregular for him to buy a slave."

"Irregular, perhaps," Rexton replied, "but not prohibited. Nowhere in the written regulations governing Slave Week is the legal overseer enjoined from purchasing a slave. Is that not the case, Riddell?"

The auctioneer mulled that over with a frown. Grudgingly, he said, "I believe you are correct, my lord."

The gentlemen applauded that ruling; the slaves exchanged smiles.

"I have forty thousand guineas from Lord Rexton," Mr. Riddell intoned. "Do I hear—?"

"This is outrageous," Dunhurst exclaimed. "A fucking travesty."

"Do I hear—?"

"Fifty thousand." Dunhurst glared at Rexton, jaw outthrust, as if daring him to go that high.

"Sixty." Rexton took a nonchalant sip of brandy.

Baring his teeth, Dunhurst spat out, "Seventy."

With a weary glance at the ceiling, as if this were all an enormous bore, Rexton said, "One hundred thousand guineas."

Dunhurst's mouth fell open. The room erupted in excited conversation, with a few whoops and exclamations of "Bravo, Rexton!" and "That's the spirit!"

Lord Dunhurst, his face purpling, jabbed his walking stick into the air and said, "One hundred ten thousand guineas."

The viscount smiled as if at a blustering child. "Yes, well, unfortunately, old man, you're not at liberty to bid that high."

"The devil you say!"

Rexton said, "Based upon the evaluation of your financial wherewithal conducted by my partner, Sir Charles Upcott, the maximum sum you are permitted to bid is one hundred thousand guineas."

"I . . . I'm afraid that is the case, my lord," said Mr. Riddell.

Stabbing a finger at Rexton, Dunhurst said, "Sir Charles didn't snoop into *his* finances. Who's to say *he* should be permitted to bid a hundred thousand?"

Riddell said, "I daresay every man here is aware of the value of the Rexton estates and holdings."

This statement was greeted with a chorus of affirmation.

Raising his voice to be heard over the cacophony, Mr. Riddell said, "One hundred thousand guineas is bid by Lord

Rexton. Is there any advance upon that sum?" After a moment
of silence, he muttered, so softly that only Caroline could hear,
"No, I should bloody well think not." His gavel struck the
podium with a crack like a gunshot. "Sold for the extraordinary sum of one hundred thousand guineas to David Childe,
Viscount Rexton."

A roar of approval resonated through the hall. "Well done,
old man!" "Good show!"

"Your slave, my lord," said Mr. Riddell as he ushered
Caroline by her leash to the steps at the edge of the dais.

Rexton drained his snifter, straightened up, and walked
over. When he ignored the leash and reached instead for
Caroline's hand to help her down the steps, Riddell lowered
his voice and said, "By the leash, my lord. It is required."

With a sigh, Rexton took her leash and led her to the console table. There, he executed several documents before wit-
nesses, including a note of indebtedness to "Miss Caroline
Keating of London, England" for the sum of ninety thousand
guineas.

Ninety thousand guineas. It didn't seem real. None of this
seemed real.

Mr. Riddell blotted his face with his handkerchief, then
turned toward the door to the courtyard and called out, "May
we have the enchanting Lili, please?"

⁂

Lord Rexton swung open a heavy oak door on the second
floor of the castle's west range and gestured Caroline into a
magnificent, candlelit bedchamber *moderne* decorated to look
like something out of a Roman villa. The walls were marble

with gold candle brackets and gilded bronze bas relief in the form of lyres, laurel wreaths, and winged horses. The furniture was gilt and ebonized wood, the draperies and bedclothes scarlet damask embroidered in gold. Against the back wall stood an opulently draped bed, each post of which was in the shape of a tall gold urn. A pair of glass-paned doors stood open, revealing a balcony furnished with a wicker chaise longue heaped with cushions.

On a blanket bench at the foot of the bed sat the worn old leather satchel Caroline had brought with her from London, looking grotesquely out of place amidst all this stylized splendor, alongside a rectangular, black leather case about the size and shape of a large gun box. A handsome wardrobe case with *Rose* inked on its tag stood next to an ornately carved clothespress. Nearby sat a big leather-covered trunk secured with an iron padlock.

"They call this room *la Chambre Romain*," Rexton said as he crouched next to the trunk, setting his writing box on the Aubusson-carpeted floor next to it. "A bit too archly imperial for my taste, but make yourself at home as best you can."

"Thank you, my…" My lord? Should she still call him that?

"You would do well to address me as 'master' outside of this room," he said as he twisted a key in the padlock. "Oliver Riddell has never cared for me. He would leap at the excuse to snatch you away and auction you off to someone else—unless, of course, you would prefer that."

He stowed the writing box in the trunk, retrieved from it a square green bottle labeled GORDON'S SPECIAL DRY LONDON GIN, and relocked it. "I can do with some fresh air," he said as he rose to his feet. "You needn't wait up."

"My lord," said Caroline as he strode toward the door.

He turned and met her gaze for the first time that evening.

She held out her hands, still linked together. "Do . . . do you suppose . . . ?"

He unlatched her wrist cuffs and left.

Caroline stared at the door. He hadn't locked it, but she knew better than to go wandering about the castle by herself. She'd come too far to be sent home at this juncture, especially with ninety thousand guineas at stake.

A man's angry, muffled voice drew Caroline's attention to the open glass doors. There came a pause, and then he spoke again in a harsh tone, but still she could not make out the words.

She took off her slippers and padded silently onto the balcony. A balmy breeze fluttered the leaves on the surrounding trees, through the branches of which glowed a three-quarter moon.

"I said *strip,* you insolent cunt."

The voice, which came from the large open window of the adjacent chamber, was that of the Marquess of Dunhurst, who had succeeded in purchasing Lili after losing Caroline to Lord Rexton. Caroline had been horrified on her friend's behalf, but Lili had smiled and winked at her as the Flogster led her away.

Lili's voice was so much softer than Dunhurst's that Caroline could barely hear it. "Nakedness can be so banal, don't you think?"

Caroline edged farther out onto the balcony until she had a partial view of the dimly lit room, which had floral-stenciled walls and a half-tester bed. A figure crossed in front of the window—Dunhurst, shirtless and with a perforated wooden paddle shoved into the waist of his breeches. He pulled something out of his pocket as he disappeared from view—a key, Caroline realized when she heard it turning and the door lock.

He reappeared, facing away from the window as he rooted around in a black leather box identical to that in Rexton's room, which sat open on the foot of the bed. His naked back was like a side of beef, dense with muscle.

"Just the thing." He produced a rod of gleaming steel about the size and thickness of Caroline's forearm, rounded on one end and with a handle on the other. Looking toward Lili, he said, "Have you ever been fucked in the arse?"

"Why, yes, I have, my lord." Her relaxed tone astounded Caroline.

"*I am your master,*" he bellowed, the blood rising in his face, "*and you will address me as such!*"

"Yes, master." It almost sounded as if Lili were trying not to laugh.

"Yes, of course you have, you shameless trollop. I'll bet you loved it, too, getting bent over and having a big, hard stiff shoved up your bung."

"Very much so."

Caroline shook her head in confoundment. She couldn't imagine taking pleasure in such an act.

"Yes, well you won't like getting buggered with this. I'm going to ram it in till you scream and bleed." He gave the big phallus a fierce thrust in illustration. "That'll teach you to be smart with me."

"I daresay it would."

"Strip and kneel down," he commanded, pointing to the edge of the bed. "And get that nice round bum of yours good and high."

What can I do? Caroline thought, her heart thumping wildly. *How can I help her?* Even if she could get into that room, she had no weapon with which to fend off the brawny Dunhurst.

"*Do it!*" he screamed, yanking the paddle out of his breeches, "or I'll make you sorrier than you can possibly imagine."

"You won't need that, my lord," said Lili as she sauntered up to him. "But *I* might find it useful."

"What the devil is that supposed to—"

"*Sittu.*" She touched his forehead.

His eyes closed; his arms went limp. The paddle and the phallus thumped onto the floor.

What just happened? Caroline wondered. He looked as if he had suddenly fallen asleep standing up.

Lili stroked his forehead, murmuring something in a language Caroline had never heard before.

Dunhurst opened his eyes, blinking in evident bewilderment.

"Unbutton those." Lili pointed to the fall flap of his breeches. "And untie your drawers."

He did her bidding without hesitation. Caroline had read about mesmerists, who could induce a trancelike state with certain words and actions. Somehow, Lili must have learned how to do that.

"Push them down to your ankles," she said, "then clasp your hands behind your neck."

He did so. His masculine appendage was entirely flaccid, which Caroline wouldn't have expected. From what she'd been told about men like Dunhurst, it aroused them sexually to incite fear and pain and humiliation, which was what he'd been doing until just a few seconds before.

Lili regarded the limp little organ with interest. "Of course. I should have known. Can't raise the old sail, eh?"

Dunhurst, looking sheepish, lifted his meaty shoulders.

Lili cracked her palm across his face.

Caroline gasped.

"Answer your mistress when she asks you a question. Are you impotent?"

"Y-yes, mistress."

"Other men suffer from that malady without turning into a brutish hound like you." She picked up the phallus and paddle and walked around him, appraising him up and down as the slaves had been appraised during Inspection. When he looked at her over his shoulder, she smacked his backside with the paddle, making him yelp. "Eyes forward, dog."

"Yes, mistress." As he was turning his head, his gaze lit on Caroline, and he paused.

"Forward!" Lili whacked him again.

He obeyed her. Caroline fretted for a moment about his having seen her watching him, but given his mesmerized state, he probably wouldn't recall any of what was happening here.

With a wicked little smile, Lili said, "Await."

He hesitated.

She whacked him again. "You heard me."

He bent over, bracing his hands on his knees.

Setting the paddle aside, she retrieved a little green jar from the leather box, opened it, and scooped up a dab of something that looked like cold cream. "Have *you* ever been fucked in the arse?" she inquired as she spread the unguent over the phallus.

"Yes, mistress."

"Yes? Who was it, some older schoolmate?"

"Yes, mistress."

"But not since then?"

"No, mistress."

"Then I should say you're overdue." She spread the cheeks of his arse with one hand, while positioning the steel rod with the other.

Dunhurst flinched, looking apprehensive.

"Don't clench," she said. "It will only make it hurt more." She shoved the phallus in a few inches, making him howl. "You see?"

"Y-y-yes, mistress."

"At least I've greased it up for you," she said as she twisted it this way and that. "That's more than you would have done for me, is it not?"

Dunhurst groaned hoarsely, his face contorted in pain.

"Is it not?" Lili grabbed the paddle and brought it down hard on his reddened rear end. "Answer me, dog."

Through a pained moan he said, "Y-yes, mistress."

She continued paddling him as she worked the phallus in deeper and deeper, using quick, hard thrusts. "You need this," she told him. "You should thank me for doing this."

"Th-thank you, mistress."

"When I get it all the way in," she said, "I'm going to strap it onto you so that it stays in, and then I'm going to chain you to that bed and make you lick me till I've come a dozen times. If you do it well, I shall remove the silver truncheon. If not, I shall leave it in until you weep and beg to have it out. Do you understand?"

"Yes, mistress."

"Am I fucking you hard enough, or do you need it harder?"

"H-harder, mistress." He groaned as she jammed the rod in forcefully.

"Do you still need the paddling?" she asked.

"Yes, please, mistress. Make it hurt."

Caroline backed off the balcony and closed the double doors, drawing the curtains over them, which muffled his rhythmic grunts and servile utterings, but didn't silence them entirely.

She turned and regarded the black leather box warily, speculating on its contents with both apprehension and, if she was honest, lurid curiosity. On the lid was a tooled orchid and chain design like that on the cover of the *Floral Compendium*. She flipped open the latch and lifted the lid.

The interior of the big box was lined in gold satin with indentations shaped to accommodate their contents. One niche, a round one, was empty. The others contained a dizzying variety of items. Many were phalluses, with the steel rod, what Lili had called the silver truncheon, being the largest. Three others—crafted of whalebone, wood, and tortoiseshell—resembled erect penises in every particular, including size. Two, one of bronze and the other silver, were much smaller, with wide bases. And then there was a very curious one made of black India rubber with two separate phalluses, one a bit thicker than the other. There was a small rubber ball, a handful of padlocks, a little polished stone egg, a string of onyx beads with a little handle on the end, two steel balls a little larger than marbles, several curious clips and rings, some black silk cravats, the jar of cold cream, and a bottle labeled OLIVE OIL.

These items were housed in what Caroline realized was a removable tray. When she lifted it out, she found the bottom of the box divided into three sections. One held coils of chain, another a number of leather straps with buckles, and the third a large black velvet pouch with little golden clasps all around the open end. Upon closer inspection, she discovered that there were two slits in the pouch, which were finished all around with gold thread, like oversized buttonholes. One was about three inches long and lined with little hooks and eyes, the other half that length and with no means of closure. Caroline turned the pouch this way and that, stumped as to what prurient use it might be put—until she held it up with the open end on the bottom. The holes were for breathing, she realized, the larger one for the mouth and the smaller for the nose.

Don't think about all this, Caroline told herself as she stuffed the hood back into its compartment, returned the tray to the box and relatched it. *Wash up, go to bed, and . . .*

And await Lord Rexton's return.

There was no washstand in the room, but there was a door in the corner, and perhaps a bathroom of some sort behind it. Caroline opened the door to discover an elegant, classically inspired room with a round bathtub sunk into the center of the marble floor and satin couches tucked into little alcoves. The walls were lined with painted wall panels depicting naked men and women engaged in all manner of obscene acts, making it seem as if this lavish *salle de bain* had been lifted right out of Pompeii. A sink in a gilt cabinet stood against one wall next to a separate little room that housed a Brahmah water closet, a modern luxury that Caroline had never even seen until her arrival at Grotte Cachée. When she built her new house, she would have Brahmahs installed on every floor, and lovely sinks and bathtubs, with water piped down from rooftop cisterns, as it was here. Why not indulge herself a bit? She would certainly have earned it.

She washed off her face paint and brushed out her hair,

then opened the tall wardrobe case to see whether night-clothes had been provided for her. There were hats, bonnets, gloves, slippers, half-boots, fans, parasols, a drawer full of paste jewelry, and several décolleté gowns of salacious design. Noticeably absent was the periwinkle silk frock she'd been given at Lord Rexton's, and in which she'd arrived here. There were quite a number of sheer negligees, a silken wrapper, a riding habit, and all manner of underpinnings. Most of the latter were lasciviously fashioned of transparent netting and lace. There was, however, one surprisingly modest cotton shift that she decided would serve nicely—though whether Lord Rexton would approve remained to be seen.

"Every morning after your bath, every evening before dinner, and every night before retiring," Mr. Llewellyn *had instructed them, "you are to seek your master's instructions as to your manner of dress—or undress, as the case may be—and follow them to the letter."*

As Caroline set about pulling the Inspection gown off over her head, she was impeded by the leash dangling from the front of her collar. She didn't relish the notion of getting into bed with it on, but dare she unclip it herself? The answer really depended on Rexton's intent in purchasing her. His advising her to call him "master" outside of this room, which implied that she needn't do so within it, was no guarantee that he didn't mean to use her as the other slaves would be used. Perhaps he simply considered it silly to be addressed that way by someone with whom he was already acquainted; he appeared, after all, to be a confirmed cynic. He did, however, pledge one hundred thousand guineas for the right to dominate her, sexually and otherwise, for the coming week. Would any man, especially a self-indulgent libertine like Viscount

Rexton, part with that kind of money without claiming what he'd paid for?

In the end, Caroline left the leash in place, donned the shift, and blew out the candles. She got into bed, keeping to one edge so as to leave room for Rexton. The sheets were cool and smelled of green grass and clear blue skies. She closed her eyes, trying to imagine herself lying in a field of clover with white linen sheets flapping in the breeze, but her fretful mind couldn't be soothed, and sleep eluded her for some time.

Caroline awoke to the creak of door hinges.

At first, she couldn't recall where she was...and then she remembered. She lay on her side, trying not to breathe too loudly as she watched the tall form of a man backlit by moonlight—Viscount Rexton—opening the double glass doors. He was slow and deliberate in his movements, but clumsy nonetheless.

He stepped out onto the balcony rather unsteadily and undressed with his back to her, leaning for support on the stone balustrade and letting his clothes lay where they fell. Nude, his silhouette put her in mind of an engraving she'd seen of Michelangelo's *David*—broad-shouldered, lean-hipped, long-legged.

He turned.

Caroline closed her eyes, but not before catching a glimpse of his privates, which shifted heavily as he moved. She heard the faint squeak of a floorboard beneath the carpet as he approached the bed. He stood still for what seemed like an eternity as Caroline feigned sleep, her heart jittering.

Something nudged her collar very slightly, which was when she realized he'd leaned over and was touching it, manipulating something. She smelled the gin on his breath. It took all her self-control to keep her breathing slow and somnolent as he unclipped the leash and carefully gathered it up.

Caroline sensed him walking away, and slitted her eyes open just enough to follow his movements. She froze inside when he opened the leather box and perused its contents. He lifted the silver truncheon, gave it a bemused look that she could see even in the semidarkness, and replaced it. Coiling the leash around his hand, he tucked that into the box—no doubt into that round compartment that had been empty. He closed the box and set it on the floor, along with Caroline's satchel. Raising the lid of the bench, he withdrew a folded blanket, which he took back onto the balcony, hissing a curse when he stubbed his toe on something.

From where Caroline lay, she could see the top half of the wicker chaise, which was backless, with a scroll arm on either end. Rexton rearranged the cushions, tossing some onto the stone floor, wrapped the blanket around himself, and lay down. It took him some time to accommodate his long body to the too-short chaise, the wicker griping squeakily as he tried out different positions. He finally settled down reclining on his side, facing away from her. Caroline knew he must be uncomfortable, but she just couldn't bring herself to invite him into bed with her.

She closed her eyes and tried to return to sleep, but she couldn't stop wondering what matter of libertinage she would encounter tomorrow, the first official day of Slave Week. Some of the veteran slaves had spoken of a veritable festival of ribaldry, with acts of unspeakable lechery conducted right out in the open, but Caroline suspected they were merely having a bit of fun at the novices' expense.

She *hoped* they were.

They weren't, as she discovered the next morning.

S_{ix}

SIR ALBERT NICKERSON, sitting to the left of Caroline at the long, damask-draped table in Grotte Cachée's oak-paneled dining room, tore off a shred of his brioche and slathered it with butter and Auvergnat fruit paste. He clicked his tongue at the naked Holly, sitting next to him on the Savonnerie rug, hands dutifully clasped behind her.

She looked up and opened her mouth, whereupon Sir Albert fed her the little morsel.

"Get it all," he said, smiling in approval as the veteran slave licked and sucked the butter and fruit paste off his fingers with sensual relish.

Reaching down, he pulled her onto his lap so that she was sitting astride him face-to-face. He unbuttoned his breeches flap, prompting Caroline to concentrate fixedly on her plate of shirred eggs, but she could still see him as he scooped a dollop of butter out of the pot and reached between them, his hand working busily.

"Take your time," he told her as she lowered herself onto his rigid, greased organ. "Aye, that's it. That's it." He let out a deep, luxuriant sigh.

With the exception of Lord Rexton, sitting in glum silence to Caroline's right, the gentlemen at their end of the table watched this performance with open interest. Two or three of the slaveless Unattached Gentlemen—identifiable by their lack of the Black Heart pendant—reached under the table to stroke themselves.

Monsieur Pomerleau, sitting across from Caroline, spoke softly to the dark-haired Poppy, standing next to him. She wore a pink-checked dimity frock that would have looked innocently pastoral but for the two lace-trimmed cutouts on the bosom, framing a pair of creamy breasts with crimson-rouged nipples. She unclasped her hands from behind her and crawled under the table as her master leaned back in his chair, his languorous gaze on Sir Albert and Holly.

Of the half-dozen slaves in the dining room, Caroline was the only one who had been permitted to fill a plate at the sumptuously laden, marble-topped buffet and take a seat at the table. Three had been made to sit on the floor so as to be fed like dogs, the other two to stand in attendance and apparently not be fed at all. They were either entirely unclothed but for their shackles, or lewdly attired in accordance with their masters' wishes—except for Caroline. After bathing this morning, refreshing her sponge, and applying her creams and powders, she'd asked Lord Rexton what he would have her wear, only to be told he didn't give a damn and would rather not be pestered about such things.

She'd chosen a gown of filmy white lawn worn over layers of petticoats so as to render it opaque. Laughable though such an attempt at modesty was after her de facto nudity in front of everyone the night before, it gave her some comfort. Of course, her attire contrasted absurdly with her golden shackles and the leash Rexton had been obliged to clip onto her collar before bringing her down to breakfast.

Rexton's breakfast consisted of a cup of coffee spiked with brandy from his flask—the hair of the dog, of course. He'd slept past ten out on the balcony and awakened sallow and forbiddingly dour. Caroline was surprised at how well turned out he looked after washing up, shaving the morning stubble off his jaw, and getting dressed. In lieu of knee breeches, he wore trousers, as did most of the younger men. However, he was the only one aside from Mr. Brummel, whom Caroline had spied leaving the dining room as they were entering it, who had forsaken the cutaway for one of the new military-inspired coats that buttoned all the way down the front.

"Dunhurst! You look like hell," greeted Lord Gatleigh as the puffy-eyed marquess trudged over to the table—the end opposite Caroline's, thank the saints—with a plate of eggs and ham in one hand and his walking stick in the other. He set the plate on the table, dragged out a chair next to Gatleigh's, and eased himself into it, wincing.

"Long night, eh?" asked Sir Edmund Byrde, the silver-haired gentleman who had examined Caroline so clinically, teeth and all, but who had failed to purchase a slave the night before.

"Bloody right," the marquess grunted as he cut off a chunk of ham and pierced it with his fork.

Caroline wondered if he actually remembered any of it, given his mesmerized state.

"Let's feel you come," urged Sir Albert as Holly writhed atop him with increasing urgency. "Tell us when you're ready."

"Yes, master."

Caroline stole a glance at them, amazed that Holly, veteran or no, could be so abandoned before all these leering strangers. It didn't appear to be a performance. Her movements were hectic, her face and breasts darkly flushed.

"Are you close?" inquired her master, as breathless as she.

"Yes, master," she rasped.

Caroline didn't want this shameless ribaldry to arouse her, but it did. What would it be like, she wondered, to perform a sexual act in front of others? It would be mortifying—to Caroline. Rose, on the other hand, might very well relish the experience.

Lord Gatleigh elbowed Dunhurst. "Gave that luscious little heathen a taste of the old dilly-whacker, what?"

"In every hole. I might've made some new ones."

"Did you bend her to your will? Did you make her grovel?"

"Had her begging for mercy, even as she was begging for another good, hard boning." Dunhurst shoved a forkful of ham into his mouth, chewing it with a cocky sneer—until a particularly dramatic groan from Holly drew his attention to Caroline's end of the table. His jaw ceased its grinding as those hard little black eyes lit on her; hot color stained his cheeks.

He abruptly looked away and lifted his teacup, its contents sloshing over the rim to stain the tablecloth. "God's bones!"

He did remember, Caroline realized—all of it, including her having witnessed his debasement at Lili's hands. Dunhurst knew that she knew it was he, not Lili, who had begged and groveled—and, worse, that he was incapable of having penetrated Lili even the once, never mind "in every hole."

Remembering Dunhurst's impotence made Caroline wonder about Rexton's having slept outside on the balcony rather
than in bed with her, where she would have had no choice but
to grant him the sexual privileges he'd purchased fair and
square. She thought back to the night they'd met, and his having rejected her grudging offer to sleep with him in return for
his having saved her from the madhouse. Was it possible that
Rexton was impotent, too? She'd heard that could happen
from overindulgence in drink.

"I'm coming, master," Holly gasped, her body taut and
quivering. She let out a series of little gasps as Sir Albert arched
beneath her, a low, strangled sound rising from his chest.

"Dunhurst, old man," Sir Edmund said conversationally, as
if this lewd scene were not playing out just down the table
from him. "Where's your Black Heart? We're to wear them at
all times. If that little fop Llewellyn sees you, he'll report you to
Riddell, and there will be a black mark next to your name."

Glowering at his plate, the marquess said, "Little twat wasn't
worth a shilling, much less what I would have ended up paying
for her. I'd rather be unattached than be saddled with the likes
of her."

❧

Oh, bloody hell, Rexton thought. What had made him think
he could nurse his blinding morning head in peace?

He lowered his coffee cup and leaned forward so as to have
a clear view of Dunhurst. "What have you done to her?"

Dunhurst snickered bitterly. "Your concern is quite moving, Rexton, but that one's not the type of chit that warrants
fretting over."

"Where is she, then?"

"How the hell should I know? She was gone this morning when I woke up. Left a note saying she was done being my slave."

"*Una donna astuta*," murmured the unattached Conte Montesano, sitting to Rexton's right. Catching Rexton's eye, he said, "A smart one, eh?"

"*È molto astuta*," Rexton replied.

"I think I saw her heading toward the bathhouse a little while ago," offered Lord Madderly, also sans slave. "She was with Cutbridge and that slave of his, the magnificent blonde."

Pointing his knife at Rexton, Dunhurst said, "I expect you to tear up my note of indebtedness. I don't owe her a bloody penny now. *And* I expect you to send the wench packing. Ship her back to Turkey, or Egypt, or wherever the bloody hell she came from. She's got to go."

"I'm not so sure about that," Rexton said.

"*What?*"

"It's not as if she violated the terms of her contract."

"Of course she did. She…she…" The marquess glanced around at his breakfast companions. "She…"

"To hear you tell it," Rexton said, "she allowed you to 'bend her to your will,' which would indicate that she lived up to her end of the arrangement. However, it would appear that she has chosen to voluntarily sever it and sacrifice the money simply to get away from you."

There were snickers from some of the gentlemen at Rexton's end of the table. Even Dunhurst's two old chums, Gatleigh and Sir Edmund, appeared to be trying not to laugh.

Dunhurst stared daggers at Rexton. "Voluntary or not, it amounts to the same thing."

Rexton shook his head. "Not according to the terms of the contract. Since she terminated it, I *will* tear up your note, Dunhurst, but I've got no legal right to expel her if she wishes to stay."

"To stay?" Dunhurst exclaimed. "As what? She won't be a slave anymore."

"Re-auction her!" cried Sir Edmund, a sentiment echoed by his fellow Unattached Gentlemen.

"Only if she desires it," Rexton said. "Otherwise, I must permit her to remain here as a . . . well, I suppose she'll be an Unattached Lady."

"There *is* no such thing," Dunhurst said.

"There is now," Rexton replied. "If the lady wishes it."

"You son of a bitch," snarled Dunhurst, his big hands curling into fists as he glared at Rexton down the length of the table. "You've had it in for me ever since last summer, when that fucking Dahlia started maligning my good name. You took the part of a slave against her master. Oh, yes, I know all about it. I know you were the one who made them search my chamber for that imaginary stick of hers, as if I were some common—"

"This conversation is becoming tedious," said Rexton as he pushed his chair back and rose.

"I know you sent her home with sixteen thousand guineas she hadn't earned and didn't deserve," Dunhurst spat out.

"Come along, Rose," said Rexton, pulling her chair out.

"Don't want to hear it, do you?" Dunhurst sneered as he hauled himself to his feet. "Don't want to remember what a dupe you were, handing over sixteen thousand guineas of your own money to a lying little baggage like that."

Gripping Caroline by the arm, Rexton strode toward the open doorway to the rose garden on the west side of the castle.

"And I know you tried to have me banned from Slave Week," shouted the enraged marquess, spittle flying. "But Sir Charles and Oliver Riddell knew what I could afford to pay for a slave, and they wanted their cut of it. Not you, though, eh, Rexton? You don't need my money, you've got enough of your own—enough to part with a hundred thousand guineas for that one"—he stabbed his walking stick in Caroline's direction—"just to keep me from having her. Why else would you have done it? It's not like she's anything special, just another greedy little jade like all the rest of them...."

He continued raving as Rexton led Caroline along a brick path lined with cast-iron benches, one of which was occupied by Beau Brummel and his slave, the gamine Jessamine, locked in carnal union. Jessamine, wearing nothing but a man's shirt, knelt on the bench facing the backrest, her hands and feet chained to the cast-iron scrollwork. She winced with every thrust of the dashingly attired Brummel, who stood behind her with one hand clutching her boyishly short hair and the other holding her shirt bunched up so that he could observe the juncture of their bodies.

They were coupling in the Greek manner, Rexton observed. So, evidently, did Caroline, who blanched and looked away as they passed the couple.

She started struggling against his grip as he ushered her down the path to the bathhouse.

"My lord, I beg you," she implored. "You're hurting me."

He stopped walking and released her arm, grimacing at the

livid marks his hand had left. He pulled his flask from inside his coat and took a drink.

"Is...is it true?" she asked as she rubbed her arm. "About you giving Dahlia the sixteen thousand—"

"You are forbidden to speak except to answer a question or acknowledge an order, remember?" He capped the flask and tucked it away.

"But..." She looked around them in every direction. "There's no one within earshot, and I thought you didn't care about...you know. The rules."

"Except for the one about you keeping your mouth shut. I'm rather partial to that one."

Caroline looked up at Rexton with those big, quiet eyes for a moment that felt interminable to him.

"Yes, master," she said—not in a mocking manner, nor subservient, of course, but with a sardonic nuance that he couldn't help but admire.

"Impudent chit." He grabbed her leash and continued down the path, tugging her along with him.

He didn't want to admire her. He didn't want to have anything to do with her, but here he was, forced into lockstep with her for the entire goddamned week. Dunhurst was right. He *was* a dupe. First Dahlia, now this one. They were his Achilles' heel, these bloody damsels in distress. His compulsion to play the savior was the one vulnerable spot in the otherwise impenetrable armor he'd been piling onto himself these past two years. It made him weak; it made him foolish. It was a shortcoming he must endeavor to rectify for his own peace of mind.

"Oh, my word!" she said when they rounded a curve in the path, and she saw the bathhouse for what was apparently the first time. "Oh, it's exquisite. Was it really built by the Romans?"

On a sigh, he said, "You've no intention at all of shutting up, do you?"

"Sorry—I forgot."

"Well, if you forget in front of the wrong person and end up being auctioned off to the likes of Dunhurst, it won't be on my head."

As they approached the bathhouse, Rexton noticed Gilles Bertrand and his naked slave, the tall, plumply pretty Jonquil, standing against a tree at the edge of the nearby woods, embracing—or so he thought until he got closer and saw that Jonquil was facing the tree with Bertrand behind her, grinding away slowly. Another alfresco buggering; must be something in the air.

Caroline looked away sharply, much as she'd done when they passed Brummel and Jessamine on the garden bench. He would have thought she was just priggish in general, but for her ill-disguised fascination with the bawdy goings-on at the breakfast table.

"Consumed with shock already?" he asked as he led her by her leash toward the entrance to the bathhouse. "The week has barely begun."

"I'm...I'm not shocked." She looked genuinely offended.

He gave a dubious snort.

"I'm *not*. I may not be as...experienced as some, but I am a good deal more worldly-wise than you give me credit for."

"Sir Charles told me you nearly swooned when he started showing you his little portfolio of smutty pictures."

Avoiding his gaze, her face bright pink, she said, "Yes, well, I've accustomed myself since then to the existence of different

tastes and predilections in . . . such matters. But some things . . ."
She gave a little nod in the direction of Bertrand and Jonquil
while keeping her gaze safely averted. "They're just not natural."

"There is nothing unnatural about sexual pleasure," he
said. "Short of it involving livestock, I suppose."

"A man might take pleasure in such an act, but a lady? I
think not."

"You think too much. Have you never just flung your mis-
givings aside and surrendered to a new experience just to . . .
well, just to *experience* it?"

"Not if it strikes me as wrong," she said. "We are blessed
with our powers of moral judgment for a reason."

"Spoken like a true rector's daughter," he muttered as he
led her toward the entrance to the bathhouse.

Her nose twitched at the sweetly scorched aroma wafting
toward them. "What is that I smell?"

"They don't smoke opium in St. Giles?"

"That's *opium*?" Her eyes widened, and grew wider still
when she stepped into the smoke-hazed bathhouse and saw
what was transpiring there. So much for her "worldly wisdom."

The marble floor surrounding the pool was mounded with
silken pillows on which were strewn a dozen or more bodies,
some in repose and some writhing in masses, all naked or in
extreme dishabille—with the exception of the fully dressed Li
Menshang, who sat with a lacquered tray near the cave entrance, twirling a spindle tipped with bubbling brown paste
over the flame of a spirit lamp. Lifting a bamboo smoking pistol, he used the spindle to knead the dab of cooked opium on
its knoblike bowl, letting the flame kiss it from time to time to
prevent it from stiffening. It was a complicated operation, one
that had taken Rexton himself quite some time to master.

When he was satisfied with the opium's consistency, Li inserted it into the little hole on the bowl, withdrawing the spindle with a deft twist. Leaning over, he handed the pipe to Inigo, reclining on his side with Li's beloved mistress, Tulip, curled in his arms front to back. Inigo was naked from the waist up, with his trousers unbuttoned. He flexed his hips slightly, and that was when Rexton realized he had that gigantic cock of his buried inside her.

Inigo took the pipe, astounding Rexton by thanking Li in the Chinaman's native tongue. *"Fei chang gan xie."*

"Bie ke qi." Li sat back against the wall of rock and tugged gently on the leash of his own slave, Violet, who'd been lying at his feet lazily frigging herself with an ivory dildo. She wore the same expression of languid euphoria as did her master, Inigo, and Tulip. No doubt they had been passing that smoking pistol around for some time.

"In the French manner, if you please," Li told her in his heavily accented English as he unbuttoned his trousers.

As he drew on the pipe, Inigo, who had formed a friendship with Rexton the year before, caught his eye and nodded in greeting. Rexton nodded back, grateful that Inigo's mouth was occupied, so as to preclude conversation. He didn't think he would ever get used to chatting with other men while they were doing a bit of business, although most of the men who attended Slave Week seemed to think nothing of it.

"Can one become drunk on opium just from breathing air in which it's been smoked?" Caroline asked Rexton softly, so as not to be overheard by the others.

"You feel it, too?" A sense of woozy unreality had overtaken him from the moment he'd entered the bathhouse. Then again, he'd felt much the same the day before, during his solitary predawn bathe, and there'd been no opium being smoked then. The feeling had intensified when he'd ventured into the cave, so much so that he'd turned back before he'd gone a hundred yards.

Taking in the salacious satyr-and-nymph statues, she said, "It's almost as if this were all a fantastic dream."

Rexton nodded as he watched the smoke from Inigo's pipe drift toward the pool and up through the open roof, glittering in the wash of sunlight.

Several people were taking the waters at present, including Lili, Elle, and Rexton's old army acquaintance and the hero of Vitoria, Jack Compton, now Baron of Cutbridge. His lordship was standing waist-deep in the water facing away from Rexton, rousting Elle as she leaned back with her arms braced on the side of the pool, her spectacularly long legs wrapped around his waist. Lili stood behind Cutbridge manipulating something under the water, possibly one of those little arse-sized dildoes from the black leather box that had been delivered to each of their rooms. She stroked Elle's leg lingeringly, affectionately. Elle met her friend's gaze with an intimate smile, the kind of smile lovers shared. It had never occurred to Rexton that the two women might be sapphists.

Wanting to gauge the temperature of the water, for he'd been told it could vary dramatically from day to day, or even hour to hour, he crouched down and dipped in his hand. Arousal slammed through him like mortar fire. He gasped and bolted to his feet, instantly erect. Thank God he'd had the foresight to wear a coat that covered him in front. He would hate to be going about with an obvious cockstand all day, like some of these randy dogs in their snug breeches and cutaways—although none of them seemed to mind.

Glancing at Caroline as he brushed off his trousers and coat, he saw her unblinking gaze shift from one tangle of bodies to the next, and the next...

"A penny for your thoughts, Miss Kea—" He glanced around. "Rose. Or should I say a hundred thousand guineas."

Stiffening her back, she said, with studied nonchalance, "I was thinking, what a remarkable level of activity for so early in the day."

He chuckled and shook his head, prompting her to turn away with a self-conscious little smile that tickled him in the center of his chest. How the devil could he have failed to recognize, upon their first meeting a fortnight past, what an incredible beauty she was? Yes, she'd been panicky and bedraggled, with snarled hair and a sodden frock, but still he had not recalled the next day those big, disarming eyes, the delicate nose, the lush mouth. He must have been drunk as an owl. Would that she didn't feel the need to disguise her appearance with henna and face paint. He did remember that her hair in its natural state was very blond, more so even than Natalia's.

Thinking about Natalia jolted him out of his reverie.

Caroline's expression sobered. "Well, I suppose it couldn't have lasted forever."

"What?"

"You were smiling. I'd never seen you smile. You looked..."

"Like a grinning idiot?"

"What? No. No, of course not."

He *felt* like an idiot, having gawked at her like a callow schoolboy. More the fool he, for dropping his guard, however briefly. Nothing had changed in the past two years; *he* hadn't changed.

Don't let her get to you, he told himself. She's nobody, a river rat, just another St. Giles harlot offering to spread her legs for the highest bidder. He should remember what she was, and treat her accordingly, not let her worm her way under his skin.

Yanking on her leash, he said, "Let's get out of here. And from now on, keep your fucking mouth shut."

∂৫

That night, Rexton chose once again to sleep on the balcony, after sitting out there alone with his gin bottle for about an hour. And once again, Caroline lay awake half the night, her mind far too busy to settle into sleep.

"*From now on, keep your fucking mouth shut.*" This, not ten seconds after he'd stood there smiling into her eyes in a way that had made her feel even more light-headed than she'd been.

In the middle of the night, she heard a faint sound coming from outside, almost too faint to hear. She lay very still on her back, not even breathing, to concentrate on it. It sounded rather like fingers briskly rubbing a wool blanket.

Slowly, so as not to make a sound, Caroline turned onto her side facing the balcony. The night was clear and her eyes had gotten used to the dark, so she had no trouble making out the chaise with Rexton lying upon it—or rather, reclining with his back propped up on pillows, because his body was too long to lie flat. She could see him down to his thighs, around which the blanket was bunched, leaving him otherwise naked. His eyes were closed, but his right arm was moving briskly, as if he were scratching his lower belly—except that his hand was fisted. It didn't take long for her to figure out what it was fisted around.

She knew she should close her eyes and give him his privacy, but her attention was riveted, and all she could do was lie there and watch. He stroked faster and faster, the muscles of his arm hard and corded, hips flexing.

His left hand appeared, clutching something white—a handkerchief, Caroline realized when he shook it out. This he pressed to the end of his sex as he squeezed and pumped. He arched his head and torso off the pillows, his entire body shuddering for several long seconds. There came a long exhalation from deep in his lungs, and then he sank back bonelessly onto the pillows. He lay still for a moment, his chest heaving, gazing up at the sky. And then he turned and looked toward Caroline.

She closed her eyes, consciously slowed her breathing.

There was no sound for some time, and then she heard him sigh. She heard a slight rustling, and then the muted squeak of the cork popping out of the gin bottle.

Lord Rexton must have his reasons for not bedding her, Caroline reflected, but clearly impotence was not one of them.

Seven

THE NEXT MORNING, Caroline emerged from a long, hot bath in the Pompeian *salle de bain* to find Rexton standing before the cheval mirror in his shirtsleeves, tying his long, voluminous white cravat. The nearly empty gin bottle stood open on the dressing table next to him.

David Childe, Lord Rexton, was a singularly complicated man—erudite, yet dissipated, ruthless yet generous, and indecently beautiful. She wished he didn't fascinate her. She very much wished she hadn't lain in that steamy, rose-scented bath until her fingertips shriveled, revisiting in her mind the sight of him relieving his pent-up lust by his own hand. Never had she imagined that she might find such a thing arousing, yet the very memory of it had excited her passions to an almost excruciating degree. She might have resorted to slaking her lust as Rexton had slaked his, had she not forgotten to lock the bathroom door. The prospect of him walking in on her as she pleasured herself was too mortifying to risk.

He eyed her reflection in the mirror, his gaze lighting on her damp hair, her fresh-scrubbed face, the gilded steel slave collar, and her breasts, their contours all too apparent beneath her thin silken wrapper. He met her gaze, and for a fleeting moment she saw a glimmer of heat in his eyes before they went cold and opaque, as if a shade had been pulled down over them. He'd been much the same yesterday, except for that brief moment of rapport in the bathhouse.

"Shall I choose my own clothing, my lord?" she asked.

"Is that not what I told you to—shit!" He yanked at the knot he'd just made, unwrapped the cravat, and flung it to the floor. "Shit, shit, shit."

He'd sworn liberally in her presence since yesterday afternoon, as if she'd somehow been demoted in his mind from lady to trollop.

Caroline picked up the cravat, which she folded just to have something to do while Rexton paced across the room and back again, the balls of his hands pressed against his forehead.

"Do you have a headache, my lord?"

"No. And I don't recall giving you leave to speak."

Since yesterday, he had demanded that she keep her counsel even in private.

He sank into a red leather chair, leaned forward on his elbows, and scrubbed his hands over his face. Perhaps, she thought, it would lighten his mood if she were to say what she'd wanted to say to him ever since she woke up that morning.

"My lord, if I might just—"

"Shut up!" He bounded up from the chair and stalked

toward her until she felt one of the urn-shaped bedposts at her back. Hovering over her, flushed with fury, he yelled, "Can't you just fucking shut up?"

Say it. Just say it. It will help. "I just wanted to thank you," she said tremulously, twisting the cravat in her hands.

He looked at her as if she were mad. "Whatever for?"

"I know that you bought me as a kindness, to keep Lord Dunhurst from having me."

"Has it occurred to you that he may have been right when he accused me of buying you just to spite him?"

She shook her head, which held strangely wobbly on her neck; her hands were trembling. "You did it for me. You want people to think you're cold and uncaring, but you can't hide your true nature. You have a good heart, a compassionate heart."

"This is all the heart I've got," he said, holding up the Master's Pendant that hung around his neck. "It's all the heart I want. And if you think otherwise, you're a fool."

"Then, I'm a fool, because I know what's in here." She pressed a hand to his chest, a wall of warm, solid flesh beneath cool linen. "I can feel it beating. It's the most real and vital part of you."

"Can you feel this?" Seizing her hand, he pulled it downward, molding it to his sex through his trousers. "This is a damn sight more real and vital than that lump of meat in my chest."

Caroline tried to pull away, but his grip was far too strong. He pressed it harder to his member, which swelled and stiffened as he rubbed her palm up and down its length. She turned her head and closed her eyes, trying not to think about what she was doing, what he was making her do—and how it was making her feel, God help her, to be touching him this way. The arousal she'd felt in the bath came rushing back with breathtaking force.

Rexton seized her by the chin and jerked her head around to face him. She opened her eyes and saw *his* eyes, black and hungry and so close that she felt as if the sun had winked out, turning day into night.

He said, "I'm not what you think I am. The sooner you learn that, the better off you'll be."

He reached for the sash that secured her empire-waist wrapper.

Bewildered by this sudden turn of events, she instinctively tried to push him away. Rexton captured her hands, raised them over her head, and snapped the wrist cuffs together through one of the handles on the urn.

He untied the sash and whipped open the wrapper, leaving her naked and exposed. With one hand, he kneaded a breast; with the other, he unbuttoned his trousers. The shock of his hot, rough palm on her bare flesh made her sex throb wildly. Being bound was a relief, just as it had been during the Inspection of the Slaves. This would happen with or without her cooperation; she was helpless to resist.

"Tell me to stop." He crushed her to the bedpost, his erection like hot steel against her belly, its tip damp.

Oh, God, don't stop, she thought as she struggled not to rub against him. *Don't stop, don't stop.*

"You bought me, my lord," she said shakily. "You may do as you wish."

"What do *you* wish?"

"I . . . I have no wishes."

He slid a hand down her belly, and lower still. She sucked in a breath as he glided a finger between the lips of her sex and along the inflamed, slippery flesh within. Her hips jerked forward of their own volition.

"I think you do have wishes," he murmured into her ear as he caressed her. "Dark desires you're too cowardly to confess, even to yourself. You'd rather play the slave than sully yourself by admitting them. Is that not right, Miss Keating?"

"I . . ." She hadn't thought it through like that. She'd been reacting, not thinking.

"Answer me." He lifted her, holding her against the post as he stood in the cradle of her thighs, his sex nudging hers. "You want me to take you, use you, as a master uses his slave. Don't you? *Answer* me."

Damn him for doing this to her—and damn *her*, for letting him crawl into her mind this way.

"No indignant denial, eh? Well, then, if you are my slave, Miss Keating, that would make me your master, would it not?"

"Please, my lord. P-please, I . . ."

He pressed into her just slightly, enough so that she could feel the broad, smooth head of his organ stretching her open. "Do you want me to fuck you, slave?"

It wasn't a *want*, it was a *need*. She was consumed with it, shaking with it.

"*Say it*," he commanded.

"Don't make me. Please don't make me."

"That's answer enough." He drove into her hard, sheathing himself with one lubricious thrust. She cried out at the abrupt impalement, feeling a burning, impossible fullness, a sense of utter possession.

He took her with deep, grinding thrusts that she met eagerly, hips bucking against his. Every sharp plunge forced a low, feral growl from his chest.

"Don't look at me," he panted.

She turned her head. "Yes, my lor—"

"Don't talk to me. Don't make a fucking sound."

She bit her lip to keep from moaning as her pleasure mounted higher, higher... The enforced silence seemed to amplify it, so that when her climax hit, she screamed with the force of it.

He shouted hoarsely, his fingers digging painfully into her flesh. She felt spasm after spasm as he shot his seed, and then he collapsed against her, limp and damp, his hair stuck to his forehead. He sucked in air as if he'd just finished a footrace. One of his breaths emerged as a faint groan that struck Caroline as being filled with misery.

He straightened up, his gaze lighting on hers. He looked away quickly, but Caroline had seen something raw and unguarded in his eyes that provoked in her a grudging pity, despite how he was treating her.

When he uncoupled, it felt as if her insides were being pulled right out of her. He lowered her legs, buttoned his trousers, donned a double-breasted gray waistcoat over his shirt, rinsed off his face, and combed his hair. Only then did he detach her wrist cuffs so that she could lower her arms.

Caroline tugged her wrapper closed and knotted the sash with unsteady hands. Rexton retied the cravat, getting it right on the first try this time, put on a coat similar to the one he'd worn the day before, and crossed to the door. "I'm going down to breakfast. Be dressed when I get back."

He swung the door open and stood with his back to her for a moment, his hand on the knob. "Wear the lace chemise. With nothing under it."

He slammed the door so hard it felt like a punch in the stomach. Caroline heard the click of his key in the lock.

Eight

"TODAY'S *DIVERTISSEMENT* WILL be blind-man's buff," Mr. Llewellyn announced at the conclusion of afternoon tea in *le Salon Bleu*. "All are welcome to join in, however masters should be advised that any slave who takes part may be enjoyed by one or more gentlemen during this little frolic. Participating slaves are therefore required to wear the Black Hearts to indicate their availability. They are also required to be unclothed, although they may retain their stockings, slippers, and gloves if it pleases you."

From the corner of his eye as he reclined on an indigo velvet armchair with his cigar and snifter of brandy, Rexton saw Caroline, sitting on the floor with her hands clasped behind her neck, steal a furtive glance at him. He ignored her so as to let her fret for a few moments. Llewellyn's afternoon games always devolved into an orgy of one stripe or another, and being made to serve other men was Caroline's worst fear.

Two days ago—it was the afternoon of their second day as master and slave—they'd come upon a hooded slave tied to a garden arch, the Black Heart dangling from her collar. Two men were taking her fore and aft, while a third knelt before her, fucking her mouth hard and fast. The man on top of her slapped her arse with every thrust; the one below squeezed her breasts as if they were putty. Four other men stood and watched, stroking themselves through their breeches as they waited their turn.

"My lord!" Caroline had exclaimed, in rare defiance of the injunction against speaking out of turn. "Do something. Make them stop."

"I've no call to. They don't appear to be abusing her."

"That's not abuse?" She was shaking in outrage.

"She agreed to this sort of treatment when she signed her slave contract—as did you."

"Yes, but I never realized it could be so . . . so . . ." She shook her head, evidently at a loss for words to express her revulsion. "I can't imagine what that poor woman is going through right now."

"If I know her, she's in heaven," Rexton said. "That's Lady Beckinridge. Narcissa," he added in response to Caroline's puzzled look. He would recognize that lissome alabaster body anywhere. "I happen to know she likes it rough—very rough. I wouldn't be surprised if she specifically requested this."

"Impossible."

"Oh, look," Rexton had said. "I do believe she's coming."

Next to being shared with other men, buggery was what Caroline most feared Rexton would demand before the week was over. With those two exceptions, there didn't seem to be much in the way of sexual activity that Caroline found genuinely distasteful. Over the course of the past three days, he had subjected her to the kinds of acts that most men only experience in their darkest imaginings.

He had made liberal use of the contents of the black leather box and of the various commands she'd been taught to obey, starting the day he'd fucked her against the bedpost. That evening after dinner, he told her to strip, then to lay a blanket over the bed. "Wouldn't want to ruin that beautiful counterpane." He delivered this command calmly, quietly, having cooled down considerably from his earlier wrath. She did as commanded, albeit with a good deal of reluctance as regarded the disrobing. Her modesty was absurd, of course. She had an exquisite body, with a tiny waist and full, high breasts. "Supine," he ordered, pointing to the bed.

Once she was on her back with her legs spread, he retrieved four lengths of chain and four padlocks from the black box and secured her hand and foot to the bedposts. He took a silver tray from the drinks cabinet and laid it out with a few carefully chosen selections from the box—the tortoiseshell dildo, ivory cock ring, nipple pinchers, and olive oil. This he set on the bed between her outspread legs, and then he took his time undressing and washing up as she lay there trembling. He didn't mind the trembling, but he didn't much care for the way those big, nervous eyes followed him around the room, so he blindfolded her with one of the black silk cravats before he uncorked the bottle of oil. She shook in earnest then—until she discovered that that which gave him pleasure served her in equal measure.

They both slept in that big bed now, but he'd taken to

ordering her to turn in while he sat on the balcony and drank himself insensible; it was the only way he could get to sleep anymore. When he awakened during the night, always with a fixed bayonet despite his lingering drunkenness, he would roll her onto her back, or more often, onto her stomach with her arse propped up on pillows and her legs spread as wide as he could get them—though last night he'd simply straddled her face and shoved his cock in her mouth.

She kept him in a state of constant, excruciating arousal. He took her three, four, five times a day. He'd taken her in the bathhouse, the woods, and various rooms of the château, though never in the company of others. Twice, he'd made her kneel and fellate him through the mouth hole of the black velvet hood, after hooking it onto her slave collar. He often employed the leather bindings and chains, and almost always the hood or a blindfold, except when he was taking her from behind.

On no occasion, no matter what he did to her, had Caroline resisted him. Once she—and for that matter, he—had gotten over the initial strangeness of regarding each other as master and slave, it was as if she had surrendered not just her body, but all those ladylike inhibitions and scruples that she had lugged here with her. She embraced his escalating sexual demands with a level of enthusiasm that Rexton found fiercely arousing—but unnerving as well. It was starting to feel almost as if she could anticipate his desires, feel what he felt, be exactly what he wanted her to be. Were she some vacuous little nit, he might think she was just being blindly obedient, but she was far from vacuous, and her reactions were not those of a mindless slave, however much she purported to embrace the role.

Theirs was a complex and increasingly intimate relationship, and that was the problem. The last thing on earth that
Rexton wanted was a relationship of any kind, much less with
a woman who consumed his every waking thought, who inspired him to do things he'd never imagined he would do, to
act upon desires that, until now, had been hiding in the darkest recesses of his mind. It was he who should be wielding the
whip hand, not she.

He didn't like it. Over the past couple of days, he'd found
himself contriving excuses to mistreat her in the hope of driving a wedge through the center of this *thing* that held them in
its grip.

Yesterday evening, he'd ordered her to "await," then left her
in the room while he went downstairs to dinner. When he
came back and found her no longer bent over with her hands
on her legs, he'd put her over his knee and spanked her till that
pert little ass of hers was scalding pink and they were both on
the verge of spending. He made her beg him to fuck her, and
then, to prolong her punishment, he refused. Instead, he ordered her to "kneel down," clipped her wrist cuffs to her ankle
cuffs, and stood over her while he worked himself off. He'd left
her there, with his come drying on her back, while he joined
some of the other men in a game of whist that lasted past midnight.

"Our blindman's buff differs from the childhood pastime
with which you are all familiar," said Mr. Llewellyn as a team of
footmen moved the furniture to the edges of the big room. "In
our version, the blindfolded player is always one of the gentlemen. The order of play is determined beforehand by choosing
cards. The slaves are the blindman's prey, and they are permitted, in fact encouraged, to attempt to elude him. One by one,

each blindman will endeavor to capture a slave other than his own, whom he must then attempt to identify by whatever means he chooses to employ."

Rexton regarded Caroline with a look of feigned speculation as he idly fondled his Black Heart. She kept her gaze fixed on Mr. Llewellyn, Rexton having trained her never to look directly at him, but rather to keep her eyes lowered when they were speaking. She could see him, though. She would be wondering if the time had come when she would finally be compelled to publicly disrobe and allow other men to have their way with her.

He hadn't yet forced her to get naked in front of the others, although the attire he chose for her was invariably, in his estimation, a damn sight more provocative than simple nudity. This afternoon she wore nothing on top but rattling masses of faux pearl and diamond necklaces, which more or less concealed her breasts. From the waist down, she was clad in pantaloons of transparent black netting fashioned, like lady's underdrawers, with the crotch split from front to back. However, unlike the open slit in drawers, it was secured with a row of little ball buttons about the size of pearls, made of black jet glass.

"At no time during this game," Mr. Llewellyn continued, "are the slaves permitted to speak, even if one of the gentlemen asks her a direct question. As I said, a slave may use every means at her disposal to avoid being captured, but once the blindman touches her, she must immediately surrender and obey his every command. The blindman, who must retain his blindfold, has ten minutes to identify his prey by name—ten minutes and no more. To make things a bit more interesting, every gentleman who manages to correctly name the slave in question when his ten minutes are up will have his own name put into a hat. After dinner, I shall choose one of those names, and that lucky gentleman will have the use of the entire corps of participating slaves as his private harem for two hours following dinner tonight."

The roomful of men murmured excitedly as they placed bets with one another as to who the lucky sultan would be.

Holding up his pocket watch, Llewellyn said, "I shall keep track of the time. The game will be over when every gentleman has taken his turn. And now, will the participating slaves please remove any garments they might be wearing and gather in the center of the room?"

Rexton said, "Rose." He still called her "Miss Keating" in private, and she addressed him by his title. He preferred this, lest she find comfort in hiding behind a false identity.

Her gaze shot to him, then dropped to the floor. "Yes, master," she said in a soft, slightly trembling voice.

"Come." Setting aside his brandy and cigar, he patted his leg. She leapt up with a look of relief and sat on his lap. He drew her back against his chest, where she settled with her head on his shoulder. The only other nonparticipating slave in the room was Elle, lounging on a silken couch next to Jack Compton, Lord Cutbridge, while Lili lay with her head in his lap. Lili had elected not to be re-auctioned after taking her leave of Dunhurst, choosing instead to form a ménage à trois with Cutbridge and Elle that had made Cutbridge the envy of the other men.

The man who chose the ace of spades, and therefore the first man to wear the blindfold, to the jubilation of his fellow Unattached Gentlemen, was Sir Edmund Byrde. His friend, Lord Dunhurst, offered words of encouragement as Llewellyn tied the blindfold over Byrde's eyes.

Dunhurst himself had been prohibited from taking part in any more games, either as a player or a bettor, after the slaves' footrace two days ago. He had wagered a thousand quid on the tall, sturdy Saffron to win, but hampered by the ill-fitting men's riding boots that Thomas Quirk made her wear, she came in fourth. Dunhurst raised that ridiculous walking stick of his with the aim of striking the poor girl with it, but she was too quick for him, and sidestepped the blow. The incident nevertheless enraged Quirk, who prevailed upon Rexton to ban Dunhurst from all future group activities. Rexton had been only too happy to oblige.

Byrde made his way haltingly toward the middle of the room, arms stretched in front of him, as the slaves stumbled over each other to get away. After a few minutes of this, several of the men, in an effort to hurry things along, started shouting out clues as to the whereabouts of the slaves. "About six feet in front of you, Eddie." "They're mostly to your left." "Right behind you!" Byrde turned and snatched a handful of Iris's coppery mane.

His audience cheered and applauded as he squeezed her bum and fondled her breasts. "Who the devil *are* you?" he asked, although she was, of course, forbidden to answer him, and none of the other men was about to enlighten him; why increase competition for the harem? By now, Byrde had a stiff that so strained the fall front of his breeches, it was a wonder the fabric didn't split from the pressure.

"You're quite a slender thing," he said, "so you might be Angelique. If so, you'll have a nice, tight, wet little notch. I've heard your master singing its praises. We shall see about that. Kneel down—facing away from me."

She lowered herself to the floor with her cheek on the

carpet, her hands clasped behind her neck, and her dainty little arse raised high. Dropping to his knees behind her, Sir Edmund felt about until he located her quim, which he probed thoughtfully.

Rexton shifted Caroline a bit so that she wasn't pressing uncomfortably against his own erection. Her breathing had quickened, he noticed, and that telltale flush of arousal was forming on her chest. He rested a hand on her sex, which felt hot and swollen through the tissue-thin silk of her pantaloons.

She stiffened as if she might try to rise up. He banded an arm around her waist to prevent that. She'd gotten used to his not touching her like this where others could see—not that anyone was paying any attention to them tucked away in the corner, given the afternoon's entertainment. "Shh." He stroked her slowly, as if to soothe a beloved pet, enjoying the contrast between the cool jet beads and her warm flesh.

"You slicken up right quick, I'll give you that," Sir Edmund told Iris. "But as for size, well, there's really only one proper gauge for that."

The other men applauded as he freed his straining cock and pressed in.

"Five minutes, sir," said Mr. Llewellyn as he consulted his watch.

"What say you, Eddie?" someone called out. "Is it Angelique whose measure you're taking, or one of the others?"

"Hard to say," Sir Edmund answered a little breathlessly, gripping her hips as he pulled slowly out of her, then pushed back in. "Perhaps if she came, and I could hear her voice. Is Angelique the noisy type, Soames?"

"You'll have to see for yourself," replied Soames in a

deliberate effort to mislead Sir Edmund as to the identity of his prey.

Leaning over, Sir Edmund reached between Iris's legs, causing her to thrust her hips and moan.

Caroline's pantaloons were already soaked through where Rexton was caressing her; she quivered from head to foot. It was those little jet beads rubbing against her clit that had driven her so close, so fast—that, and what was transpiring in the middle of the room.

Caroline climaxed when Iris did, but whereas Iris bucked and cried out rather theatrically, much to her audience's delight, Caroline strove not to move or make a sound. She shuddered deliciously as he held her tight, her head thrown back on his shoulder, her fingers digging into the arms of the chair.

Sir Edmund yanked himself out of Iris with a groan and milked his cock, fetching all over her. To ejaculate inside another man's slave was considered discourteous.

Buttoning his breeches as he gained his feet, he said, "You're not Angelique at all, are you? I've heard her come, and she does it in French. I'll wager you're Iris." He pulled off his blindfold, crowing in triumph when he saw that he'd guessed correctly. "Put my name in the hat, Llewellyn. Who's next?" he asked, holding up the blindfold.

Inigo was next. The slaves elbowed each other aside with breathless giggles to put themselves in his way.

Rexton cradled the spent Caroline in his arms, enjoying the weight and softness of her. He caught himself absently rubbing his cheek against her hair, and grimaced. She was a slave, for pity's sake, not a lover.

He shoved her off his lap and grabbed her leash. "Let's go."

When they got to their chamber, Rexton started changing into riding clothes, and instructed Caroline to do the same. She hadn't yet worn the riding habit she'd been provided, which consisted of a short spencer jacket of bright blue silk twill over a full-skirted dress of the same fabric. It struck her as oddly conservative hanging next to all those indecently sheer gowns and negligees—until she removed the jacket from the hanger and got a good look at the dress.

The neckline, which was trimmed, like the collar and sleeves of the jacket, in thick gold braid, wasn't just low; it scooped all the way to the high empire waist, with no fabric whatsoever in the area of the bosom, which was clearly meant to be displayed in its entirety. Caroline put it on with her back to Rexton, then quickly donned the jacket, which was double-breasted, with big gold buttons.

"Turn around," he said.

She did. He looked dashingly sporty, having changed into snug buckskin riding breeches, a fawn waistcoat, and a handsome brown riding coat. Caroline was almost grateful that he made her keep her gaze lowered. If she were permitted to look directly at him, she was all too certain her admiration would be emblazoned on her face, which would shame her deeply.

What was happening between them was not about admiration or affection or anything of the kind. She was his property, nothing more, a thing to use and then discard at the end of the week. Little would she have suspected when she first came here that the arrangement would suit her as much as it seemed to suit him. Rexton had been right when he accused her of playing the slave because she was too cowardly to admit her "dark desires." As a slave, she could satisfy those desires without having to acknowledge them as her own.

He looked her up and down, then produced a white neckcloth from his trunk and handed it to her. "Ladies generally wear one of these when riding. And I trust there are proper boots and gloves in there—and a beaver hat."

"There are." She stood in front of the cheval mirror fumbling with the cravat until he came up behind her and did it himself.

"A hunting knot, I think," he said as he wrapped the swath of starched white linen around her throat, over the slave collar. He crossed it in front, tucking one end under her jacket and smoothing it down. He stilled, his hand cupping her left breast over the cravat. He gently squeezed her, then nudged the cravat aside and caressed her bare flesh, her nipples tightening as his warm palm grazed them.

"What a very interesting garment," he murmured, meeting her eyes in the mirror for a fleeting moment before they both looked away. "And how very naughty of you, Miss Keating, to try to hide this particular detail from me." He gave her nipple a reproachful pinch that drew a sharp gasp from her. "You were wrong to have done so. You know that, don't you?"

"Yes, my lord."

"Every aspect of what you do or say or wear or *think* is to be governed by me," he said as he finished tying the cravat. "You forgot that for a moment. You need to be reminded who your master is, I think."

He brought a pair of tall riding boots out to the balcony and sat on the pillow-covered chaise to tug them on. Caroline laced up her half boots, wondering with a mixture of dread and anticipation how he meant to prove his mastery over her.

"Open the black box," he told her, "and fetch the rubber dildo and the jar of cold cream. Oh, and the *rin no tama,* those little steel balls. Bring them out here."

Nine

CAROLINE'S STOMACH CLUTCHED at the mention of the two-pronged rubber dildo, but she did as Rexton had commanded. The balls felt hollow, with something heavy that rolled around inside them, creating a faint tinkling sound.

"I'll take the *rin no tama*," he said, holding out his hand. "You are to open the jar of cream and coat the narrower of the two phalluses. Don't be stingy with it. The more you use, the easier this will go for you."

Reminded of what she had witnessed that first night between Lili and Dunhurst, she obeyed him unhesitatingly, but with a fair measure of trepidation, holding the loathsome object by a fat knob at its base.

He took it from her. "Lie across my lap."

Caroline did so, positioning herself according to his directions so that her back was arched and her bottom canted up.

As if he'd read her mind, he said, "I'm not going to spank you this time. You seem to fancy being spanked, and I don't care to make this unnecessarily pleasurable for you."

He pulled her skirts up, not seeming to care that they covered her head—or perhaps that was deliberate. "Widen your legs as much as you can while keeping them on the chaise," he said as he parted the crotch slit of her knitted silk drawers, opening it so wide that her bum was almost completely bared.

She felt his fingertips at the mouth of her sex, and then something cool and smooth that he slipped into her—one of the steel balls. The second ball followed the first. She felt them inside her, weighty and warm, having instantly absorbed her body heat.

"You will keep these inside until I remove them," he said. "Clench yourself shut if you have to."

She tensed as he parted her bum, knowing what was coming. He had never touched her there, nor inserted anything.

"Yes, I know you don't want this," he said. "That is, after all, the point."

The tip of the greased phallus nudged the tight opening, while the larger phallus slid part of the way into her sex. He gave it a shove; she flinched at the thick intrusion into both orifices. The smaller phallus was as slender as a man's thumb, but it felt massive and vaguely wrong inside her.

Rexton said, "Relax, Miss Keating. The worst of it is over."

He eased the device in slowly, working it this way and that, until both phalluses were plunged deep. The one in her sex pressed against the little steel balls, creating a pressure that aroused her intensely, notwithstanding Rexton's disregard for her pleasure. He slid the device in and out of her at a maddeningly unhurried pace, until she couldn't help but grind against his thigh, aching for release.

He slowly withdrew the devilish instrument, saying, "Not this time. This was merely a demonstration—or the first part of it. What I wish to do to you, I will do. What you want or don't want interests me not in the least." He lowered her skirts and lifted her off him. "Put on your hat and gloves, Miss Keating. We are going for a ride."

The first part of it.

Caroline wondered about that promise—or threat—as she and Rexton entered a path in the woods sharing the same slowly walking horse, she sitting in front on the oversized saddle he'd requested of the stableman, along with his calmest, most imperturbable gelding.

She didn't have to wonder long. When they were about a quarter mile along the path, shadowed by primordial trees alive with the chittering of birds, she felt his free hand moving behind her; he was unbuttoning his buckskin breeches. A thrill of excitement coursed through her at the prospect of finding relief from the red hot lust that held her in its grip. It was those *rin no tama* balls. Whatever it was that was rolling around inside them vibrated with every thudding footfall of the big animal. The effect was extraordinary. She'd been teetering on the edge of climax ever since they started riding.

Rexton said, "Take the reins, Miss Keating, and be careful not to pull on them. Sèbastien swears the beast will simply follow the path at a walk no matter what, but no point in testing that, is there?"

"No, my lord."

"He fancies you."

Caroline couldn't have summoned a response to that even if it were permitted.

"While he was saddling the horse, he whispered that I was a lucky man, because you are the prettiest of all the slaves."

It surprised Caroline that the taciturn Sèbastien should have said such a thing. The young stableman, who had no English, had spoken very little when she and Rexton came for the horse. He was solidly built and nearly as tall as Rexton, with a certain rough-carved beauty to his face and a quiet, watchful manner. Were he garbed as the viscount was, in a riding suit and kid gloves, he would have had no trouble passing for a gentleman, but a man's clothing defined him to the world; a rough homespun jacket and fingerless leather work gloves did not a gentleman make.

"Put your feet in the stirrups and rise up," Rexton said.

This she did, heart thumping. Before they left the room, he'd pocketed something from the black box, but she hadn't seen what it was.

He lifted her skirts in back, resting the mass of silk and linen and lace on his arms as he widened the slit in her drawers. "Ease yourself down—slowly," he said, guiding her with a strong hand on her hip.

She felt him conducting his manhood between her bottom cheeks until its head pushed against that aperture which had never accommodated anything until that rubber phallus—a phallus that was considerably narrower than the one between Rexton's legs. She jerked forward instinctively.

"None of that." He pulled her back easily and pressed his hips forward, lunging into her. She cried out.

At first, she thought he'd buried himself to the root, but then she realized little more than the head was inside her.

"Sit back down and take your feet out of the stirrups," he instructed, gripping her hips with both hands to steady her. "And keep yourself limp if you don't want this to hurt."

He returned his own feet to the stirrups, using them for leverage as he slowly penetrated her. It felt like a wooden club being shoved inside her inch by inch, but the discomfort was not what she had feared, in large part because she was so slippery inside—which, in retrospect, was almost certainly Rexton's reason for having used that cold cream–slathered dildo on her.

When he was fully buried inside her, with her tucked up comfortably against him, he took the reins back, curling his other arm around her waist. Having overcome the shock of being so unnaturally breached, Caroline actually found herself relishing the sense of deep and absolute invasion. Every step the horse took on the twisting, turning path jarred them a bit, causing him to shift back and forth inside her and jostling the little steel balls.

"Oh!" Caroline exclaimed when she suddenly realized she was about to climax. She came hard, bucking and crying out. Spasms gripped him rhythmically where they were joined.

He groaned. The muscles of his thighs tightened into stone; his fingers dug into her waist. She thought he would finish then, too, but he seemed to be trying to resist.

They continued on, his breath shuddering, and hers, too, as the little steel balls worked their magic and another orgasm detonated. His groan was more ragged this time as her body squeezed his. She felt his chest pumping against her back; his entire body was rigid.

She spent again, and this time it was Rexton's undoing. He roared as his seed discharged in pulsing waves that wrested a jolting climax from her just as the other had been winding down.

"My God," he whispered amid gulps of air. It took them both some time to catch their breath. When he withdrew from her, she found that she actually missed having him inside—especially given that the *rin no tama* were maintaining her in a state of heightened arousal.

They continued in silence along the path, which snaked through the vast, sprawling woods along a circuitous route that seemed to have no rhyme nor reason. After a while, Rexton pulled on the reins, turning the horse down a narrow track through the woods that was so overgrown, Caroline would never have noticed it on her own.

He said, "You may speak as you wish, Miss Keating." It was not a privilege he granted often, or lightly.

Caroline said, "You are a very wicked man."

His chest shook with a little gust of laughter—and then he sighed. Caroline didn't need to see his face to know that those shades had been drawn down over his eyes again.

"I trust that experience was not painful," he said.

Caroline hesitated, not sure how to answer that, for there had been some discomfort in the beginning.

"*Was* it?" he asked, sounding almost worried.

Caroline chuckled.

"Did I say something amusing?"

"No, my lord. It's just that the real you so rarely breaks through that façade of cold indifference you affect."

"It is no façade, Miss Keating. You think that because, like most people, especially women, you are blinded by sentiment. You want to believe that all people are good and caring deep inside. But they aren't, and I am a case in point."

"You say that not because you don't feel," she said, "but because you do, and it unnerves you. I wish I knew what happened to you to make you so afraid of letting people get close. Was it a woman?"

"Resume your silence."

This must be the Nemeton, thought Caroline as they dismounted in a grassy clearing surrounded by huge, oddly misshapen oaks. It was late afternoon, but the days were very long this time of year, and the sun was bright, casting sharp black shadows across the clearing.

"How far will you ride?" the stableman Sèbastien had asked Rexton in French.

"Only as far as the Nemeton," Rexton had replied.

Sèbastien had given him a look of surprise. "You know of this place?"

Rexton had said, "I happened upon it last year, while I was exploring the woods."

Secluded though the clearing was, the groundsman was obviously tending to it, given the close-cropped grass. A rectangular stone table carved from lava stood in the center of the clearing next to a stone-rimmed fire pit that looked as if it hadn't been used in a very long time. The top of the table was eroded with age and carved in a complex design of circles and knots surrounding the words DIBU E DEBU.

"It's an altar," said Rexton as he looped the horse's reins over a tree branch. "The Celts who once lived here regarded oak trees as sacred. This was a holy place to them. They used it for orgiastic rituals, among other things."

Orgiastic? Caroline would have questioned him about that, had she been permitted to speak. During the short time she'd known him, Rexton had displayed, despite his debauched nature, an impressive fund of knowledge that indicated he had taken his studies seriously—at one point.

He said, "The druid, or high priest, would have sat over here."

Caroline followed him to the largest and most bizarrely gnarled of the surrounding oaks. At the base of it, to one side, sat a squarish boulder.

"You shall sit here." He patted a bulge on the trunk at the juncture of two thick branches growing parallel to the ground at right angles to each other.

Before she could process that, he lifted her and set her on the shelflike bulge, which was perhaps three and a half feet off the ground.

"What are you—" She bit off the rest when he shot her a look.

"Do not make me punish you, Miss Keating." He stretched each of her legs along one of the splayed branches, hiking her skirts up so that he could spread them that wide. "I daresay this little interlude will be trying enough on its own. And no, this is not a punishment. It is merely the second part of the demonstration I began before we left the château."

Ah, yes. *"This was merely a demonstration—or the first part of it,"* he'd told her as he was sliding that blasted rubber phallus out of her. What he was doing to her now, whatever that was, represented a continuation of his instructive display of mastery over her. *"What I wish to do to you, I will do. What you want or don't want interests me not in the least."*

He had already sodomized her. That he'd made her enjoy it didn't negate the fact that he'd done it against her express wishes. What further indignities did he have in store for her?

He peeled off his gloves, unwrapped his cravat, bit the end, and tore it lengthwise, producing a long, narrow strip. Walking around the tree, he pulled both of her arms behind her so that they were hugging the massive trunk and lashed her wrist cuffs to each other with the band of linen. He must have pulled it tight; she could barely move her upper body. Ripping the remnants of his cravat in two, he bound her legs to the branches on which they rested, tying the strips over her stockings between her knees and her garters.

The viscount removed her hat and set it on the boulder, then withdrew from inside his coat the small rubber ball from the black box; so that was what he'd retrieved from it before they left the room.

He said, "Open your mouth, Miss Keating."

She stared at him.

Gripping her jaw, he pried her lips open and shoved the ball in. It filled her mouth, forcing her tongue back so that speech would have been impossible even if she'd had the temerity to attempt it.

He removed her cravat then, and tore it into two strips, one of which he tied around the lower part of her face to hold the ball in place. The other, he tied over her eyes.

She felt his hands on her spencer jacket, undoing the buttons. He opened it to expose her breasts, then pushed up her skirts and petticoats as far as they would go and parted the slit in her drawers. Caroline's lack of vision seemed to intensify the sensation of his fingers brushing her most sensitive flesh. The little hairs there tickled; the arousal that had consumed her earlier came rushing back.

Caroline flexed her hips in a wordless plea.

He said, "Sorry, but I'm headed back to the room to take a nice long bath, wash off the dust of our little ride. But perhaps one of the other gentlemen will oblige you." There came a rasp of metal on metal that Caroline recognized, with a surge of horror, as a padlock being opened.

She shook her head wildly as he locked the Black Heart onto her collar. His only response was to slide two fingers inside her and scoop out the little steel balls. "Wouldn't want you enjoying it too much," he said, and then she heard him walking away through the grass.

She stopped moving and listened, trying to figure out where he was, what he was doing. There came a creak of leather as he settled himself into the saddle, then a soft click-click of his tongue and the slow, retreating hoofbeats of the horse.

Caroline thrashed against her bindings, trying vainly to cry out. *He won't leave me like this for long,* she thought desperately. *He's just trying to teach me a lesson.*

It was a dramatic one. He'd shown her not only that he could wield absolute power over her, but that he didn't care one bit whether other men were intimate with her. She felt like Reenie Fowls, lying sprawled in that doorway for any randy goat to use as he wished—except that, in Reenie's case, she'd been blessedly unaware of her debasement.

Tears welled in Caroline's eyes, but her blindfold absorbed them before they could run down her cheeks. She gulped back the urge to cry, but she couldn't seem to stop shivering.

She heard a soft thump, and froze. *Please be Rexton. Please...*

A cat mewed from somewhere just off to her right. That gray cat she occasionally saw roaming about must have jumped onto a branch.

She heard a low feline rumble as he drew near. He settled down very close to her head; she could almost, but not quite, feel his heat and the tickle of his whiskers. There came a soft rasping sound, and she knew, because she'd grown up with cats, that he was rubbing his head against the rough bark of the tree. He sat there for some time, purring and keeping her company. His presence soothed her. *At least someone cares about me,* she thought giddily.

After some time, she heard a soft shudder as he stretched head to toe. He mewed again, as if to say good-bye, and then padded away.

Caroline felt calmer after the cat left, stronger. There was nothing to be afraid of, not really. Rexton would come back for her soon. He had to.

He didn't. Time stretched on. It was difficult, in her present circumstances, to estimate how long it had been since he'd left; it felt like an eternity. Her most helpful clue was the quality of the light filtering in through her white linen blindfold, which dimmed considerably as the sun dipped behind the looming mountains. The air cooled, and a symphony of chirrups and trills rose up all around her.

It was dusk, and so far she had managed to remain unmolested. Of course, the Nemeton was hidden deep in the woods, and evidently it was not a place of which the château's visitors were routinely aware.

Rexton knew no one would happen upon her here, she realized. He just wanted to scare her, to prove a point.

She heard hoofbeats on the dirt path through the woods. He was back. Thank God he was back.

He dismounted, and a few moments later she heard, or sensed, his footsteps in the grass as he walked toward her.

Her scalp prickled. Why was he approaching so slowly? Why would he, unless he was looking her over, absorbing the sight of her bound and gagged and tied with legs widespread to this tree . . . as if it were the first time he was seeing her like this?

Her foreboding intensified as he came near. Rexton had a certain subtle but distinctive scent, warm and pleasant. The man now standing between her legs carried with him a whiff of something earthy, even perhaps a bit rank. There was a hint of the barnyard—or the stable.

He squeezed her breast with a hand that felt oddly beast-like. His palms were covered in leather. He was wearing thick gloves, she realized—fingerless gloves.

God, no, she thought as he unbuttoned his trousers, the gloves and his coarse-textured coat grazing her inner thighs. *This can't be happening. Please don't let this happen.*

Ten

CAROLINE THRASHED AND bucked, whipping her head wildly as he pushed into her. She tried to scream, but of course no sound emerged. He clutched her thighs as he took her, his thrusts starting slow, and growing sharper, deeper.

A sob shook her chest, but the gag rendered it silent. She wept as she struggled, her blindfold soaking through with tears; no doubt her ravisher didn't even realize she was crying. Each spasmodic breath she took became increasingly shallow because of the congestion in her nose. Panic seized her as her air supply diminished. She felt the same wild desperation as when she'd been drowning in the Thames.

The stableman grew still, and then she felt his hands on her gag, yanking it down. She spat out the ball and gasped for air.

He withdrew from her abruptly; she felt his gloved hands brushing her thighs as he rebuttoned himself. There came a tugging on the strip of linen securing her left leg as he fumbled with the knot. She heard a soft click, then the cold slide of steel against her stockinged thigh as he sliced the binding off. He freed her right leg, as well, then circled the tree and did the same to her hands.

Caroline pulled off her blindfold and lowered her legs, which gave out the moment her feet touched ground. She collapsed in a heap, sobbing uncontrollably.

Sinking her face in her hands as he came to stand before her, she pleaded, in a hoarse, watery voice, "Go away. G-go away. *Laissez-moi tranquille. Je vous prie...*"

"Miss Keating."

She looked up sharply.

Lord Rexton hiked up his trouser legs and crouched so that they were at eye level. He reached toward her with a handkerchief.

She recoiled until her back hit the tree. He was wearing the stableman's homespun jacket, his fingerless work gloves. She shook her head in outraged disbelief.

"I borrowed these things from Sèbastien," he said.

"What? But..." She looked down at the Black Heart on her collar, only to find that it was an ordinary padlock. "W-why?" she choked out as she rubbed her damp cheeks. "Why would you do such a thing? Just to prove that you can subject me to whatever godawful nightmare strikes your fancy?"

He sighed heavily. She thought he was going to say something, but he just offered her the handkerchief again, saying, "Here, take—"

She swatted his hand away. "Bastard. *Monster.*"

He rose to his feet, looking down upon her with a grim expression. Quietly, he said, "You see?"

❧

"This promises to be quite a show," Narcissa told Caroline that night as they sat next to each other in a corner of the candlelit dining room, their leashes looped around the legs of a dessert table laden with traditional Auvergnat sweets: Sour cherry *milliard*, walnut cake, fruit-studded brioche, apricot pâté, and sweet rye crêpes stuffed with peaches and blueberries. A few other slaves were tethered in other parts of the enormous room, while the remainder were with their masters at the long dining table.

On top of the table, amid the playing cards and liquor bottles, stood the elfin Jessamine strapping on a leather harness equipped with two polished ebony phalluses. One she'd greased up and shoved inside her; the other jutted out in front like a giant black erection.

"Where did she get that thing?" Caroline asked Narcissa. "I didn't see it in the black box."

"She brought it herself. You do know she's one of the boys, don't you?"

"Let's have her do her friend Laurel first," called out Mr. Charles Bricks, a wealthy manufacturer of steam engines who had bought Narcissa, much to her dismay. He was in trade, a nobody in her scheme of things. Fed up with her high-handedness, his treatment of her had grown increasingly rough and punishing with each passing day. It was a turn of events that had thrilled her—so much so that she'd agreed to continue their liaison upon their return to London.

"Not Laurel," Dunhurst said. "I want to see her ride a chit she's never ridden before, one who's never gotten it from another wench."

"All in good time," said Jessamine's master, Beau Brummel. "She shall begin with Laurel—providing Don Ortiz will indulge us with the loan of his beautiful slave."

"But of course." The courtly and elegant Eugenio Ortiz rose and helped Laurel to climb onto the damask-draped table.

The two women went into each other's arms with practiced ease, kissing like the longtime lovers they evidently were as they kneaded each other's bottoms.

"Not like that, for pity's sake," Dunhurst barked at Jessamine. "She's a slave. Treat her like one."

This sentiment was echoed by several other men. They looked toward Mr. Brummel, who shrugged and told Jessamine, "This will be your chance to play the master."

The two slaves met each other's gaze in brief but eloquent communion. Laurel nodded almost imperceptibly. With a smile of anticipation, Jessamine stepped back and gave the other woman two sharp slaps across the breasts. "On your knees, bitch!"

The men all snapped to attention, save for Lord Rexton, sitting toward the end of the table drinking gin and smoking a cigar. He hadn't joined the other men in their customary late evening game of whist, nor in the bawdy conversation that accompanied it. Nor did he seem very interested in Jessamine's little performance. All he wanted to do was drink. He had imbibed more that night than Caroline had ever seen him consume.

Narcissa, having apparently noticed the direction of Caroline's gaze, whispered, "David's emptied half of that bottle while we've been sitting here, and he doesn't appear to be slowing down."

David. Caroline had never thought of him by his Christian name. Of course the woman who had been his lover, however briefly, would call him that.

Turning to Caroline with a coy smile, Narcissa said, "You're quite the lucky little goose, to have been bought by the likes of him."

"You think so, do you?"

"I've shared his bed, my dear. When it comes to doing a bit of front door work, David has no equal. If only he weren't such a cold-eyed prick. He pees ice water and shits snowballs, that one."

Before this evening and that heartless charade in the Nemeton, Caroline might have defended her distant and brooding "master." Now, her assessment of David Childe, Lord Rexton, was very much the same as Narcissa's. Something had shut down in her when she realized he'd contrived to make her think she was being taken against her will. He truly was a monster. Caroline's goal now was simply to get through the next and last day of Slave Week and earn her ninety thousand guineas. Curious, how infrequently she'd thought of the money this past week. Now, it was *all* she thought about, because it was her only reason for remaining here and putting up with the likes of Rexton.

They had spoken not a single word to each other during the ride back to the château. Once they were in their room, he'd had their chambermaid bring her some wine and saffron-scented stew, and fill the bathtub. As if to prove that he hadn't requested these things out of kindness, he said, "We'll be joining the others downstairs later this evening. Wouldn't want my slave looking like some consumptive little St. Giles gutter-crawler."

"What shall I wear, my lord?"

"Black stockings and those black velvet slippers."

She waited a moment for him to continue. When he didn't, she had said, with well-feigned composure, "Yes, my lord."

Caroline had hoped all week that she would never have to be completely unclothed in front of the others. Despite the casual nudity among the slaves—and some of the masters, for that matter—she'd found the prospect excruciating. Rexton had seemed to sense that, because he'd never demanded it before. But things were different now. He appeared determined to demonstrate that her feelings were of no import to him. For her part, Caroline had resolved never again to surrender to despair as she had that evening in the Nemeton. Her mistake had been to care. For her own sake, she must be as callous and unfeeling as Rexton himself until she was gone from here.

When he'd led her into the dining room naked but for her shoes and stockings, she kept her head high and her comportment serene. Most of the men surveyed her up and down with open curiosity. She had expected that. There were a few admiring comments—nothing crude except for Sir Edmund Byrde. "See there?" he said as Rexton was tying her to the table leg. "I knew she was a blonde."

That quip was greeted with laughter, except from Rexton—and Dunhurst, who stared at Caroline in a way that made her shiver.

Rexton had scowled when, about an hour later, Charles Bricks tethered Narcissa so close to Caroline. No doubt the viscount suspected that his slave and his former paramour would end up talking about him—for conversations among the slaves were permitted when they were waiting about for their masters, so long as they maintained their prescribed positions and kept their voices low. Caroline had thought he might separate them, but he hadn't, probably because he was too soused by then to be bothered.

"Has David been on the cut all week?" Narcissa asked.

"On the cut?"

"Funneling gin down his throat. He was a lush when I was with him, but not to this extent."

"That's right, you little strum. Suck it deep." Jessamine stood on the table with her legs braced apart, clutching handfuls of Laurel's hair as the other woman fellated the big ebony phallus. With one hand, Laurel pleasured herself, on Jessamine's orders; with the other, she manipulated the phallus in a way that Jessamine appeared to find intensely arousing, given her quickening thrusts and hectic breathing.

"Was that why you broke things off with Lord Rexton?" Caroline asked. "Because of the drinking?"

"Oh, my dear, I would never have broken it off. A bastard he may have been, but he could go all night. I'd be so exhausted the next day that I wouldn't even get out of bed. No, it was he who ended it. I made the unpardonable error of telling him I was falling for him. He got out of my bed, put on his clothes, and left. I never see him anymore unless we happen to bump into each other at a ball or the opera. Of course, we see each other here, but he acts as if I'm invisible. He hasn't said a word to me all week."

Jessamine and Laurel climaxed together, to the appreciative applause of their audience. Laurel was handed down from the table and replaced with Aster. Jessamine commanded her to assume the "await" position, with her legs wide apart and her hands gripping her ankles, then took her with the phallus as she whipped her on the bottom with the end of her leash.

"Is this where you met Lord Rexton?" Caroline asked. "At Slave Week last year?"

"Oh, goodness, no. I only came here last year because I knew he would be here. It hadn't been that long since he'd thrown me over, and I suppose I wanted to know how he would react, seeing me as the sex slave of another man. I was a fool. He didn't display the slightest bit of jealousy. He hardly seemed to notice I was here, the knave. I did discover that I quite enjoyed Slave Week, though, so it wasn't a complete waste of time."

Narcissa was the type who prattled on with nary a pause. Violet had been right. She was quite the magpie.

"How did you meet, then?" Caroline asked.

"Oh, I've known David since we were young. I met him through his cousin, Clarissa Lefever, when we were children. Well, she was Clarissa Bensley back then. She and I were bosom friends, still are. We grew up on the same square in London. Clarissa's mother, David's aunt, brought him up after his mother died. Scarlet fever, you know. David came down with it at Greyton Hall, the family seat, when he was six, from breathing the night air when he'd been told not to. His mother sent the family and servants away so they wouldn't catch it, but she stayed behind to take care of him. She nursed him back to health, only to die of it herself. He was alone in the house with her body for a week because Lord Rexton—the late Lord Rexton, David's father—had been waiting for word from Lady Rexton before he brought everyone back. He eventually came home to find his wife decomposing in their bed and David huddled in a pile of straw in the stable, staring at nothing and refusing to speak. Ghastly business."

At a loss for words, Caroline looked toward Lord Rexton, who was refilling his glass with gin. He spilled some on the tablecloth as he set the bottle aside unsteadily.

"His lordship got fed up with David pretending to be mute," Narcissa continued. "A thing like that can get on one's nerves. And, too, he couldn't help feel that David was responsible for his mother's death. He told him as much, and that having him around the house was just a painful reminder of—"

"He told a six-year-old child that he'd killed his mother?"

"Well, he did, in a way. In any event, his father sent him to London to live with the Bensleys, but he kept his older brother, Alex, home with him. David didn't utter a sound the first few weeks he lived with Clarissa and her family, not one bloody word. I told Clarissa they ought to just pack the little loon off to Bethnal Green and be done with it."

"That strikes me as a rather...precocious observation from a child of that age," Caroline said. Precocious and sickeningly cruel.

"I said *David* was six. I never mentioned how old I was, nor do I intend to."

"Ah."

"A few years later," Narcissa said, "David's father sent him to Eton—Alex was already there. David followed Alex to Oxford, and then he was called to the bar and served his barrister's apprenticeship with Sir Charles Upcott. According to Clarissa, it was 'delusions of altruism' that had attracted David to the law, so he was quite put out to discover that Burnham and Upcott had no interest in scuttling 'round in the muck with draggle-tails from the Rookery or what have you who'd run afoul of the law. He bought a commission in the King's Dragoon Guards and talked his brother into doing the same.

Clarissa used to say David couldn't make water without Alex there to hold his twanger for him."

"Were you and David courting then, or did that come later?"

"Courting?" Narcissa said through a mocking little giggle. "Darling, David and I never courted, we just fucked—but not until last year. Augie was still alive—my late husband. I actually did try to interest David in a discreet little tryst a couple of years ago—he'd grown into quite the strapping specimen, as you know—but he was already betrothed to this absurd little Hungarian, with whom he was insanely besotted, so I couldn't sway him."

Jessamine let out a series of ecstatic groans, ramming the phallus hard into Aster as her pleasure crested. Aster was traded in for Angelique at Jessamine's request, Brummel having allowed her to choose her next partner, and the harness was replaced with a curved ivory column carved to look like a male organ with two heads, one at each end. Producing a little vial of oil she'd apparently brought with her along with these curious devices, Jessamine slicked it over both of their bodies, as well as the double phallus. She instructed Angelique to lie back and open her legs, whereupon she pushed one end of the phallus into the slender little Frenchwoman and lowered herself onto the other. The two women rocked their slippery bodies together with sensual abandon as they kissed and caressed, Angelique demonstrating a surprising degree of zeal. *"Oh, oui, baisez-moi! Baisez-moi!"*

Laurel, standing next to Don Ortiz, looked away with her jaw set, eyes glimmering.

"Looks as if Jessamine is in for a tongue-lashing tomorrow," said Narcissa, "and not the good kind."

"What you said before, about David being engaged..." Caroline began. "Is he...he isn't married, is he?" The possibility had never occurred to her.

"Oh, good heavens, no. The engagement ended on a rather lurid note, but until it did, David mooned over her like a schoolboy. She was pretty enough—a tawny blonde with big gray eyes—and she knew how to dress and act, but she was nobody, a commoner, and a foreign one at that."

"How did they meet?" Caroline asked.

"She was the daughter of his philosophy professor. He dropped dead one day of apoplexy, leaving Natalia with two shillings in her purse and no place to live. David prevailed upon Alex and his wife to take her in—they'd been making their home at Greyton Hall with Lord Rexton because of Alex's military obligations. David had always avoided Greyton Hall because of his father, but he started visiting more often now that Natalia was there, and finally he asked her to marry him. A few months later, he and Alex were sent to Waterloo, Alex took a bullet in the head, and David—"

"Alex died at Waterloo?" Caroline asked, sitting up.

"That is what customarily happens when a bullet enters one's head. David brought the body home. I went to the funeral. He was incredibly distraught, but in that eerie, contained way of his. Hardly spoke a word to anyone but Natalia all weekend. Clarissa overheard him telling her that she was all he had left in the world, and that Alex's death was on his head, because he never would have bought that commission if David hadn't talked him into it—which was entirely true, of course."

Caroline bit her tongue to keep from telling Narcissa what she thought of her lest she stop talking. She was learning more about Lord Rexton than she'd ever thought to learn, certainly far more than he was ever likely to volunteer.

"David tried to talk Natalia into marrying him right away," Narcissa said, "but she insisted on waiting. I knew why he was in such a hurry. Grief tends to make men rammish—women, too. I've seen it time and again. A loved one dies, and all one wants to do is fuck. David didn't want to compromise sweet, innocent Natalia before the wedding night, but he had his needs. I renewed my offer to give him a nice, discreet little tumble, but he told me he'd sworn fidelity to Natalia when they became engaged. So he returned to the Guards. A month later, he was called back to Greyton Hall. He arrived to discover that his father's heart had burst while he was taking a turn up the petticoats of some young doxy." With a conspiratorial little smile, Narcissa added, "Imagine David's surprise when he found out that the doxy was none other than his beloved Natalia."

The air drained from Caroline's lungs. She closed her eyes.

"She fell all over herself with apologies and tearful explanations," Narcissa said, "but David would have none of it. Of all the men for her to betray him with. He was crushed, furious. He ordered her out of the house, of course. Greyton Hall was his now. With Alex dead, he inherited the viscountcy. Here's where the real melodrama starts."

There was more?

"About two months later, Natalia came crawling back to David at his house in London, threw herself utterly on his mercy. Turned out the old fuckster had gotten her in the family way. She was ruined, or would be as soon as she started showing. She begged David to support her until the baby came, after which she would return to Hungary and he could

232 • Louisa Burton

raise the child as his ward, given that it would be his half sibling. He was sizzled at the time, probably, and in no humor to hear this. He told her that her problems were of her own making, and that she had a lot of cheek, coming to him for help after what she'd done to him."

"He turned her away?"

"He did. The next morning, he was summoned to the Newcastle Street Watch House. They'd pulled a woman's body out of the Thames just downstream from Southwark Bridge. She'd left a note on the bridge that had his name on it, so they were hoping he could identify her."

Caroline stared at Narcissa, thinking of the night she herself had been hauled out of the Thames. "She . . . she drowned herself?"

"Not the first ruined girl to do it. They throw themselves off those bridges in droves."

"*Oh, mon dieu!*" Angelique exclaimed as she and Jessamine writhed together like one sleek, wild little creature. "*Oh! Je jouis! Je jouis!*" She came with a series of sharp, breathy cries that Jessamine echoed as she reached yet another shuddering climax. Sitting up, she turned Angelica over and shoved her into the "kneel down" pose without either of them disengaging from the phallus. She ground against the other woman's upraised bum while reaching around to stroke her sex and breasts, both of them moaning in sensual frenzy.

Every person sitting around the table, gentleman and slave alike, stared in rapt fascination at the two lithe little oil-sheened women—except for Rexton. He sat gazing off into space like an old man who'd forgotten where he was and wished there was someone who could show him the way home.

❧

"Natalia?" Rexton said, his voice oddly slow and thick. Fucking gin.

It was dark as hell, and he was reeling drunk. He heard her sodden frock dragging on the ground, but all he could really see of her was that long, damply snarled mass of blonde hair—until she stepped into the amber nimbus of a street-lamp.

He cried out, stumbling back, at the sight of her bloated, darkly mottled face, her filmy eyes and gaping mouth. "Jesus! Oh, God. Natalia!"

"My lord," she said.

"No. God, no." He was shaking. "Natalia..."

"My lord, wake up."

She was shaking him. She was pushing at his shoulder, say-ing, "My lord. David. You're having a—"

He pushed her away and sat up, trembling and sweating in the dark. "Jesus. Oh, fuck."

He was in a bed, but he had his clothes on, except for his shoes and coat. Where the hell was he?

"My lord, are you all right?"

A woman was sitting up next to him, a shadowy form in the darkness. She reached for him.

He scrambled away from her, falling off the bed and land-ing hard on the carpeted floor. Groaning, he struggled to his feet. Despite the darkness, for it was a nearly moonless night, he gradually recognized the slowly spinning room—*la Chambre Romain*.

Rexton's stomach pitched. He lurched into the bathroom and vomited into the Brahmah.

He leaned against the wall, gasping. And then he vomited some more. When he was finally done, he rinsed out his mouth and splashed water on his face, his hands shaking like those of an old man.

It wasn't quite so dark anymore. Caroline must have lit some candles in the bedroom.

It was she who had pulled off his shoes and wrestled him out of his coat, after he'd collapsed on the bed in a stupor, he suddenly recalled. He couldn't remember much of what had transpired earlier that evening, including having come back to the room.

No, he did remember something. He remembered taking a tumble on the stairs, and Caroline guiding him the rest of the way with an arm around him as he muttered and raved and careened into walls.

"Jesus Christ." He clawed his hands through his sweat-dampened hair, recalling her cool fingers stroking his forehead as he sank into a deep, drunken slumber. He had wanted her to keep touching him like that forever, softly, tenderly, as if he were her lover.

God, you fool, Rexton. You fucking idiot. Will you never learn?

"My lord?" She was standing in the bathroom doorway in a sleeveless linen shift, looking at him with those big, all-seeing eyes. "Is there anything I can—"

"You can shut up and stop looking at me like that. Just stop...stop..." He growled in frustration and punched the wall, his fist connecting with the toilet glass over the sink, which shattered in a burst of mirrored shards.

"Oh, my lord—you're bleeding." She reached for his hand, which was lacerated across three fingers.

"Just stop!" He hauled back with his fist. "Will you just leave me . . ."

She had backed away and was staring at him, eyes wide with alarm.

"Oh, shit," he whispered. He'd never struck a female, never come close, yet here he was with his bloodied fist raised high, every nerve jumping with a crazy, gin-fueled fury. "Get the hell away from me," he said. "Get out of here. Go."

"You mean . . . ?" She looked toward the door to the hall.

"Go!" he roared, both fists clenched.

"I . . . I'll be sent home if I'm seen outside this room without you."

"Oh, fuck." He pushed past her and snatched the leash out of the black box, but he fumbled drunkenly when he attempted to clip it onto her collar. "You do it."

When she had it fastened, he grabbed it and flung open the door.

"Where are you taking me?" she asked as he tugged her down the corridor.

"Did I say you could speak?"

"N-no, but—"

"Then keep your fucking mouth shut."

Frederick Weatherall, Marquess of Dunhurst, having awakened to a crash of breaking glass next door, stood at the window of his bedchamber watching Rexton, lantern in one hand and leash in the other, half dragging that little bitch Rose across the stretch of lawn to the west of the castle. The viscount's

236 · Louisa Burton

gait was unusually heavy and awkward. Little wonder, given all the gin he'd swilled that evening.

They proceeded up the path to the north, disappearing into the darksome woods surrounding the stable and adjacent carriage house. Dunhurst poured himself a tall whiskey and drank it as he gazed into the night.

What he wouldn't give to get that little cunt alone and teach her a lesson—teach both of them a lesson, she and that meddling cur, Rexton. As if Rexton's treatment of him last year weren't outrageous enough—having his room searched, trying to get him banned from Slave Week—he had set out this year to deliberately show him up and make him a fool in front of the others. The only man here wealthy enough to out-bid Dunhurst for the coveted Rose, he had done so for the sole purpose of keeping her out of Dunhurst's hands. Dunhurst had ended up with Lili, who had somehow—he still couldn't fathom it—turned the tables and humiliated him most extra-ordinarily.

In the letter Lili had left for him to find in the morning, she'd promised to tell no one of his debasement at her hands, provided he was "a good boy" for the remainder of Slave Week. *If I even suspect that you've hurt one of the slaves,* she'd written, *every soul here will find out exactly what happened in your chamber that night.* She had warned him, after that inci-dent with Saffron losing the footrace, that she had come very close to following through on her threat, and that he'd better toe the line, or else.

The problem was, Lili wasn't the only one who knew what had happened that night. There had been a witness—Rose. Dunhurst had enough friends here to know that he would have more than likely been warned had she started telling people what she'd seen, but what would happen once they were both back in London? She would convey the juicy tidbit in a snickering whisper to some friend who would whisper it to three or four other people, and so would begin the inexorable decay of his reputation. Before long, they'd be calling him Bum Boy and Miss Freddie—behind his back, if not to his face.

A glimmer of light emerged from the woods. Dunhurst lowered his glass slowly when he saw that it was Rexton alone. The viscount started retracing his steps across the lawn, only to pause with an arm braced against a tree and his head down. He remained like that for about half a minute, then turned and headed back toward the path.

"No," Dunhurst whispered.

As if Rexton had heard him, he paused again, raking his hands through his hair. He spun around and strode purposefully back to the castle.

Dunhurst smiled.

Eleven

ONE MORE DAY, Caroline thought as she sat in the pitch-black stable amid a pile of straw. Tomorrow would be the last day of Slave Week. If she could put up with all this—with *him*—for just another twenty-four hours, she would be able to start her life anew.

Rexton had tied her leash to the ladder leading to the hayloft at the rear of the cavernous horse barn. The leash wasn't locked onto her collar, just clipped, and he had left her hands unbound. If she wanted to, she could untether herself with ease, but what would be the point? Were she to be caught walking about alone and unrestrained, she would be sent home empty-handed. And it wasn't as if the leash were causing her any real discomfort. It was long; she had room to move about, and to lie down in the straw—assuming she would be able to get back to sleep.

The horses in the fourteen stalls lining the stone-paved central aisle had awakened, nickering and fidgeting, when Rexton brought her here. Some of them were still awake—she heard hay being munched, and the occasional equine grunt—but most of them seemed to have settled back down.

The earthy barn smell was an unpleasant reminder of what Rexton had done to her in the Nemeton. The clean, refreshing anger she had harbored toward him after that had retreated somewhat in light of Narcissa's revelations—only to be renewed in full force when he dragged her here and tied her up like a dog simply for having shown him a bit of kindness.

In truth, she was grateful to him for having left her here. It was an instructive reminder of the contempt in which he held her. She had begun to weaken toward him again, after having finally learned to feel as little for him as he felt for her. She would not make that mistake a second time.

Light wavered through the gaps in the main double door at the far end of the aisle. It would appear Lord Rexton had second thoughts about leaving her here.

It doesn't matter, she told herself. *Don't soften toward him. He doesn't deserve it, and you'll only bring yourself pain.*

The door creaked open. Lord Dunhurst entered, holding a lantern in one hand and his walking stick in the other.

Caroline bolted to her feet.

The burly marquess, who was in his shirtsleeves, smiled coldly as he sauntered toward her. "You look different without the face paint," he said. "Younger. One could almost believe you're the pure, sweet little maiden you pretend to be, and not the whore we both know you are."

"You'd best leave before Lord Rexton returns," she said in

as even a voice as she could muster. "He just went to get some . . . some blankets. He'll be back any—"

"It doesn't surprise me that you are a liar." Setting the lantern on the floor, he set about unscrewing the ivory handle of his walking stick. "I must say, however, that I would have expected someone like you to be a bit more skilled at it."

"It . . . it's true," she said as she strove, with jittery fingers, to unhook the leash from her collar.

"Liar!" He pulled from within the walking stick a straight black truncheon and swung it at her arms.

Pain cracked through her; a scream filled her ears. He swung again and again, as she collapsed into the straw, covering her head. Ribs crunched. Her shoulder bloomed with pain. The horses were all awake now, several neighing in alarm and one or two kicking at their stall doors.

She looked up and saw him untying her leash from the ladder, having set aside the truncheon, which she realized was made of India rubber. This, then, was the weapon he had used on Dahlia, the one they couldn't find in his room because it had been secreted in his walking stick all along.

"You can't do this," she said as he yanked on the leash, pulling her to her feet. "I'm not wearing the Black Heart. When Rexton finds out what you've—"

"He won't." Turning, Dunhurst reached for one of the tools hanging on the wall nearby—a hay knife over a foot long.

She grabbed the hand that was holding her leash and bit down to the bone. Bellowing in pain, he dropped the leash.

Caroline sprinted toward the back door to the stable, which was only a few yards away. He seized her shoulder and turned her to face him, pressing the big knife to her throat as he backed her against the wall.

"When Rexton returns in the morning," Dunhurst said, "he'll find you gone. He'll search for you, but you won't turn up. He'll assume you had enough and ran away—they all will. They'll all go home, never suspecting they'd actually left you here, buried deep in the woods where no one will ever—"

She kneed him in the groin, sharp and hard, as Aubrey had taught her. He doubled over, but as she turned to flee, he shoved the knife into her.

Caroline staggered away, looking down in dull shock at the blade sticking out of the left side of her belly. She turned toward the door, only to feel him clutch at her hair. Summoning all the strength at her disposal, she grabbed the knife handle with both hands and yanked it out, blood spilling onto the stone floor.

Dunhurst spun her around. She lashed out with the blade. He stumbled back, howling as he covered his bloodied face with his hands.

Caroline ran from the stable, one hand pressed to the agonizing wound in her side, the other gripping the knife. By the lamplight from the stable, she could see a dirt path disappearing into dense, black woods.

"You little bitch!" Dunhurst screamed as he came after her. "Fucking little cunt!"

She darted into the woods, making her way as quickly as she could through the tangled underbrush. She stumbled along frantically for quite some time, but just as she'd concluded that he wasn't tracking her anymore, she heard him behind her, closing in. She veered off toward the sound of a gurgling stream and waded through it, reasoning that Dunhurst would hesitate to cross it in his shoes. She found a huge tree and crouched down behind it, grimacing in pain. He lumbered through the woods in the opposite direction, cursing and threatening her.

After a period of silence, he yelled from a distance, "You won't get far, with that hole in your gut. You'll never even make it out of these woods. And in a few hours, when the sun's up, I'll come back and find you and bury you good and deep."

Caroline waited a while longer, and then she hauled herself unsteadily to her feet. She knew she had to get back to the château before she bled to death, but she was so woozy and disoriented that she just ended up wandering aimlessly. Time and again, she tripped over rocks and fallen limbs, but clambered back to her feet and carried on. As dawn broke, she headed in the direction of the rising sun, thinking the château must be to the east, but the woods only grew thicker and more difficult to navigate.

She leaned against a tree to catch her breath. The knife wasn't in her hand anymore; she must have dropped it somewhere. She looked around; the trees swayed. Her head hit the ground.

Get up, she thought blearily. *Get up.* But her body was so heavy, and the ground felt oddly soft beneath her, like a feather mattress. Her heart thrummed in her chest, and she felt strangely cold. She was soaking wet—that was why.

Caroline looked down at her shift, dark with blood.

Not like this, she thought. *Please, God, not like this.*

Darius wove his way along the forest floor as the sky lightened, occasionally pausing to pull back his lips and taste the air as he homed in on the scent of blood—human blood. As the smell became overpowering, he saw a patch of something white amid a feathery sea of ferns.

It was a woman, the one called Rose who had been tied to the Great Oak in the Nemeton the day before, lying curled up on her side with her eyes closed and her arms wrapped around herself. Her skin was as pale as her linen shift, or the top half of it, the bottom being, to his feline eyes, nearly black. The source of the blood appeared to be a still-seeping wound on her left side. Livid bruising mottled her left forearm and shoulder. Her legs, and to a lesser extent her arms, were covered with scratches. Darius could see her chest moving with every rapid, shallow breath. Given how much blood she'd lost, it was a wonder she was still alive.

She wouldn't be for long. If the bleeding could be stopped, she might have a chance, but it would not stop on its own.

For Darius, cursed as he was with the power to wrest life from imminent death, there was never any right thing to do in a situation like this. To heal this woman would be to circumvent the natural course of things, which could have unforeseen consequences. Of more immediate and personal concern, however, was the possibility that his "gift" would be discovered, putting him at the mercy of anyone with an ailing loved one. It had happened before, turning him into a virtual slave trapped in a nightmare of pain and infirmity, for every healing took its toll on him; the worse the malady, the more depleted it would leave him. It was to escape such a hellish existence that he'd left his homeland and journeyed halfway around the world, where the djinn were unknown and he could live in peace and solitude. Even his fellow Follets here at Grotte Cachée had no idea that Darius could cure illnesses and mend injuries. He had learned the hard way that there was no one, human or Follet, in whom he could safely confide.

Were he to stop this woman's bleeding, he would be risking much. On the other hand, experience had taught him that if he did nothing—if he walked away and let her die—it would leave him in a torment of guilt.

Darius turned his head this way and that, focusing his hearing for any hint of a distant footfall or voice. He sampled the air for the scent of a human other than this one. Nothing.

He mewed. Rose didn't stir. He moved close to her face and let out a strident yowl. Her eyelids fluttered, then stilled.

He sat down, held his breath, and willed himself into human form. The transformation was instantaneous, and as jolting as always. He kept his eyes closed, his hands braced on solid earth, until the vertigo let up, which only took a few seconds. Filling his lungs with air, he opened his eyes, blinking at the sharp, jewel-like colors all around him.

He turned Rose gently onto her back and stroked her cool, waxen face, sensing an emptiness that told him she was, indeed, entirely unaware of his presence. Holding his hands just above her body, he trailed them downward, noting the two broken ribs he would have to deal with when he was done with the other—if he had the strength left.

The wound in her side, which had been made by a large knife, had nicked her spleen—hence the incessant bleeding. Closing his eyes, Darius concentrated all his vital energy on the ruptured vessels in the little organ, sealing them as if by cauterization, his hands growing hot and quivery as he worked. That done, he joined the incised tissues, working upward from the spleen to the skin, which sealed together quite nicely. She would be left with a scar about three inches long, but over the next week or so, it would fade away to nothing. Of course, the blood loss would leave her in a weakened state for some time, but she would survive.

He took a moment to knit those ribs, then fell back onto the ground, shaking and depleted.

❧

Rexton stood in the stable, staring in bewilderment at the spot where he'd left Caroline tied up. She was gone, with no sign that she'd ever been there except that the pile of straw he'd left her sitting in had been spread out, for some reason, over that section of the floor.

He grabbed a rake and pushed back the straw, some of which stuck to the volcanic stone blocks with which the aisle was paved. Crouching down, he touched the stone; it was wet. In a corner, he found a wooden bucket with a damp wash rag slung over it.

Where the devil was she? Why had she washed the floor? If only he hadn't gotten so bloody foxed last night. His head felt as if it were being squeezed by a pair of giant hands, making it impossible to think.

He stood up to find a gray cat watching him from just outside the open rear doorway. He'd seen it before; Inigo called it Darius. It sniffed at a leaf, one of many scattered over the dirt path that led away from the stable.

"I don't suppose *you* know what became of her," Rexton muttered as he turned to leave. He'd taken three steps, when he nearly tripped over the animal as it darted in front of him. Bloody cats. Always underfoot.

There was something in its mouth—the leaf. Darius dropped it on the floor and mewed.

Rexton had seen cats bring a freshly killed mouse or bird to a favored human as presumed tribute, but this was the first time he'd seen one make a presentation of flora rather than fauna. The leaf looked to be from either a plane tree or a maple, bright green save for a little spot of red near the stem. Rather early, Rexton thought, for the leaves to start changing, even in a mountainous region like Auvergne.

Darius sniffed at the leaf again. And then he looked up at Rexton.

Rexton knelt and lifted the leaf. He rubbed his thumb over the little red spot.

It smeared. "Jesus Christ."

The cat returned to the back door, looked at Rexton, and mewed.

Rexton stared at it in puzzlement and alarm.

It padded to the edge of the woods, turned, and mewed again.

He followed it.

Twelve

OH, MY GOD. Oh, Jesus."

Caroline struggled up from the darkness, straining to move, to open her eyes.

Something settled lightly upon her chest. She felt the tickle of hair, an ear pressing against her. "Thank God," he breathed.

There came a ripping sound, tentative fingertips touching the knife wound on her side.

He cupped her head, stroked her face. "Caroline."

She'd thought it was Rexton, but it couldn't have been; he wouldn't call her Caroline. Forcing her eyes open, she squinted at a dark form backlit by spangles of sunlight.

"What happened? Who did this to . . . ?"

Her eyelids drifted shut.

"Caroline," he said in a hoarse, strained voice. "Stay with

me. Was it Dunhurst? He has a cut. He said he fell holding his razor. Was it him?"

She tried to answer. Her mouth wouldn't work, but she found she could move her head enough to nod.

He muttered something she couldn't hear, and then he gathered her to him, and told her she was going to be all right, that everything was going to be all right, his voice fading away as she sank back into oblivion.

ॐ

She whimpered as she was lifted. Everything hurt.

"I know," he said. "I know. Soon you'll be in a nice soft bed..."

ॐ

"She should be dead."

Caroline opened her eyes and looked around. She was in *la Chambre Romain,* lying in the middle of the big, scarlet-and-gold draped bed.

"I don't understand, Dr. Coates." It was Rexton's voice. "How is it possible for the wound to have started healing so quickly?"

Caroline turned her head toward his voice, her neck feeling strangely thin and weak. She lifted a hand from beneath the covers to touch it. The collar was gone. So were her wrist and ankle cuffs.

"It's a mystery, I'll grant you that," replied the doctor, who was standing with Rexton and Mr. Riddell on the balcony, all three men leaning on the balustrade with their backs to

Caroline. "But it's hardly the first...miracle, if you will, that I've encountered as a physician. Once, I delivered a baby boy who was born with a tumor on his spine. Such cancers are always fatal—there's nothing to be done. I told his mother this, but she prayed for his recovery anyway. One morning, the little boy woke up, and the tumor was gone, just as if it had never been there. He's fifteen years old now, a healthy and robust young man."

"I don't believe in miracles," Rexton said.

"Luckily for Miss Keating," the doctor replied, "God doesn't let that stop him. She is very fortunate to have endured what she did and survived—albeit with a massive loss of blood. She will be too weak to travel for some time. And, er, I've no idea how long you intend on remaining here, my lord, but I feel compelled to advise you that the young lady is in no condition at present to participate in relations of an intimate—"

"What do you take me for?" Rexton asked.

Both men looked away.

Mr. Riddell punctured the awkward silence. "Archer tells me that Miss Keating is welcome to remain here until she is fully recovered. As to her contractual obligations, although her servitude has terminated prior to the official conclusion of Slave Week at midnight tonight, it was through no fault of her own. You do understand, Rexton, that you are still obligated to pay the entire purchase price of one hundred thousand guineas."

"Of course."

"If I may ask," Riddell continued, "was there some...particular reason you left her in the stable last night? Did she do something to displease you?"

Rexton sighed. "I was in my cups."

Liar, thought Caroline. Yes, he'd been drunk, but that wasn't why he did it. He did it for the same reason he tied her up in the Nemeton yesterday afternoon and ravished her in the guise of the stableman. He did it to push her away so that he could deal with her as a *thing,* not as a person. It was why he was always covering her face with that hood, or a blindfold. It was why he'd made her perform acts he knew appalled her, so that she wouldn't complicate things by harboring any but negative feelings toward him.

It was a lesson she'd been slow to learn, but now, at last, she had taken it to heart. Mindful though she was of the unhappy circumstances that had driven Rexton to isolate himself from others, the fact remained that he had become a genuinely distant and unfeeling man. Every gesture of warmth or caring on her part, without exception, had been cruelly punished. He was no longer capable of forming a real attachment to another human being.

"You see?" he'd said after he'd proven, in the Nemeton, what a monster he truly was.

She hadn't seen then, not really. She did now.

❧

"Then you'll do it?" asked Lili, sitting on the edge of Caroline's bed later that afternoon.

The door opened. Lord Rexton, unshaven, uncombed, and still wearing the clothes he'd slept in, entered bearing a heavily laden tea tray.

"Yes," Caroline said quietly.

"Good," Lili whispered. "You won't be sorry."

Rexton greeted Lili and set the tray on Caroline's nightstand.

It held a pot of tea and a platter of biscuits and finger sandwiches. "I filched these from *le Salon Bleu*."

"May I speak to you for a moment, my lord?" Lili asked.

He looked back and forth between the two women, his eyes wary. "Of course."

Lili kissed Caroline on the cheek and promised to return later, and then she and Rexton retreated to the corridor. She closed the bedchamber door for privacy, but they stood so close to it that their voices were audible, if muffled.

"Perhaps," Lili said, "it would be best, considering Caroline's condition and her need for rest, if you were to sleep elsewhere."

"Did she ask for this? Caroline?"

After a moment's hesitation, Lili said, "Yes, my lord."

It took him a while to answer. "Very well," he said.

There came such a long period of silence after Lili said good-bye that Caroline assumed Rexton had left as well, until the door reopened.

He crossed to her bedside without looking directly at her. Filling a little plate, he said, "You must eat if you are to regain your strength."

"I'm not hungry," she said, "but I'll have some tea."

"Just cream, right?" he asked as he poured.

"That's right," she said, surprised that he knew.

He handed her the cup and saucer and lowered himself into the red leather chair. Scraping a hand over his beard-darkened jaw, he said, "Dunhurst is dead."

She lowered the cup and looked at him.

"*I* didn't do it."

Not for want of trying, though. During Lili's visit, she'd recounted how Rexton had confronted the breakfasting Lord

Dunhurst after bringing Caroline back to the château this morning. He had hauled the marquess out of his chair and pummeled him savagely. "*If Inigo and Cutbridge hadn't held him back,*" Lili had said, "*he'd have killed the blackguard.*" Given how the two men reviled each other, Rexton had no doubt been grateful for the excuse to bloody his knuckles on Dunhurst's face.

Rexton said, "Seigneur des Ombres' Swiss Guards chained him up in the cellar with the intent of handing him over to the local authorities to be prosecuted for attempted murder. Archer told him they probably wouldn't hang him, but they might very well lock him up for the rest of his life, or most of it. He said he had no intention of rotting away in some obscure French prison, and apparently he meant it. They put him in leg irons chained to a big stone column. He demanded a chair to sit on, so they brought him one. When the guards left, he tore up his cravat to make a noose, put it around his neck, and climbed onto the chair to tie it to an iron ring embedded high in the column. Then he kicked the chair away."

Caroline nodded dazedly. She took a sip of her tea, then replaced the cup on the tray and said, "I'm tired. I'd like to sleep."

He said, "I was thinking perhaps..." He rubbed his hands on his trousers in a nervous gesture she wouldn't have expected from a man like him. "You and I became acquainted under rather singular circumstances, to be sure, but I thought perhaps..." He took a deep breath and said, "I would be very honored if you would consent to be my wife."

She stared at him, trying to fathom his reason for doing this.

He said, "You could still teach, if you'd like. I...I could

build you a school. I do realize things have been... Well, I mean, we've hardly had what one would call a normal... courtship, or anything like it. You were sold to me as a slave. It can't get much more abnormal than that. But over the course of the past—"

"Oh, my God," she murmured. "Of course. Of course. If you were to marry me, it would save you having to pay the hundred thousand guineas. Well, I suppose you would still owe the ten thousand in commissions, but it would save you the rest."

He stared at her.

"I know what marriage means to your class," she told him. "It's a contractual arrangement. It has nothing to do with love, or even affection. You'll get your heir and your aura of respectability, without having to give up anything—the gin, the opium, the whores, the mistresses..."

"Christ," he whispered, shaking his head.

"Ease your mind, my lord. You needn't bind yourself in unwanted matrimony to save the ninety thousand. I don't want it. It's yours to keep."

"You can't be serious. You would go back to the squalor of St. Giles just to keep from taking my money?"

"I'm not going back to London. I'm going to Russia."

He gaped at her as if she had said she were going to the moon.

"Lili has told me about a family with whom Seigneur des Ombres is friendly. They are related to the imperial family somehow. I believe the wife is a cousin of the Tsar. They have two young daughters, and they're looking for a governess. Lili has already discussed it with *le seigneur,* who is willing to vouch for me. She tells me the Russians are very keen on

English governesses, so if that particular family doesn't offer me a position, another surely will."

"You'd give up the money after everything you've gone through this past week to earn it?"

"It is precisely because of everything I've gone through that I'm giving it up. If I took it, it would be an eternal reminder of how I earned it, how I...how I demeaned myself, the things I let you..." She looked away, her eyes burning. "I wish to God I'd never come here. If I could give up seven years of my life to erase the past seven days, I wouldn't hesitate."

"Caroline..."

"Don't call me that!" Sitting forward, she said, in a quavering voice, "Why would you call me that? Why now, after...? *Why?*"

Her outburst seemed to leave him speechless. He raised his hands in a placating gesture and said, "You are quite right. I overstepped. But, Miss Keating...about the money, I beg you recon—"

"Please go away," she said, all too sure she was on the verge of tears and loath for him to see her weeping over him. "I'm so tired. I feel as if I've been crushed beneath a boulder. I just want to sleep." She shifted on the bed to lie down, wincing at the stab of pain in her side.

Rising and reaching for her, he said, "Here, let me—"

"Don't. Just leave me alone—please. I just want to sleep."

❦

Caroline opened her eyes, wondering what had awakened her.

A sound, something like a gasp.

She lay still in the semidarkness, for it was dusk, and listened closely, but she didn't hear it again. Gritting her teeth against the pain, she turned over, facing the balcony. The double door was closed, but through its leaded glass panes she could see Rexton sitting on the chaise facing away from her.

At first, she thought he must be laughing, because his shoulders were shaking, but then he lowered his head and clawed his hands through his hair. His whole back shook, and it didn't stop. She heard the gasping sound again.

Incredulous, she sat up too quickly, inciting a fresh stab of pain. Pressing her hand to the wound, or what remained of it, she folded back the covers and carefully got out of bed. Her silken wrapper lay across the foot of the bed; she pulled that on over her shift.

The spasms that gripped Rexton did not appear to be letting up. Caroline watched him for a minute longer, and then she opened the door and stepped out onto the balcony.

When he heard the door open, Rexton sat up and combed his fingers through his hair, covertly wiping his cheeks as he did so. Clearing his throat, he said, still without looking around, "You shouldn't be up. Dr. Coates said you're to stay in bed."

"I woke up and . . . saw you out here."

The viscount seemed to ponder that for a few seconds, and then he hunched over and rested his elbows on his knees. A little sheepishly, he said, "I haven't wept since my . . . since I was six."

"When your mother died," Caroline said.

He gave her a quizzical look over his shoulder, as if wondering how she knew that. His eyes, red rimmed and puffy, lit with revelation. Turning back around, he said, in a jaundiced tone, "Cordelia."

"Who?"

"Cordelia Beckinridge. Narcissa."

"Yes, Narcissa. She waxed quite exhaustive on the life and times of Lord Rexton."

" 'Exhaustive' sums her up fairly well, I think." He sighed and shook his head. "Do go back to bed, Car—Miss Keating. You need your rest, and I'm not fit company. God, what you must think of me."

Taking a seat on the chaise behind him—tentatively, because she wasn't at all sure this conversation was a good idea—she said, "There is no shame in giving vent to your feelings."

"I didn't mean that," he said. "I meant what must you think of me as a man, after this past week. My God, I nearly killed you."

She reached out to touch his back, then withdrew her hand. "You didn't do this to me. Dunhurst did."

"I all but handed you over to him. Look what I've reduced you to. You said yourself you've been crushed. That was my doing. You're right to loathe me. I just wish . . ." He rubbed his fists against his forehead. "I just wish I could love one bloody person in this world who didn't end up . . . Christ."

Turning sideways on the chaise so that he could see her, he said in a low, raw voice, "I'll be leaving here tomorrow. I'll stop mucking up your life, but you need to know something. When I asked you to marry me, it wasn't about the ninety thousand guineas. I understand why you won't have me—why would you? But you deserve to know that you're . . . My God, you're not the kind of woman a man wants to marry because of money, or convenience, or any of that pointless . . ." His throat moved as he swallowed; he was trembling.

"You're the kind of woman a man loses his heart to even

when it's the last thing in the world he wants, even when it terrifies him. You're the kind he wants to be a better man for, the kind he wants to keep close and protect and share his life with even when he thought he would never have any of that again, or even want it."

"Or need it," Caroline said softly. She could barely see him through the unshed tears in her eyes. "But you're human, David, just like the rest of us. We all need—"

"Say that again."

Caroline knew what he meant. She said, "David." Her throat tightened. Reaching up to stroke his face, she whispered, "David . . . David . . ."

He closed his eyes and dropped his head, his forehead coming to rest against hers. A hot tear trickled down her cheek. She didn't know whether it was hers or his.

"I'm sorry, Caroline," he said. "I'm so sorry for—"

"You don't need to—"

"I do. I need to say it. And you've bloody well earned the right to hear it." Gripping her shoulders, he said, "There is no excuse for how I treated you, and don't say it's all right, because it isn't."

"I forgive you."

"I don't deserve your for—"

"Ask me again."

He stared at her as if he couldn't believe his ears. "After I've treated you so monstrously?"

"You wore the mask of a monster, but now that you've taken it off, I find that I quite fancy the man who'd been hiding behind it."

"Really?" he said. "You . . . you . . ."

"Ask me again, David."

Taking her head in his big hands, he said, "Will you marry me, Caroline?"

She smiled. "Marry a man who's never even kissed me? I don't know if that's such a good—"

He closed his mouth over hers, and her heart stopped. The kiss was deep and long and achingly tender.

He held her tight, rubbing his scratchy face against hers, nuzzling her hair. "I can't wait until you're better so that I can make love to you—really make love, not . . . like before. I promise I'll never subject you to anything like that again."

With a mischievous smile, she said, "I suppose I would understand if you felt compelled to break that promise from time to time when I've been very, very naughty . . . my lord."

"Why, Miss Keating," he chuckled, "what a scandalous suggestion." Dipping his head for another kiss, he said, "I do believe this is going to be a very interesting marriage."

Magic Hour

By the will art thou lost, by the will art thou found, by the will art thou free, captive, and bound.

Angelus Silesius

"Magic Hour": A brief period around sunrise and sundown when the lighting conditions for cinematography change rapidly, from a warm orange glow to a clear blue that permits the shooting of night scenes before darkness falls.

One

Late Afternoon,
August of This Year

*W*ELCOME BACK TO *Château des Freaks*.

I pulled my little rented blue Renault up to
the gatehouse and lowered the side window as the guard
strode across the drawbridge.

Château des Freaks: That's what I'd dubbed Grotte Cachée
during the three-week Christmas vacation I spent there when
I was sixteen so that Mom could go to Hawaii with Doug.
It was my first and last visit; I'd refused all of Dad's invitations for a return engagement. As far as he knew, this was
because I'd been weirded out by the château and its perma-
nent guests. I'd been too embarrassed to tell him the real reason.
In any event, he finally got the hint and stopped inviting me
about ten years ago.

Until yesterday.

The guard, a hulking silverback male in a black polo shirt

and black trousers, said, *"Bonjour, mademoiselle. Êtes-vous perdu?"* It had been their standard greeting to unknown visitors for decades, possibly centuries.

I dug the little gold-edged card of entrée out of my jeans pocket, took it out of its little envelope, and handed it to him. "You don't recognize me, do you, Luc? Does this help?" I took off my straw hat and roughly finger-combed my fashionably choppy hair, which had remained the same cornsilk blond as when I was born.

"Mon dieu! Mademoiselle Archer! I am so sorry. It has been such a very long time."

"Nineteen years," I said, taking the card back. "My father asked me to come. He's home, I hope."

"But of course," he said as he opened the car door for me. "Would he invite you if he weren't going to be here?"

"I, um, I'm here earlier than he expected."

"See if you can't clear your schedule around the beginning of September," Dad had said during yesterday's call. Was it my imagination, or had that aristocratic British drawl of his sounded especially languid?

I said, *"That's like three or four weeks from now. Dad, I've been so worried about you. It's been almost a year since you've come to New York, and you usually visit me every couple of months, at least."*

"We've got several sets of guests coming over the next few weeks. It really would be best if you waited until September."

"Actually, this weekend is perfect for me. I've got a meeting in London Monday morning with some clients I'm designing a swimwear catalogue for. Today's Friday. I could fly to Aulnat Airport tomorrow and spend most of Saturday and Sunday with you, then fly to London Sunday night."

"You wouldn't want to come when we have guests. My time will be divided. Wait until next month."

Luc told me I'd probably find my father in the library, and that he'd have the car parked in the garage and my luggage brought inside.

The gum-chewing blonde standing in the hallway outside the open library door was wearing a long dress that looked vaguely Edwardian except for the plunging neckline, which displayed fake boobs of monumental proportions. Her face was thickly made up, her hair long and wavy and teased on top: Brigitte Bardot meets Edith Wharton.

I said, "Excuse me, but have you seen Emmett Ar—"

"Shh!" She held a finger to her frosted melon lips and whispered, in a Brooklyn accent, "They're shooting."

I looked through the door into the library; my jaw dropped. Three people were going at it on a table in the middle of the huge, lofty room surrounded by banks of searing lights and two men hovering with digital movie cameras on their shoulders. One woman, a redhead, was tied spread-eagled to the table with a buzz-cutted hunk on top of her, thrusting away while he licked the pussy of a dark-haired woman kneeling in front of him. The latter was the only one who was clothed, or semi-clothed, being done up in a satin merry widow, stockings, stiletto heels, and long-sleeved gloves, all black. She was slapping Buzz-Cut on the ass with a riding crop and yelling, "Harder! Faster! Put your back into it."

Lili? I hadn't recognized her at first, with all that eyeliner and the crimson lips, but that velvety, exotically inflected voice was unmistakable.

"Are you the fluffer?"

I turned to find the semi-Edwardian blonde looking me up and down as she blew a fat pink bubble.

"Fluffer?"

She popped the bubble, stuck her tongue in her cheek, and pumped her fist toward her mouth in the Universal Blow-Job Symbol. "It's the girl that gets the guys primed for their scenes. I guess you're not her."

"I'm just a guest here."

The blonde stuck out her hand. "I'm Juicy Fisher."

"Isabel Archer." I shook her hand, trying to remember if I'd packed my Purell. She didn't ask me, as people sometimes did, whether I'd been named for the Henry James character. Had she done so, I would have been astounded.

"Cut!" bellowed a man from inside the library. "Emmeline! That was your cue! What the *fuck*!"

The blonde hissed, "Shit," and stuck her wad of bubble gum on the doorjamb. "Sorry, Larry! My bad."

"Take it from, 'Fuck that bitch, ram her,' " he said.

A Goth chick with half a dozen facial piercings held a clapperboard up to one of the cameras and said, "Scene two, shot two, take seven."

"Action," Larry called.

"Fuck that bitch!" Lili said. "Ram her!"

Juicy opened a parasol and sauntered into the library.

A parasol, indoors?

"Archie!" she shrieked as a crew member held a microphone boom in her direction. "What are you doing?"

"Emmeline!" Buzz-Cut said. "I wasn't expecting you."

"Obviously. You cad! You heartless deceiver!"

"It seems our Archie has been a very naughty boy." Extending the riding crop toward Juicy, handle first, Lili said, "Naughty boys need to be taught a lesson."

"Gladly." Crossing to the table, Juicy snatched the crop from Lili's hand, hesitated, and said, "Sorry, Larry, but where do I stand again?"

"Cut!"

I stepped into the doorway to get a look at Larry, who was sitting on the edge of a writing table next to a laptop. He was thirty-something, with tortoiseshell glasses; he looked more like a schoolteacher than a porn director.

Sitting in a corner behind him on side-by-side armchairs were Elic and Inigo, chuckling as they engaged in a whispered conversation. Inigo, who wore a Betty Boop T-shirt, baggy striped shorts, orange Converse All Stars, and sunglasses, was unscrewing a bottle of tequila. Elic, in a faded black T-shirt, jeans, and bare feet, still had that golden god thing going. Like Lili, they looked like they hadn't aged a day over the past nineteen years. Must be something in the water at Grotte Cachée.

A movement from above caught my eye. I looked up to see my dad leaning over the railing of the gallery, gesturing me to join him.

I climbed the stairs in the southeast tower, pondering the strangeness of my cultivated and oh-so-proper father sitting and watching a skin flick being filmed. Stranger still, it wouldn't be happening had he not arranged it. As *administrateur* to Adrien Morel, Seigneur des Ombres, the thirty-six-year-old lord of Grotte Cachée, everything that took place at the château was ultimately Dad's doing. He had acquaintances all over the world, and during his frequent travels, he issued invitations to people who were, as he put it, "promising." He'd never explained to me what he meant by that, but I knew it had something to do with Elic, Lili, Inigo—and, oh yes, the reclusive Darius, whom I'd met only briefly during that three-week visit.

My father referred to them as "the Follets," which I took to be their last name. I assumed they were related somehow to Adrien, although Elic and Lili must have been distant relations—of each other, I mean, given how lovey-dovey they were. I thought of them as "Freak Family Robinson," marooned as they were in their isolated little valley, where they invented and played by their own rules—emphasis on "play." They'd struck me as eccentric, mysterious, and spoiled—because whatever they wanted was provided with virtually no effort on their part.

They didn't have jobs, didn't seem much interested in anything but amusing themselves. Whenever I asked Dad what their deal was, he told me he'd answer all my questions when I agreed to succeed him as *administrateur*—which would make me the ninth generation of Archers to do so, the first having been Lord Henry Archer, second son of the Marquess of Heddonshaw, who'd served in that capacity from 1742 until his death in 1801. My response was always some variation on, "Yeah, I'll move to a remote French château to babysit a bunch of rich, coddled wackos . . . when hell freezes over."

Dad had warned me that Christmas not to spend too much time around the Freaks, and never to go to the bathhouse or cave. Two-thirds of the way through that visit, I overheard him telling Inigo, "In a week, she'll be gone, we'll have amusing new visitors, and you may 'exercise your heroic dimensions,' as you put it, to your heart's content. In the meantime, I would very much appreciate it if you would cease this bloody whining about how bloody horny you are, especially around Isabel. Do you think you can manage that?" What had made this little speech memorable, aside from his use of the words "bloody" and "horny," was his testiness. With the Freaks, as with Adrien, he was never less than deferential. Indeed, so surprised was Inigo by his tone, that he burst out laughing and said, "Way to go, Arch!"

I located the door on the second-floor landing that opened onto the gallery. To my left as I looked down its length were rows and rows of bookshelves perpendicular to the castle's front wall, interrupted at intervals by windows aglow with buttery afternoon sunlight. Between the stacks and the railing to the right was a long, narrow, loftlike space with armchairs scattered here and there on Persian rugs. In one of those chairs sat my father.

Dad's smile of greeting had a baleful "what-are-you-doing-here" quality, and there were faint pink streaks on his cheekbones; clearly, he was abashed at what I'd witnessed downstairs. He grabbed the railing and stood as I approached. His once-dark hair had grayed considerably since I'd seen him last, and his ubiquitous Savile Row suit didn't seem as flawlessly tailored as usual. He was only sixty-three, but he looked a good decade older than that.

"Hey, Dad, seen any good pornos lately?" I kissed my father on each cheek, which was as physical as we ever got; he wasn't much of a hugger.

"What have you done to your hair?" he asked.

"It was two hundred dollars, so don't even start."

"It's so good to see you," he said earnestly, "but I do wish you'd waited."

"Hello, Isabel." The voice was deep, soft, and Gallic-flavored.

My heart felt as if it had been squeezed and released, very quickly. I turned and saw Adrien Morel, the reason for my nineteen-year absence from Grotte Cachée.

$\mathcal{T}$wo

$\mathcal{A}$DRIEN WAS STANDING in front of the window next to a desk piled with books and papers, including a leatherbound tome with illuminated parchment pages lying open in front of him. As soon as my gaze lit on it, he closed it and circled the desk, hand outstretched.

The last time I'd seen him, he'd been a lanky, soulful seventeen-year-old. He still had those big, heartbreaking eyes, that boisterous, seemingly uncombable brown hair, but he'd matured into a man. His face displayed a history that hadn't been there before; his shoulders were broader, thicker. He had on khakis and a crisp blue shirt with the sleeves rolled up, a far cry from his adolescent uniform of saggy sweaters and tattered jeans.

"Adrien." I shook his hand, smiling into his eyes even though I was literally reeling with the effort it took to keep my expression and demeanor neutral, my hand steady. "It's been a long time."

"It has, indeed. You speak English with an American accent now."

"Except when I'm excited," I said. "You know—angry, or ... whatever."

"Cut!" Larry yelled from below. "Emmeline, whip him harder. And, Fanny, this is where you enter. Come up behind Emmeline and rub against her as she's whipping Archie. First comes the line about how men are more trouble than they're worth, and then you unbutton her dress and take out her tits and feel them up. Make it real."

With a sigh, Adrien said, "I'm pleased to see you again, although I daresay you should have heeded your father and come at a more appropriate time."

I glanced down at the actors and camera crew with feigned indifference. "It's actually kind of interesting, seeing one of those movies made."

"My apologies, in any event," he said.

The men didn't sit until I did. That kind of chivalry lingered, so far as I knew, at only one place on the planet: Grotte Cachée. Adrien, despite his relative youth, was possibly even more tradition-bound than my father.

I asked about the porn film, and the old man told me he was actually executive producing the damned thing.

"It's based on this." Adrien chose a book from one of the stacks on his desk and handed it to me.

It was a slender volume bound in a maroon cover worn at the edges, with EMMELINE'S EMANCIPATION stamped on it in gilt. I opened it to the title page. The author was "Anonymous."

My father said, "The author, if she was who I suspect she

was, spent a few days here in 1902. The book was published by Saturnalia Press a year later. It's set in a remote castle with a Roman bathhouse. There's mention of a cave, although none of the scenes takes place there. And some of the characters, especially Tobias, bear a striking resemblance to"—he shared a fleeting glance with Adrien—"people who lived here then."

"That's a first edition," Adrien told me as I thumbed through the book. "It was offered at auction by Sotheby's in New York on the hundredth anniversary of the book's publication. Darius put in a winning bid by telephone—he collects antiquarian books. It still had the dust jacket in surprisingly good condition, so he removed that and set it aside for safekeeping."

I nodded without looking up, reluctant to make any more eye contact with him than absolutely necessary. My attraction to Adrien Morel was profound, a white-hot chemical reaction over which I had no control—and which Adrien evidently didn't share. It hadn't been one-sided in the beginning, or I hadn't thought it was. When we'd met nineteen years earlier, I'd felt as if I were connecting with the other half of me. Like me, Adrien was an only child coping with a world that had been turned upside down.

The previous winter, his parents and their *administrateur,* my grandfather, had died suddenly when the Morels' private jet crashed in the Swiss Alps. At sixteen, Adrien inherited the *seigneury* of Grotte Cachée, while my father, recently retired from the RAF as a flight lieutenant, found himself Adrien's *administrateur* years before he'd expected to assume that position. We lived in the Chelsea district of London, where my American mother, a self-styled "goddess-worshipping psychic" named Madeleine Lamb Archer, played new age fortune-teller to the likes of Princess Diana and her Sloane Ranger hangers-on. When my father informed her that we would be moving to an isolated valley in the most backwater district of France—and it would probably be best if I attended boarding school until college—she promptly filed for divorce. Within a month, we'd moved back to her native New York, where she took up with a former boyfriend, Douglas Tilney; they were married as soon as the divorce was finalized.

When I came to the château that Christmas and met Adrien, he struck me, despite his youth, as an old and somewhat melancholy soul. Because his parents had deemed it inappropriate to expose him to the goings-on at Grotte Cachée, they'd brought him up in a luxurious hunting lodge tucked away in the woods some distance from the castle. Having been educated by private tutors rather than in a school, he'd formed few friendships with other young people.

I was similarly lonely at the time, having found it difficult to make friends at the snooty, cliquish private school in which my mother had enrolled me. Adrien and I immediately recognized each other as kindred souls and spent all our time together, talking, hiking, cross-country skiing, and listening to music. I sketched his portrait and gave it to him, and he seemed genuinely moved by that. He told me it was the most personal and beautiful thing anyone had ever given him.

One night, while we were sitting in front of the fireplace in the great hall, he took my hand and held it. I sensed that he wanted to kiss me, but didn't have the nerve, so eventually I girded my loins and kissed him. There was a gray cat that used to come and go like a ghost, and just then it mewed really loudly and sat down in front of the fireplace, staring at us.

Adrien seemed a little rattled by it, and told it to get lost, but it wasn't budging. The mood was broken, and he seemed ill at ease, so eventually I just went to bed.

The next morning, Adrien turned inexplicably cool toward me and stayed that way for the remaining three days of my visit. When I wanted to hang out, he was usually busy. When we did talk, he never sat next to me, but on a chair some distance away. He didn't want to walk in the woods or ski or do any of the other things we'd been doing together. Once, I caught him looking at me, and I thought I might have seen a shadow of something bleak in his expression before he turned away, but he remained as distant as before. I was mortified at having misinterpreted his interest in me as more than friendly, and furious with myself for having ruined what we'd had. The morning I left, as my father was loading my luggage into the car, I noticed the curtains part in the window of Adrien's study on the top floor of the gate tower. I looked up; they fell shut.

"Isabel?" Adrien said. "Would you?"

"I'm sorry?"

"Would you like to borrow the book? You seem quite absorbed by it."

"Oh. Um, sure. Thanks."

Dad said, "It was Inigo's idea to turn the book into a movie starring the Follets. Well, not Darius, of course. He would never have anything to do with something like this. But Elic and Lili thought it sounded like great fun. The fellow I hired to direct it, Larry Parent, has been trying to transition from adult films to mainstream. There's a quirky little movie he wants to make, but he can't get funding for it because of his X-rated background. I offered to finance his indie film if he would agree to direct *Emmeline's Emancipation* in and around the château, with Inigo, Elic, and Lili cast in their roles of choice. He didn't take me up on it right away, because he'd promised himself he would never make another hard-core film—he really hated the idea—but eventually he came around. He's almost done filming. It only took a couple of weeks."

Adrien said, "Inigo has chosen to play the Tobias character who...tutors Emmeline in the arts of love. His friend Erik will be played by Elic, and the antagonist's mistress, Lucretia, by Lili."

"I'm confused about something," I said. "Dad, remember when I came here that Christmas, and I brought my camera, but you took it away from me till I left to make sure I wouldn't photograph the Follets? You said they hated having their pictures taken, and even when I promised I wouldn't shoot them, you said you couldn't risk it. Which I still don't get, but whatever. What I want to know is how come people who hate to be photographed are willing to be filmed *having sex,* especially since this movie will presumably be distributed on DVD, which means all kinds of people will see it?"

"It won't be a problem," he said.

"But—"

"If you'll both excuse me," said Adrien as he rose to leave, the illuminated book under his arm, "there are things I must attend to. So good to see you again, Isabel. I hope you'll stay with us for a while."

"Thanks, Adrien, but I'm actually flying to London tomorrow night."

"I'm sorry to hear it. *Adieu.*"

My father watched until Adrien had ducked into the stairwell, and then, as if he'd been waiting, he let out a series of hoarse coughs.

"Dad, are you all right?"

"You shouldn't call him Adrien."

"Oh, please."

"You should call him *mon seigneur,* as I do."

"It's obsequious."

"It's respectful. And when you're *administrateur* you'll be expected to address him that way, so you may as well begin now."

"Dad, please don't start with that."

He looked down and rubbed his jaw pensively. "Come," he said as he pushed himself up from his chair. "Walk with me back to my rooms."

It wasn't a very long walk, but by the time we got there, he was wheezing. The first thing he did when we entered his apartment, which had a clubby, leather-and-mahogany thing going on, was to open a closet and wheel out something that looked at first like a portable sewing machine in its case, only taller. He sat down and uncoiled from it some plastic tubing, at the end of which was a nasal cannula. This he inserted into his nostrils and wrapped around his ears before turning on the machine, which produced a low drone. He sat back with his eyes closed, breathing deeply.

I lowered myself onto his couch and sat with my head in my hands until he turned off the machine and removed the cannula.

Looking up, I said, "Talk to me, Dad."

"It's called idiopathic pulmonary fibrosis," he said matter-of-factly as he wound up the plastic tubing around his hand. "Idiopathic means they don't know what caused it. Essentially, my lungs have become extremely inflamed, with scarring that makes them stiff. I'm being treated on an outpatient basis at

Clermont-Ferrand University Hospital, where they've dosed me with corticosteroids and immunosuppressants, which have had absolutely no effect. I'm too old for a lung transplant—the cutoff is sixty. They tell me mine is an exceptionally aggressive case, and that I shall turn up my toes within the year."

"*What?*"

"According to my pulmonologist, my longevity will be in inverse proportion to the level of stress and strain in my life. He wants me to stay relaxed, keep my traveling to a minimum—"

"Oh, my God," I said, my eyes stinging.

"If you begin to cry," he said softly, calmly, "I shall have to ask you to leave. I can deal with my own emotions much more successfully than I can deal with yours."

"Oh, fuck." I dragged in a deep breath in an effort to get ahold of myself. I wanted to go throw myself into his arms, but I knew better.

"Isabel, my dear, must you swear like a cutter?"

"Dad, what the hell is a cutter?" I demanded, a slightly hysterical edge to my voice. "I mean, you've been saying that all your life, and I still have no idea what the fuck a cutter is."

"One who cuts. Also one who swears in excess."

"Adrien doesn't know, does he? Or anyone else."

"God, no. One doesn't need that sort of drama. The only reason I'm telling you is that you need to prepare yourself for the responsibilities ahead of you."

"Oh, my God," I moaned, slumping over as it all became clear to me—why my father had called me here, what this visit was all about. "Dad... oh, my God, I love you so much, and I wish... I wish I could tell you what you want to hear, that I'm ready, willing, and able to take over as *administrateur,* but it's just... it's not in the stars, Dad. It's not going to happen. I'm sorry, I really am, but you're going to have to make other arrangements. I'll help you. I'll find someone—"

"Archers have served as *administrateurs* to the high druids of Grotte Cachée since—"

"The high what?"

"You know what I mean."

"*Druid?* As in Celtic priest? Do you know Mom has started calling herself a druidess? So fucking embarrassing, I can't tell you."

"Just think about it, please. I beg you."

"Dad . . ." I shook my head. "I won't change my mind. I have a life in New York. I have friends, a successful freelance career, and I'm subletting the most awesome rent-stabilized apartment in Manhattan."

"All I'm asking is that you think about it. Will you do that for me?"

I nodded and told him what he wanted to hear. "Okay. All right. I'll think about it."

Three

$\mathscr{I}$ SAT IN THE pool that night, basking in the calming water and the moonlight from the open roof of the bathhouse, wondering how to help my father, what to tell him about this whole *administrateur* business, what to do to make this all better. Despite the divorce and my mother getting custody, I had always felt closer to my father. We had a rapport that I didn't share with my mom. I understood him, and I always felt as if he understood me. He was the linchpin of my world.

My throat started to close up, my eyes to burn. Dad might accept his impending death in his typical blasé manner, but I couldn't imagine what I would do without him. The prospect of losing him created a kind of black abyss inside me. I already felt bereft.

In the darkness beyond the bathhouse, I saw a tiny orange dot getting closer and closer. Presently I heard the sound of feet clad in flip-flops, and a moment later, Adrien materialized in the doorway.

He paused, staring at me. "Isabel. Hi." He was shirtless and wearing the same khakis he'd had on earlier, which rode low enough on his hips that I could see the top of a pair of gray briefs. His torso was solid and beautifully proportioned, his chest lightly furred. A black cigarette was burning in his hand. I wrapped my arms protectively around myself, even though I was wearing a tank suit, thank God, instead of bathing *au naturale,* as I'd considered doing.

"You—" My voice caught. I swallowed and said, "You smoke?"

He nodded and crossed to an ashtray on a wrought-iron table to stub it out. "Filthy habit, I know. I'm sorry to have disturbed you. I'll go back and let you—"

"That's ridiculous, Adrien. I'll go back. There's no reason you should have to—"

"Isabel?" He came to the edge of the pool, that quiet, penetrating gaze fixed on me. "Are you all right?"

"I'm fine, I just..." I scraped my wet hair back, striving for control. "I, um, I'm tired, I guess."

Crouching down, he dipped a hand in the water. He looked up sharply. "He told you? About his lungs? It *is* his lungs, isn't it?"

"You...you know? How...?"

"Let's just say it's hard to keep that kind of secret from me. Is it very serious?"

I nodded, my chin quivering. "He's...he's..." On a sob, I said, "He's dying."

"*Mon dieu.*" Adrien kicked off the flip-flops, jumped into the pool in his khakis, and gathered me in his arms, whispering, "Shh, shh. Don't cry. Oh, God, Isabel, I'm sorry. I'm so sorry."

He held me as I sobbed, stroking my arms and back, whispering soothing things.

As I quieted, I became aware of how intimate it was to be curled in his embrace like that in the balmy water beneath the moonlight, feeling his skin against mine, his warmth, his breath. The mournful void inside me transformed into something palpable, an emptiness not just of the soul, but of the body.

He rubbed his face against my hair, breathing my name. I felt a hot tickle on my scalp as he kissed my head. His prickly jaw grazed my temple, followed by the soft, electric brush of his lips. I kissed his throat.

He grew still, only his chest moving. I rested a hand over his heart and felt it thudding like a drum. I kissed his throat again, and then the edge of his jaw.

Banding an arm around me, he cupped the back of my head to tilt it up and closed his mouth over mine. The kiss was hard and hungry, tasting of salty tears and tobacco, grief and regret. I felt him grow hard, and sat astride him, pressing against his body as if to merge it with mine.

It all happened so quickly, with a kind of blind, anguished ferocity. He tugged at the straps of my bathing suit; I unbuttoned his pants, gasping as the smooth column of his erection sprang up between us. Impatient with the process of peeling my suit down, he yanked the crotch aside with one hand, grabbed my hip with the other, and pushed.

Tears pricked my eyes again as he entered me, banishing the emptiness. His thrusts were deep and vigorous, almost violent, and I found myself meeting them with equal fervor. Water sloshed from the pool onto the marble deck. He gripped my head and kissed me, groaning into my mouth with each lunge as they grew swifter and more urgent. My heart swelled painfully as the pleasure mounted, until I felt as if it might explode. When I realized he was about to come, I came, too. It was like being zapped with a thousand volts of electricity.

He held me, shaking and panting, as the tremors diminished and our hearts and lungs resumed their normal rhythm.

"I didn't use anything," he said, a little breathlessly. "Protection."

"I'm on the pill," I murmured into the crook of his neck.

He nodded. "I, um, I'm healthy. You know."

"Me, too."

"Still . . ." He shook his head slightly.

I lifted my head to look at him.

Without meeting my gaze, he brushed the damp tendrils of hair off my forehead and cheeks, pulled the straps of my swimsuit back up. Reaching between us, he withdrew from me and buttoned up his khakis.

"You think this was a mistake," I said.

He looked as if he were trying to compose a response.

I levered myself off him and got out of the pool, struggling against the urge to burst into tears again. What had I thought, that after nineteen years, he'd suddenly developed feelings for me?

Hastily donning my terry-cloth robe, I said, "Just please

don't tell me this was a pity fuck, even if it was. I couldn't take that right now."

"God, Isabel." Wading to the edge of the pool nearest to me, he said, "How could you think that?"

"Why would I not?" I turned and left.

Four

"I READ *EMMELINE'S EMANCIPATION* last night,"
I told my father the next morning over tea and
scones at a little table on the balcony of his apartment, which
overlooked the castle's central courtyard.

"Oh, yes? What did you think?"

"It's dated."

He lifted his cup and blew on his tea. "It was written over a
hundred years ago. It nevertheless has its amusing moments, I
think."

"Even if unintentionally. The movie doesn't seem to be following the book very closely. In the book, when Emmeline
walks in on Archie and those two women in the library, she
flips her shit."

"Isabel, can't you say, 'She becomes upset'?"

"Fine, she becomes upset. So fucking upset that she faints

dead away, one of like eleventy-seven times that happens. She's this totally naïve, terrified virgin when Tobias takes her under his, uh, gigantic wing, and it's not till the very end that she becomes Mistress Emmeline, She-Wolf of the Château."

"Your point?"

"When I saw that library scene being filmed yesterday, it took her about two minutes to go from, 'Archie, you cad!' to this red-hot girl-on-girl scene. What's that about?"

He sat back in his chair, shrugging. "Larry adapted the screenplay from the book. I gave him free rein to take whatever approach he chose, so long as the Follets got their chosen roles."

"Speak of the devil." I nodded toward the courtyard below, which I was facing. Dad looked over his shoulder to see Larry Parent, his crew, and a gaggle of robe-clad actors—Elic, Inigo, and Lili among them—trooping across the courtyard to the central fountain.

Turning back around, he said, "I believe that's the next to last scene on the schedule. They film them out of sequence, you know. This afternoon they'll do the cave scene, and then they'll wrap."

"There's no cave scene in the book."

"I suggested it a couple of days ago. There's an exquisite crystal pool about a half mile in from the entrance, and I told Larry I thought it would make a splendid setting for a scene between Emmeline and Tobias. Orange juice?" he asked, lifting a little cut-glass pitcher.

I nodded, pushing my glass over.

Out with it, I told myself. It was a white lie, not a real lie, and if it helped him to live longer and more contentedly, where was the harm? *"According to my pulmonologist, my longevity will be in inverse proportion to the level of stress and strain in my life.*"

"Um, Dad, I've been thinking about what we discussed yesterday, me taking over as *administrateur* after, um ..."

Leaning forward, he said, "Yes?"

"I, um ..." Unable to meet his eyes, I lowered my gaze to my glass of juice. "I'll do it."

"Oh, Isabel." He reached over and squeezed my hand, which stunned me. I couldn't remember his ever having initiated a gesture of that sort. "You can't imagine what this means to me. This has been weighing on me so heavily. It pained me so much to think of anyone other than an Archer serving as *administrateur* after all these years. And I had no idea how I would go about finding a replacement if you decided not to do it."

"I know, Dad. You can relax now. It'll all be taken care of."

"There's so much to tell you, so much to fill you in on. I daresay you'll be as incredulous as I was when I first learned the history of this place and how the Follets came to be here—and why Adrien Morel and his ancestors have been safeguarding them for the past two-thousand-plus years."

I cocked my head. "Two-thou—?"

"Action!"

I looked down into the courtyard to find a scene of orgiastic revelry taking place in the fountain as the cameras rolled. The redhead from the library scene was bent over the lip of the pool taking it doggy style from Elic as he kissed Lili, kneeling next to him with some other guy screwing her from behind. Inigo, standing on the base of the statue, was sucking on a tequila bottle while "Fanny" sucked on him. She, meanwhile, looked to be taking it in the ass from the guy playing Archie.

I said, "It's supposed to be raining in that scene."

"The weather hasn't cooperated," Dad replied as he pushed himself up from the table, "so Larry's decided he can live without the rain. He just wants to wrap. Come with me. I want to show you something."

❧

"Don't you think you should knock first?" I asked as Dad, breathing harshly from the walk, used one of the myriad keys on a large key ring to unlock the door to Adrien's gate-tower study.

"He'll be in Lyon till this evening," he said breathlessly, "meeting with an architect about some renovations. And lest you think I'm trespassing, I have free access to his study—I alone." Swinging the door open, he said, "No civilian other than the *administrateur* must ever enter this room."

"Civilian?"

"The ungifted."

"Um . . ."

Ushering me inside, he said, "The only reason I'm letting you in here is because you're my heir apparent."

Oh, man. "Dad, I really don't know if I should . . . Wow," I murmured, looking around.

It was a large room with windows on all four sides. Through those on the south wall, I saw the road leading to the gatehouse, atop which this room was situated. Those on the north wall overlooked the courtyard. The walls were of raw stone, imparting a medieval aura, although little could be seen of them given the scores of paintings, drawings, photographs, and tapestries hung right up against one another.

One of the drawings was that pencil sketch I'd done of Adrien that Christmas. It was under glass in a gorgeous gold leaf frame with triple matting. Go figure.

There were numerous bookcases and cabinets, a timeworn leather sofa, and two long worktables at right angles to each other in the northeast corner. One table held a desktop computer, a laptop, a printer, a photocopy machine, an oversized scanner, and a more esoteric machine that I recognized from the office of one of my clients as a perfect binder, the function of which was to produce professional-quality paperback books. Tucked diagonally into the corner between the two tables stood a standalone automatic commercial paper cutter. The other table was neatly laid out with a number of ancient-looking manuscripts and parchment scrolls, a stack of books—the top one was *Mass and Electric Charge in the Vortex Theory of Matter*—and a pile of spiral notebooks. On the cover of the top one was written, in black marker:

ÉTÉ 14 A.D.
L'ARRIVÉE D'INIGO
BÂTIMENT DU BAIN PUBLIC
LA MORT DE L'AUGUSTUS

"Summer, A.D. 14," I murmured. "Inigo's arrival, building of the bathhouse, the death of Augustus." I walked closer to check out the notebooks under that one. The second was labeled: 1500S–1600S, DOMENICO VITTURI/COURTISANES; The third: 18TH C., HELLFIRE CLUB; and the fourth, most eye-catching of all: VISITATIONS PAR DES VAMPIRES.

There was a massive walnut desk strewn with books and papers at the east end of the room. On the opposite wall stood a glass case housing an age-burnished walking stick made out of a gnarled oak branch and a heavy gold neck torque that looked like it should have been in a museum.

Leaning on the desk, my father said, "Those belonged to Brantigern the Protec—" His words were swallowed by a sharp coughing fit. When it was over, his eyes looked unfocused.

"Dad, are you all right?"

He nodded. "A little dizzy. It will pass."

I helped him over to the couch, where he sat heavily, slumping against the backrest. "Here." Handing me the key ring, he pointed with a slightly palsied hand to a glass-fronted bookcase and said, "Open that and take out the first volume."

The books inside were trade-size paperbacks titled VOLUME I, VOLUME II, VOLUME III, and so forth.

My father said, "The books on the second shelf are my English translations, if you'd prefer not to have to read them in French."

I withdrew the first volume in English and relocked the bookcase.

"Adrien's ancestors were chieftains and spiritual leaders in this valley since before the time of Christ," he said. "When the Romans took over Gaul, a young druid named Brantigern stayed behind along with a small group of his tribespeople in order to protect Darius."

"That hermit guy?"

"He's lived here for well over two millennia," my father said. "He's a djinni."

"Um, like, *I Dream of Jeannie*?"

Giving me *that look,* he said, "No. Not like *I Dream of Jeannie.* He's from an ancient and venerable race, as are Elic, Lili, and Inigo, who arrived here later. Elic is a Nordic elf who is also, because of a genetic mutation, what we call a dusios, which means he's sequentially hermaphroditic."

"A *hermaphrodite*? 'Cause I saw him in the altogether just now, and his parts all appear to be pretty masculine—and in good working order, I might add."

"The operative word is 'sequentially,' meaning he has the ability, like certain animals, to shift genders for reproductive purposes. Lili was the Goddess of the New Moon in ancient Babylonia, but through most of her life, she's been considered a witch or a succubus. And Inigo is a satyr."

"Okay, don't satyrs have like furry haunches and hooves and horns? And tails?"

"He had the tail surgically removed, his horns are very small, and if you look at the earliest Greek depictions of satyrs, you'll see that they have normal humanoid legs."

"Oh, well, that explains it."

"Most people consider Follets to be sexual demons, incubi and succubi—or they used to when they believed in such beings—because their carnal needs are all-consuming. Well, not Darius so much, unless he happens to touch a human and absorb *their* carnal needs—he has his own cross to bear. That's why, when he's around people, he's usually in the form of a gray cat. Sometimes a blue rock thrush, but usually a cat."

"Uh-huh. So he's like a shape-shifter, too?"

"To the ancient, pre-Islamic Semites, the djinn *were* shape-shifters. As I say, he avoids humans, but the others thrive on sexual encounters, literally, the more intense the better. Doing without would be like doing without food and water, and no sooner do they appease their hunger than it returns, keeping them in a fever pitch of lust until they can find another human with whom to mate."

Had my reserved and decorous father just said, "fever pitch of lust"? Did he really believe all this hoo-hah about gender-bending elves and *satyrs,* for crying out loud? Were we actually *having* this conversation?

"If they're so horny all the time, why can't they just..." I made a stroking motion near my crotch in the Universal Masturbation Symbol.

"Inigo can find release that way, but not Lili or Elic. In fact, Elic's physiology makes him particularly vulnerable. He would almost certainly die if he were deprived of human women for an extended period. They have to be human—he can't mate with Follets. Inigo and Lili would probably go insane if chastity were enforced upon them for very long. This is why, as *administrateur,* it will be your duty to provide carnal nourishment to the Follets on a regular, ongoing basis. For the most part, this means securing as houseguests humans with whom they can engage in powerful sexual encounters."

"Serving as their pimp, in other words."

My father's eyes frosted over the way they did when he was quietly seething, which wasn't often; he was a pretty laid-back guy in general. "Your use of that word is an insult to me and to the Follets, whose guardianship is no less than a sacred calling. To properly care for them, you must think of them as gods and goddesses who derive sustenance from sexual energy, which happens to be a natural and beautiful life force, except perhaps to mouth-breathing Philistines."

"I'm sorry, Dad. I didn't mean to insult you." *Gods and goddesses...* He was losing his mind. It was the disease, it had to be. The lack of oxygen to his brain...

In a gentler tone, he said, "I know it takes some getting used to, this notion of living gods, because no one believes anymore. I think of the Follets as being akin to princes and princesses of a deposed royal family. They have no official royal status, they govern no one, but they nevertheless have royal blood flowing in their veins."

"Dad, um…" I shook my head helplessly. "Have you discussed all of this with Adrien?"

He smiled. "Who do you think taught me about this? When Adrien's parents died, along with my father, and I took over as *administrateur,* I knew very little about the Follets or the Morel lineage. But Adrien did. He had learned it from his father and from the written accounts of the *gardiens* who had gone before him—which he is now endeavoring to turn into a single, all-inclusive document, the *Histoire Secrète de Grotte Cachée.*"

"This?" I said, indicating the book in my hand.

"That is the first of what will be many volumes before he's done. In addition to learning the history and lore of this place, Adrien also had special tutors to prepare him for his priestly calling. They helped him to recognize and develop The Gift."

"What gift?"

"It's actually a bundle of gifts, extrasensory abilities inherited from his druidic ancestors, which help him to protect and care for the Follets."

"Extrasensory? Like psychic?"

"He can't read minds, if that's what you mean, but he can sense things about people through their auras, which are quite vibrant to him. He receives extraordinary insights through his dreams, and there are also certain spells he can employ— phrases in the old Gaulish tongue—to effect, for want of a better word, magic. In olden days, he would have been called a seer and recognized for the priest that he is, which is why he refers to himself and people like him as druids and druid-esses."

"Like Mom?" I said with a little roll of my eyes.

"Your mother *is* a druidess."

I could not for the life of me figure out how to respond to that.

"She was born with The Gift," he said. "Some people are, usually because both of their parents are gifted, because it's a recessive gene. If only one parent is gifted, the likelihood of having gifted offspring is quite dim. In any event, with your mother, the problem was that she never had any proper training, as did Adrien. Her gifts are unfocused and ill-developed, but she senses their presence on some level. Most gifted people don't, because our culture is too arrogant and skeptical to acknowledge the existence of abilities beyond the patently obvious. They're generally in such denial that even an exceptionally gifted druid who's been trained to read auras, like Adrien, won't recognize them as his own kind. In any event, that's why your mother's gotten caught up in all that Tarot-reading, crystal ball–gazing mumbo jumbo."

"Oh, yeah, *that's* mumbo jumbo, but this business about satyrs and elves and djinnis—"

"Djinn," he said.

"What?"

"The plural of djinni…" He let out a few more strident coughs, then sat back wearily. "Read the book, Isabel. It will tell you everything you need to know."

Five

*A*ND SO DO I, *Brantigern Anextlomarus, record the lore of our people, not for Roman eyes, nor for the eyes of any man, but for the gods and goddesses alone. Always have our rites and secrets been safeguarded from those who would burn our gods and mock our truths. Always shall it be so.*

Thus concluded my afternoon reading, Volume I of Adrien's *Histoire Secrète de Grotte Cachée*, in which the druid Brantigern recounts the beliefs and history of his Celtic tribe from their settlement in the valley through the Gallic wars and the initial decades of Roman occupation.

I closed the book and set it on my lap, holding it firmly to make sure it didn't slide into the bathhouse pool, in which my

294 • Louisa Burton

legs were dangling. It was intriguing stuff, that book, but a little distressing, too, especially the parts about the tribespeople
serving as guardians to "gods" with whom I'd met and inter-
acted. First, there'd been Darius, their "god of fire" from some
unknown foreign land who had lived deep in their "enchanted
cave" for centuries. Then came Elic, "a benign dusios from the
North," and finally Inigo, who'd been recruited by the Vernae's
Roman conquerors to pose for the bathhouse statues. There'd
been no mention of Lili. She must have come later.

The history itself might have simply been the product of
research, but that business about Darius, Elic, and Inigo . . . It
wasn't that they worshipped gods; they had dozens of them.
It was that these particular gods were still living at Grotte
Cachée. I'd met them, for heaven's sake. Was I honestly supposed to believe that they weren't people, but divine, sex-
obsessed beings thousands of years old?

"You lied to your father."

I turned to see Adrien standing in the doorway wearing a
silver-gray suit and a tie of the same color, his hands in his
pockets. He must have just gotten back from his meeting in
Lyon. I wondered how long he'd been standing there.

"You have no intention of succeeding him as *administrateur*," he said in a gently chiding tone. "You just told him that
to ease his mind."

"What makes you so sure of that?"

"I wasn't at all sure until I came here and saw you. I admit
I'm relieved. It's for the best." Glancing at the book as he
shrugged off his suit coat, he said, "A bit much to take in all at
once, I should think."

His manner was relaxed and composed, studiously so, as if

in an attempt to erase what had happened in this very spot the night before. If it had been hard to meet his gaze yesterday, today it was agonizing.

Holding up the book, I said, "What is it, like some epic multivolume fantasy novel that mixes actual history with mythological—"

"It isn't fiction." Adrien pulled a pack of Sobranie Black Russians and a gold lighter from an inside pocket of his coat before laying it over the back of an upholstered iron chair. He sat, loosening his tie.

"So, you're saying it's all true? Even the part about the Follets?" Christ, I thought, this whole thing was a delusion of Adrien's, and my formerly rational father had somehow gotten completely sucked into it. But considering his fragile health, and the knowledge that stress would only worsen his condition, was it worth trying to talk sense to him, or should I just let him keep believing what he believed?

Adrien said, "That book is a factual and straightforward account of the life and history of the Vernae as written by Brantigern the Protector. I merely translated it from the original Gaulish into French, which your father subsequently translated into English."

"It doesn't worry you that a mere 'civilian' is privy to this oh-so-secret document?"

"You would never disclose what you've learned here," he said with calm certainty.

"What, you know that from my aura?"

"I know that because you're a dependable, trustworthy person who's far too devoted to her father to betray what's important to him, even after he's gone."

"You aren't going to tell him that I don't really intend to succeed him, are you? He's so sick. He doesn't need that kind of—"

"Of course not. But it's good that *I* know. This way I can begin making inquiries as to a replacement. Do you mind?" he asked as he flipped open the Sobranies.

I shook my head. "Don't tell him that you know about his illness, either—please. Not until he volunteers the information. He's such a private man, so proud and self-contained."

Adrien lit a gold-tipped black cigarette and said, on a plume of smoke, "I first realized something was wrong with your father about a year ago, when his aura began to darken. I mentioned something once or twice in passing, and he brushed it off, so I abandoned the subject. I know him well enough to know when to keep my mouth shut."

"I'm grateful for that. Thank you." Checking my watch, I said, "I've got to leave in less than an hour for the airport. Since Dad can't travel much anymore, I'd like to come visit him every few weeks, if that's all right with you."

Adrien lowered his cigarette, a hint of something raw and desolate in his eyes. "It pains me that you even have to ask that. I'm..." He lowered his gaze, his jaw tight, shaking his head slightly as if to admonish himself not to say too much. Looking up, he said, "You are always welcome here, Isabel. Always. You never have to ask."

I nodded, looking away. He took a drag on his cigarette, and then another one.

Gesturing toward the cave entrance in the craggy rock face that formed the back wall of the bathhouse, he said, "How long have they been shooting in there?"

"Since before I got here, so over an hour."

"I should check up on them. Your father was going to do it, but I knew it would exhaust him to walk all the way here from the château."

He looked toward the cave, his eyes narrowed slightly, as if in concentration.

I said, "What are you—"

He held up a hand to shush me. A few seconds later, he smiled and said, "It would appear this little project is at an end."

"What, so you're like Superman, you can see through solid rock?"

"Not through rock, no, and certainly not at this distance. They're pretty far into the cave, although they're heading back this way. Voices are a different matter, though. They can travel a very great distance, through all kinds of material."

"Okay, Adrien, obviously you've somehow gotten Dad to play Demons and Druids with you, but I'm not quite as susceptible to parlor tricks—especially crappy ones that don't prove a damned thing."

"How's this one?" Adrien waved a hand in the direction of the cave and said, *"Uediju rowero gutu."*

"...lost the flash drives? You lost the fucking flash drives?"

"I didn't lose them, Larry. I put them in my camera bag last night, like I always do, but this morning they were gone. I was gonna go into town and get more, but—"

"Then why the fuck didn't you?" Larry screamed. *"They were our only fucking backup."*

"Because you needed me behind the fucking camera all day!"

"We're fucked! We are totally fucked! Do you realize how fucking fucked we are?"

Adrien waved his hand again. The conversation snapped off as if he'd pushed a button.

"How was that one?" he asked.

"That one was much better," I said dazedly.

"Inigo calls it, 'surround sound.' So, Larry's got his *culottes* in a twist because, while he was filming the crystal pool scene just now, the electromagnetic vortex in the cave erased all of the digital images in the cameras and his laptop. He had the footage backed up on two different flash drives, but they appear to have disappeared. Everything he shot since he's been here is gone." He waved a hand airily, then took a puff of his cigarette. "*C'est la vie.*"

"An electromagnetic vortex?"

"You've heard about the vortices at Sedona, Arizona, and Machu Picchu?"

I nodded.

"They're often associated with volcanoes, and also with magnetic meteorites buried in the earth. In the case of Grotte Cachée, we happen to have a meteorite buried almost directly beneath an extinct volcano." He cocked his head toward the wall of rock. "The deeper one ventures into that cave, the more profound the effect of the vortex."

Still reeling from Adrien's demonstration with the voices, I said, "You knew if he shot a scene in that cave, it would wipe out everything he'd filmed up till then. And I assume the disappearance of those flash drives is no coincidence."

Adrien shrugged and smiled as he stubbed out his cigarette.

"Of course," I said. "The Follets get a novel and exciting form of 'carnal nourishment' without sacrificing their privacy. Very clever of you, *mon seigneur.*"

"It was all your father's doing. I don't know that I would have thought of the vortex ruse on my own."

"...the fuck are we supposed to tell Archer when he asks where his movie is?" It was Larry Parent's voice, unenhanced by "surround sound," approaching from within the cave. "Oh, we are well and truly fucked, my friend."

"*Bonjour,*" greeted Adrien as Larry, his crew, Inigo, and Juicy Fisher emerged from the cave, ducking to pass through the low opening.

Larry, his expression grim, sent the others on ahead. "Hey, Mr. Morel. Is, uh, is Mr. Archer around?"

"If this is about the footage disappearing from the cameras and laptop, you can discuss that with me."

Larry stood with his mouth open for a second, then closed it. "You know?"

"I overheard."

Looking toward the cave, Larry said, "Yeah, but—"

"There is an electromagnetic vortex deep in the cave," Adrien said. "We should have known better than to suggest that you try to film in there. It is really entirely our fault."

"That's ... well, that's really understanding of you, but, um ..."

"But you are distraught to have lost a creative product into which you put so much time and effort."

A *yeah, right* sneer escaped from Larry ever so briefly before he schooled his features and said, "Yeah. Right. There *is* that, but there's also ... I mean, I don't mean to sound mercenary here. I *am* an artist and all, but—"

"You assume we won't finance your independent film because you have no movie to give us. Please have no fears on that account, Mr. Parent. I think I can safely speak for

Mr. Archer when I say that this little mishap will not affect your payment."

"*Really?*"

"As I say, we are entirely to blame. What is the American expression? My bad."

After Larry had left, I said to Adrien, "I'd been worried that my dad was off his rocker. Now I'm thinking maybe it's me."

Leaning forward on his elbows, he said, "Why would you think that?"

I chewed on my lip for a moment. "The 'surround sound,' it was for real?"

"It was."

"And . . . and Elic and Lili and Inigo and Darius . . ."

"Follets. And no, that is not their last name."

I shook my head. "Holy shit."

"Has anyone ever told you you swear like a cutter?"

"So Darius is like really a cat?"

"When he chooses to be."

"That night, during my Christmas visit, when we were sitting in front of the fireplace in the great hall, and that cat came in and creeped me out till I went to bed . . ."

He nodded. "Darius. He, um, assumed his human form after you left, and had a little conversation with me about duty. He wasn't censorious, in fact he was quite kind, but he did ask me if I wanted to be 'launching into something serious' with someone I could never . . . Well."

Rising from his chair, he grabbed a towel off a stack on a bench and brought it over to me. "Here, dry your feet off. They must have shriveled up to nothing by now."

"Thanks." I set the book aside, lifted my legs out of the water, swiveled around on my butt, and took the towel.

Adrien crouched down, picked up the book, and said, soberly, "Did you read this all the way through?"

I nodded as I scrubbed the towel over my calves and feet.

"Then you know that it's critical to the welfare of the Follets that their *gardiens* be druids—that is to say, gifted. Every *gardien* since Brantigern has had The Gift, and that is because their fathers, or in some cases, their mothers, took gifted spouses. In compiling *l'Histoire Secrète*, I've come across quite a few instances in which a *gardien*, out of sacred duty, set aside the woman he loved and married instead the gifted woman who had been chosen for him."

I stopped drying my feet and looked up. "That's...My God, Adrien, that's so sad."

He just looked down.

I said, "It's as if the *gardiens* are slaves. They're completely caged by tradition and duty, prisoners of this damned château."

"I was reared, as were all my ancestors, to dedicate my life *dibu e debu*—to the gods and goddesses. They must always come first. They are my reason for being."

Looking back down, I said, "Who does the choosing? Of the wives?"

"As with any arranged marriage, it's usually the parents. If the parents are deceased, that duty falls to the *gardien's administrateur*. He—or she—is generally quite well traveled, with connections all over the world, whereas we *gardiens* tend to stick close to home."

I stood up, folding the damp towel just to have something to do with my hands. "So, um, my father's been looking for a wife for you?"

He stood, too. "For some time, but gifted women tend to

302 · Louisa Burton

be difficult to spot. Perhaps my next *administrateur* will have better luck."

No wonder he'd said he was relieved when I confirmed that I would not be succeeding my father as *administrateur*. My chest felt as if someone were sitting on it. I drew in a deep breath and said, with forced bonhomie, "God, Adrien, your life is positively medieval. I couldn't hack it. Makes me glad we never can, you know... 'launch into something serious.' "

"Liar," he said softly.

I met his gaze.

He said, "I can see your aura, remember?"

"It's not fair," I said, a little hoarsely. "I can't see yours."

"That's probably a good thing."

⁂

"Be careful driving to the airport," my father said as Adrien loaded my little carry-on into the trunk of the Renault. Glancing up at the blushy peach sky, he said, "Night falls quickly here. It's the mountains. They swallow up the sun."

"I'm an excellent driver, night or day," I told him. "You worry too much."

"He's right," Adrien said. "You're not used to driving on mountain roads, and in the dark—"

"I'll be fine, you guys. Jeez." I looked at my watch. "I've got to get going. I'm supposed to be halfway there by now."

"Go, then," my father said. "You don't want to miss your plane."

"Bye, Dad." We did our continental kiss-kiss thing. It may have been my imagination, but I think he held on to my shoulders a little longer than usual, and maybe a little more firmly.

"Adrien." I extended my hand. He shook it. It was excruciatingly civilized.

"Don't wait another nineteen years to visit us again," he said.

"I won't."

He opened the car door for me. I got in, blew my dad a kiss, and pulled away.

He'd been right about the sun setting quickly. As I was driving down the long stretch of gravel road leading out of the valley, the sky turned violet, then an ethereal blue tinged on the horizon with just the faintest indigo stain.

I looked in my rearview mirror. The castle, which had always appeared so dark and forbidding to me, seemed to take on a bronzish glow against that otherworldly sky. A single figure stood on the drawbridge, gazing in my direction: Adrien.

I watched him watch me drive away until I rounded a curve in the road and the château disappeared from view.

ABOUT THE AUTHOR

Louisa Burton, a lifelong devotee of Victorian erotica, mythology, and history, lives in upstate New York. Visit her website www.louisaburton.com.

If you loved

Bound in Moonlight

Read on for a sneak peek at the next
Scintillating and erotic novel from
Louisa Burton

Whispers
of the
Flesh

Coming Fall 2008

One

OCTOBER 1829

"You want him," Elic murmured into Lili's ear in the French that had long ago replaced the languages of their birth.

Lili, lounging next to him on a damask and gilt chaise in *le Salon Ambre,* lifted her after-dinner brandy to her lips with a silky smile that was answer enough. "Shh . . . He'll hear."

Elic glanced across the candlelit room at the object of their attention, a dark, gravely handsome young Englishman with large, watchful eyes. At the moment, he was rhapsodizing in his native tongue about the "rich volcanic soil" of la Vallée de la Grotte Cachée while Archer listened raptly and Inigo, ever the peacock in a green and gold brocade waistcoat, his mop of springy black curls riotously unbound, stifled a yawn.

When their visitor paused to take a breath, Elic said, in English, "Do you speak French, Beckett?"

He blinked at Elic, took a puff of his cigar, and said, "I confess, I never studied it in school."

"How very curious," Lili said in that velvety, exotically accented voice that still, after all these years, sent a hot shiver of desire humming along Elic's veins. "I thought all gently bred Englishmen knew French—not that I've any objection to conversing in English. It is quite as beautiful a language, in its own way."

"You're fucking him with your eyes," Elic told Lili in French.

"Can you blame me?" she replied, still smiling at their guest.

"Can't quite see the appeal." It was a lie. Of a goodly height, David Beckett had a lean but stalwart physique set off to damnable advantage by a well-cut black tailcoat. And there was a certain stillness about him, a quiet intensity, that imparted an aura of mystery.

"Such lies are beneath you," Lili murmured to Elic. "And your jealousy is absurd, my love, considering how many bedmates we've shared over the years." Before Elic could respond to that, she apologized to Beckett, in English, for having conducted that exchange in a language he couldn't understand.

The young man met Lili's eyes for an electric moment, then lowered his gaze to his brandy, which he swirled in a way that was meant to look thoughtful—though to Elic, it bespoke a deep discomfiture. He actually appeared to be blushing, though it was difficult to tell in the golden, wavering candlelight.

From the moment David Beckett had been introduced to Lili upon his arrival that afternoon at Château de la Grotte Cachée, he had seemed gripped by a sort of uneasy entrancement. It was hardly an unusual reaction among male visitors to the château. Ilutu-Lili, with her lustrous black hair, slumberous eyes, and easy sensuality, had a bewitching effect on men. She had certainly bewitched Elic; for eighty years he had been caught in her spell. Tonight, with her hair secured by a diamond-crusted comb in a knot of loops and tumbling curls, her shoulders bared by the wide, sloping neckline of her gown—a confection of garnet chine silk with billowy puff sleeves and a handspan waist—she looked the very image of the goddess she truly was.

"What language *did* you study?" Elic asked Beckett.

"I've taken classes in Latin, Greek, Italian, and Hebrew, though of those tongues, the only one in which I am truly fluent is Italian."

"Quite the well-schooled gardener," Elic said.

The taunt earned him a look of surprised amusement from Inigo, and scowls from Archer and Lili. Beckett's gaze lit on Lili before returning to Elic, whom he studied for a long, pensive moment.

"I say, Elic." Shifting his lantern jaw uneasily, Archer said, "I would, er, hardly call our guest a gardener, given the scope of his expertise and the rather ambitious nature of his work." Bartholomew Archer had just the year before succeeded his father as *administrateur* to Théophile Morel, Seigneur des Ombres, the elderly lord of Grotte Cachée. Nearly as tall as Elic, and thin as lath, the timorous Brit had yet to grow comfortable in his role as steward of Grotte Cachée; Elic wondered if he ever would. "I should think Mr. Beckett would be more correctly termed, er...a horticulturist."

Beckett said, "I infer no shame in the title of gardener. Humphrey Repton, who gave me my initial instruction in this field, styled himself a 'landscape gardener.' I am content to be called the same."

"Humphrey Repton trained you?" Archer said. "I'm impressed."

"Never heard of him," said Inigo, who, having a remarkable facility with languages, spoke English with no trace at all of an accent. Of Greek extraction, he traveled all over the known world before being recruited in 14 A.D. to pose for the salacious bathhouse statues at Grotte Cachée; he'd made his home there ever since.

Archer said, "Repton was famous for designing, or redesigning, the grounds of some of the finest estates in Britain. How came you to apprentice with him, Beckett?"

"I would hardly call it an apprenticeship," Beckett replied. "I was twelve years old at the time. My father had engaged him to devise a plan for improving the park and gardens at the country house he'd just purchased, which had been neglected for decades. This was in the late summer of 1816, two years before Mr. Repton went to his maker. He'd been injured in a carriage accident, so he needed a wheelchair to get around, and I used to push it for him while he sketched panoramic vistas. His aim was to create a natural but picturesque landscape, and he had impeccable instincts. He turned twelve-hundred dreary, overgrown acres into a veritable paradise. Whole areas were excavated and transformed, hundreds of trees were cut and planted, terraces were built, flower gardens installed."

Archer said, "I've seen Repton's work at Blaise Castle—extraordinary."

"How did he manage such rigorous work, being in a wheelchair?" Inigo asked.

"Oh, he didn't actually execute his designs," Beckett replied. "He was more of an advisor, coming up with the plans and leaving it to his clients to arrange for the actual work."

"Mr. Beckett works in much the same manner," Archer told the assembled company. "During his stay with us, he will inspect the grounds surrounding the castle, devise a scheme for improving them, and leave us a book of notes, plans, and pictures."

"It is a method I've borrowed from Mr. Repton," Beckett said. "For each client, he created what he called a 'Red Book,' because it was bound in red leather. The book would contain descriptions of what should be done, including detailed illustrations in watercolor depicting the grounds as they then existed, with vellum overlays showing how that particular area would look if his suggestions were implemented. When he discovered my aptitude for drawing and painting, he allowed me to help him with that end of things, and

I found it fascinating. For years after that, I read everything I could get my hands on that had to do with botany, floriculture, architecture. . . . And I painted landscapes, as Mr. Repton had advised, to help develop my sense of natural aesthetics."

"You studied these things at university, I suppose?" Lili asked him.

He averted his gaze from her and took his time rolling the ash off the tip of his cigar. "I confess I did not. It had always been assumed that I would read theology."

Elic hated the way Lili gazed at Beckett, her eyes glinting darkly, her color high. He didn't blame her for her hungers; she could no more ignore them than he could ignore his own. But when the object of that hunger held her in such utter thrall, when there was little doubt just how desperately she ached to possess him, it incited in Elic a primal, almost human covetousness. There was no restraining her when her lust for an exceptionally desirable male—a *gabru* in her extinct Akkadian tongue—ran this hot, no way to keep her from stealing into his bedchamber during the night and ravishing him as he lay immobilized by one of her ancient Babylonian spells. Were Elic capable of making love to Lili—really making love, not just bringing her off by hand, or with his mouth—he might have some chance of keeping her for himself. As it was, the most he could hope for was to be there on occasion when she took her human prey, to caress her and kiss her and whisper his love into her ear as she writhed for hours atop her groaning, shuddering, lust-maddened *gabru*.

"Theology, eh?" she said. "You would be the second or third son, then, Mr. Beckett? Destined for the ministry?"

"The, er, priesthood, actually."

"Ah—my apologies," she said. "One tends to think of all Englishmen as Anglican. A thoughtless presumption."

"Not at all." He still wouldn't look directly at her.

"You seem to have managed to forge your own way despite

parental expectations," Inigo observed. "Are they miffed that you didn't join the Church?"

Choosing his words with seeming care, Beckett said, "They are content with the path I've chosen."

"So, Beckett," Elic said. "I can't help but wonder what your connection to the archbishop might be."

The young man stilled in the act of lifting his snifter to his mouth, his gaze darting toward Elic and then away. Frowning into his brandy, he took so long to compose his thoughts that Archer answered for him.

"As I understand it," the *administrateur* began, "Archbishop Bélanger retained Mr. Beckett's services on the advice of friends in England, so the connection would be professional rather than... shall we say, convivial." It was at a formal dinner recently hosted by Monseigneur Bélanger for the local personages of note that Archer, who'd attended in Seigneur des Ombres's stead, had made the acquaintance of David Beckett. Intrigued by the young Englishman's proposal for enhancing the archbishop's property, and nostalgic for the lush and artless gardens of his homeland, Archer had convinced *le seigneur* to invite Beckett to Grotte Cachée.

"When I spoke of a connection to the archbishop," Elic said, "I meant the Archbishop of Canterbury under Henry the Second. It occurred to me that there might be a relation between Thomas Becket and our Catholic gardener of the same name."

"I'm afraid I can claim no such illustrious association," Beckett said.

"How long will we have the pleasure of your company, Mr. Beckett?" Lili asked with a smile that made Elic's teeth throb.

"I... well, I suppose that remains to be seen," he replied. "Tomorrow afternoon, I shall conduct a thorough tour of the grounds, and that will give me a rough idea of the areas that might benefit from a more picturesque approach. It could take a week or a month to prepare a book of plans for *le seigneur*. It all depends on the extent of the renovations."

"I can't imagine there's very much at Grotte Cachée that wants improvement," Elic said. "You'll find little to keep you here, I think."

Lili, clearly vexed by his tone, moved away from him in a subtle but stingingly eloquent gesture. She and Inigo shared a look. Such petty sniping was out of character for Elic.

Archer said, "It might help to have a bit of guidance on your tour, Mr. Beckett. I've other obligations tomorrow afternoon, but I could show you 'round in the morning."

Shaking his head, Beckett said, "I must go to Clermont-Ferrand in the morning in order to mail a letter."

"Give it to me now, and I'll have someone mail it tomorrow," Archer said.

"It...it isn't written yet," Beckett said. "I'll write it tonight, and...I've other business in town, in any event, things I must buy—more vellum, another sketchbook..."

"Very well," Archer said. "I must caution you, though, should you care to explore our cave, as many guests do, not to venture in too far—no more than a quarter mile or so, where the lamps are. Past that, it becomes...rather forbidding, I'm afraid."

"I shall bear that in mind, Mr. Archer. And now, if you will all forgive me," Beckett said as he rose to his feet and bowed in Lili's direction, "I regret that the hour has come when I must retire to my chamber. The letter of which I spoke will be a lengthy one, and all I really want is a good night's sleep."

"May you get your wish, Mr. Beckett," said Lili, her gaze following him as he crossed to the door. "Pleasant dreams."

12 October, 1829
Grotte Cachée, Auvergne, France

My Lord Archbishop,

This dispatch will serve, I trust, as an account of the progress thus far of my clandestine inquiries on behalf of your Grace and of our superiors in Rome and here in France. You will be gratified, I think, to know that I am presently ensconced in a guest chamber of Château de la Grotte Cachée, having successfully drawn upon the horticultural expertise I acquired before entering seminary to adopt the guise of a landscape gardener.

My preliminary investigation into claims of demoniacal activity in and around this château transpired much as we had planned. This fortnight past I enjoyed the hospitality of Archbishop Bélanger at his own remarkably beautiful château in the region of Auvergne, where his secretary made me privy to allegations dating back nearly four centuries of strange happenings in and around Grotte Cachée. Notable among these were reputed acts of extraordinary wickedness and lechery committed there by certain individuals identified on occasion as demons or possibly those possessed by demons. Such accusations have generally been regarded as heated imaginings, and therefore rarely committed to writing save for the most cursory of notations. As a consequence, there exist but three pieces of written evidence detailed enough to be of use for our purposes, which in the interest of discretion I was enjoined from copying. These I shall summarize for you frankly and without expurgation, as you have directed, with the caveat that such writings, by their very nature, must needs describe carnal encounters of the most impure stripe.

The earliest of the written accounts, dated 6 May 1461, is a description by a parish priest of events related to him—not, I hasten to add, under the seal of confession—by a young woman who served briefly as a chambermaid at Château de la Grotte Cachée. She gave distraught testimony of having witnessed a libidinous interlude involving *"actes déplorables de sodomie"* between a man and two women, one of the latter having afterward uttered words of enchantment that turned her into a male. Thus transformed, this *"abberration de nature"* proceeded to climb the exterior wall of a tower with naught but his bare hands and feet, whereupon he stole into the bedchamber of a female visitor to the château. The priest sent this report to the Bishop of Clermont (under the *Ancien Régime*), who transferred it to the Archbishop of Bourges, who dismissed the matter, having judged the young woman, sight unseen, to have been bereft of reason. It is worth noting that it had been the longstanding practice of the seigneurs of Grotte Cachée to make frequent and generous donations of land and monies to the Church.

The archbishop's secretary also showed me an age-worn velvet-bound book titled *Una Durata di Piacere,* an erotic memoir by a Venetian nobleman named Domenico Vitturi, which was privately published under a nom de plume for the author's intimate friends in 1609. Several chapters thereof concern visits to Grotte Cachée by Vitturi and favored courtesans for the express purpose of training them to pleasure men in exotic and unorthodox ways. This instruction was carried out with considerable zeal by two men fictitiously named Éric and Isaac, who schooled the courtesans in extraordinarily obscene forms of sexual congress. They were taught to employ various objects, devices, furnishings, and even implements of torture, for the purpose of exciting lust in themselves and their bedpartners. They became adept at such debaucheries as sapphotism, coitus oralis, coitus analis, *le vice anglais,* such punishments as spanking and slapping, ménage à trois, the use of bindings, blindfolds, and gags, and other practices of an even more debased nature. A notable aspect of these depictions of fornication was the prowess of the two trainers, which strikes one as exceeding the natural abilities of the mortal male. By Vitturi's account, Éric could perform the act of copulation a dozen or more times in brisk succession. Isaac, while possessed of a more conventional, though still remarkable, sexual vigor, boasted a generative organ described as *"come il penis dello stallion."* Furthermore, one of the courtesans claimed that Isaac possessed both a tail and a pair of stumpy, hornlike protrusions on his head, which his thick, curly hair effectively concealed. This book was brought to the attention of high personages at the Vatican, who handed the matter over to the Archbishop of Bourges, who declared that Vitturi's reminiscences were simply too fantastical to warrant investigation.

The third document in Archbishop Bélanger's possession was the letter that prompted this investigation, which was sent this past June from a lady in New York City to an old friend summering at her family's château in Lyon. It was this letter, retrieved by a laundress from the hidden pocket of a skirt belonging to the recipient, which made its way to the archbishop, who being of a more inquisitive humor than his predecessors, resolved to prove or disprove with finality the existence of diabolical forces at Grotte Cachée. You have asked me to relay the contents of this letter, and this I shall do to the best of my recollection. Upon greeting her friend with the curious salutation, "From one little red fox to another," the correspondent proceeded to reminisce about a "slave auction" they had attended at Château de la Grotte Cachée twelve years earlier. Having been "sold" to dissolute libertines for one week's sexual servitude, they subsequently—if one is to credit this shameless account—engaged in activities of the most appalling degradation. Reference is made to collars, cuffs, and leashes, as well as to casual nudity and public acts of sodomy too perverse for me to detail here. What caught the archbishop's eye was the mention of "that curly-haired devil with the lovely smile and colossal cock." It is in relation to this man that the lady writes (her actual words may have differed slightly), "I do not, as you accuse, credit the existence of satyrs, but I tell you I did briefly espy, in the course of bathhouse disportments, what looked to be a tail—and I was only very slightly tipsy from the opium. Perhaps his mother, while in a delicate condition, received a fright from a beast with such a tail. Is it not through such maternal impression that some babes are cursed with birthmarks resembling animals, or even more monstrous disfigurements?"

As I say, these three documents represent the only meaningful written accounts of unnatural doings at Grotte Cachée. There was, however, one additional source of information. It seems that in August of 1771, a young carpenter by the name of Serges Bourgoin was hired by Lord Henry Archer, the English *administrateur* to the lady who was then mistress of Grotte Cachée, to replace a door and a pair of window shutters. About a week later, as Bourgoin and another carpenter were doing some work at the home of a local physician, the physician's wife overheard him whispering to the other man of the bizarre and ungodly things he'd experienced at Grotte Cachée. She urged him to report these things to their parish priest. When he refused, she did so herself. Given the nature of her allegations, the fact that they were hearsay, Serges Bourgoin's reputation for overindulgence in wine, and the lady's own reputation as a gossip and intermeddler, the priest penned a brief memorandum about the conversation and pursued it no further.

When I was informed that Bourgoin was still alive, I made arrangements to visit him. At eighty-five, he lives with his daughter in a nearby village, and still enjoys his wine—having been told this, I brought him two bottles of an excellent local vintage. At first, he denied having ever been to Grotte Cachée, but after I explained that I was attempting to confirm or refute the presence of evil spirits there so as to determine the necessity for exorcism, and that I would share his tale only with trusted ecclesiastical personages, he saw fit to confide in me. I confess, it was helpful to my purposes that he was already somewhat inebriated when I arrived that afternoon.

The substance of what Bourgoin related to me is this: He arrived at Grotte Cachée to replace the door and shutters, only to be led up a heavily wooded mountainside to a cave entrance in a rocky outcropping. The opening, although irregular in shape, was fitted out with a door that was old and weathered, its green paint peeling. Next to it was a gap in the dark volcanic rock to which had been attached a pair of window shutters in the same condition. The cave chamber within, he describes as *"une petite salle confortable,"* furnished with a bed, a rug, and bookshelves. There were more bookshelves, many more, he tells me, in a larger chamber adjoining the smaller one. He claims that when he removed a book from its shelf to look at it, it was wrested from his hands and shoved back in place by an unseen force. Unnerved, he installed the door and shutters as dark clouds filled the sky. By the time he was finished, a violent thunderstorm was lashing the valley, forcing him to delay his return home. He spent that night in a room in the servants' quarters, and when he awakened the next morning, he recalled having been visited in the wee hours by a black-haired female, a *"démon feminine,"* who ravished him in exceptionally sinful ways while a very tall man with long, golden hair sat and watched. Sometimes this man would propose things that she should do to him, unimaginably depraved things. Other times, he would pleasure her, but although he was clearly aroused, she never touched him intimately and he did not attempt to have carnal relations with her. Many times over the intervening years, Bourgoin told me, he had tried to convince himself that it had been a dream, but in his heart, he felt it had really happened. When I asked whether he had been drinking that night before he retired, he admitted that he had, but he insisted that he wasn't so drunk as to have invented such an experience out of whole cloth.

During my stay with the archbishop, he issued an invitation to the local gentry to dine with him, as a pretext to throw me together with the present Seigneur des Ombres, Théophile Morel. *Le seigneur,* being of advanced years and ill health, sent in his stead his administrator, Bartholomew Archer, who is the grandson of the previously mentioned Lord Henry Archer. Since Mr. Archer is known to make inquiries regarding those whom he intends to invite to Grotte Cachée, I introduced myself to him as "David Beckett," Beckett being my middle name—it was, in fact, my mother's maiden name. This, I felt to be an acceptable alternative to an entirely fabricated name. You are well aware, my lord, of how deeply I take to heart the Wisdom of Solomon on the subject of lying—truly, the mouth that belieth killeth the soul. I shall endeavor, during the course of this investigation, to avoid outright untruths, although I concede that lies of omission have been unavoidable, and will continue to be so, from time to time.

In any event, the ruse was successful. Mr. Archer left his Grace's dinner party intrigued with the notion of revamping the grounds of Grotte Cachée in accordance with the picturesque ideals in vogue in Britain, and ten days later he sent a Barouche to fetch me here.

The occupants of the château, aside from Seigneur des Ombres and Mr. Archer (who actually lives in a hunting lodge in the surrounding woods with his wife and infant daughter) are one female and three males, all evidently unrelated. At dinner this evening, I was introduced to the woman and two of the men by first name only—Lili, Elic, and Inigo. The third man, Darius, who was described to me as "something of a hermit," was not present. During our postprandial conversation, I overheard a brief, whispered exchange in French between Lili and Elic—you have remarked yourself on my acute hearing. Their words, which concerned myself, had clearly not been intended for my ears. When asked whether I understood French, I replied misleadingly that I had never taken a course in the subject, which is true. I declined to mention that my father was from France, as were my nanny and nursery governess, and that I had a thorough command of French before I was speaking full sentences in English.

As for the castle itself, it is of a quadrangular configuration with corner towers, and appears to have been built several centuries ago of dark lava rock. It is tucked deeply into a heavily wooded valley beneath an extinct volcano that houses a cave which I am eager to explore despite Mr. Archer's admonition that I not venture too far within. When I do so, I will of course attempt to locate the curious little bedchamber described by Serges Bourgoin.

Given my disinclination to entrust my correspondence to the hands of strangers, this will very likely be the last communication your Grace receives from me until I return to England to make a full report in person.

> Until then, I remain
> Your Grace's devoted and humble servant,
> David Beckett Roussel